Books by Harry Crews

The Gospel Singer
Naked in Garden Hills
This Thing Don't Lead to Heaven
Karate Is a Thing of the Spirit
Car
The Hawk Is Dying
The Gypsy's Curse
A Feast of Snakes
A Childhood: The Biography of a Place
Blood and Grits
The Enthusiast
Florida Frenzy
A Grit's Triumph
Two
All We Need of Hell
The Knockout Artist

HARRY CREWS

BODY

POSEIDON PRESS

New York London Toronto
Sydney Tokyo Singapore

Poseidon Press
Simon & Schuster Building
Rockefeller Center
1230 Avenue of the Americas
New York, New York 10020

POSEIDON PRESS is a registered trademark
of Simon & Schuster Inc.

POSEIDON PRESS colophon is a trademark
of Simon & Schuster Inc.

Designed by Karolina Harris
Manufactured in the United States of America

Library of Congress Cataloging in Publication Data
Crews, Harry, date.
  Body / Harry Crews.
    p. cm.
  I. Title.
PS3553.R46B6   1990
813'.54—dc20   90-37459
                                                      CIP

ISBN 0-671-69576-2

BOMC offers recordings and compact discs, cassettes
and records. For information and catalog write to
BOMR, Camp Hill, PA 17012.

This book is for my son
Byron Jason Crews

AUTHOR'S NOTE

This is a work of the imagination. None of this ever happened anywhere except between the covers of this book. My friends in the world of bodybuilding will recognize that I have borrowed elements from both amateur and professional contests and brought them together to make something that does not exist and has never existed. Said another way, bodybuilding has been forced to serve the needs of fiction rather than the other way around. Consequently, any resemblance to persons living or dead is purely coincidental and not intended.

Walking the wire is living.
The rest is just waiting.

—KARL WALLENDA, *in conversation
a few weeks before he fell to
his death in 1978*

O N E

She was called Shereel Dupont, which was not her real name, and she had missed her period for the last three months running, but she was not pregnant and knew it. No, it was much better and much worse than that. It was partly due—even her name that was not her name—to pumping iron and starving to death on nothing but vitamin packets and protein powder and broiled flounder without butter or salt. But it was mainly due to Russell Morgan, called Russell Muscle, but only behind his back, never to his face. Russell was the one who had found her and trained her and named her, changed everything about her, even the way she talked, demanding that she lose her Georgia accent, as he forced her toward some ultimate shape that only he could see. He was not a man to talk much, but he had always made it clear that he was the only one that needed to see, that needed to know.

In the gym after the third set of prone presses with a hundred and fifty pounds on the bar (she competed at one hundred twenty-four) her pectoral muscles, lean and long as a swimmer's, but as sharply layered and defined as if they had been etched with acid, her pecs under her breasts—each the size of a hard-boiled egg—burned like fire. Still it was not enough to achieve his secret vision of what they ought to be. It was never enough.

"Another set," Russell said.

"It burns," she said. "Jesus, I've got the burn."

He watched her where she stood, her breathing rapid and shallow, hurting, the sound of other bodybuilders snorting and grunting all around her, the noise of iron plates clanging through the air heavy with motes of dust under the fluorescent lights.

For a half minute he watched her, nothing showing in his face, then: "I'll tell you when you burn."

"I hurt, Russell," she said.

"I'll tell you when you hurt," he said.

And she would go back onto the bench under the weighted bar for another set, for whatever was still required of her.

Well, at least after the contest Saturday night she would have a little layoff, whatever Russell gave her, from the gym. She would be able to take more carbohydrates, more calories, and as a little body fat came back, so would her periods, which, strangely, she missed.

She got off the bed where she had been lying, trying to block out the shouts and squeals of laughter coming from the hotel pool below her window, and went to stand naked in front of the mirror. She could not believe herself. She turned slightly and could not believe the smooth sliding of muscle against muscle cleaving tautly to her fine bones.

It was only when she was among other worldbeaters—like those down by the pool waiting this final day before contest just as she was—it was only then that she could believe herself. No other woman in the gym where she trained (Russell's Emporium of Pain), and no other woman in the city where she lived, could quite make her believe what she had done to herself.

It was only when she came together with the mysterious others, all of them coming from far cities, to stand nearly naked in front of a thundering audience—it was only then that she fully realized what it was to be special, special in her blood and flesh and sweat and most of all her pain.

A key scraped in the lock of the door. It was Russell Morgan, six feet three inches tall, two hundred and forty pounds, no longer competitive at the age of forty-five but the sight of him even now with a thirty-three-inch waist and a fifty-two-inch chest sometimes caused people to do unseemly things like run their cars off the road.

He was wearing a pair of swim trunks and he was absolutely

hairless. He used Nair on his body because the absence of hair made the cuts between his muscles show better.

His pointed calves were diamond shaped and the great lobes of his chest stood separate and distinct.

When he started to go bald at forty, he shaved his head and kept it shaved. All or nothing, that was Russell Morgan. He demanded of himself the same kind of discipline that he demanded of those he trained.

He stood in the doorway watching Shereel, naked before the mirror. He had a bathroom scale in his right hand.

"You look heavy," he said.

"Russell, I need a drink of water," she said.

He looked at his wristwatch. "In two hours, you can have four ounces of water or four ice cubes to suck on, whichever you prefer. I'm a reasonable man."

He closed the door behind him, walked to her, and set the scale on the floor.

"I'm so dry I can't even spit," she said.

"You don't need to spit, you need to dry out. Dry, dry, dry. Dehydrated. Coming in at a hundred and twenty-four, you'll win it all. And you *will* come in at a hundred and twenty-four." He paused. "Get on the scale."

"Aw, Russell," she said, but she got on the scale.

He bent to watch the needle swing. He was utterly still, staring at the scale. She saw the muscles tighten across his shoulders and the tendons stand in the back of his thick neck, and she knew.

In a flat, frightening voice, all the more scary because it was so soft, he said: "Suffering Mother of God, one twenty-five. Forty-eight hours to show time and you're a goddamn pound over."

"I can't make it, Russell."

"You'll make weight. I'm here to make you make it."

He walked over to the room air conditioner and turned off the fan. Then he turned the thermostat to high heat. When he came back to her, he slipped out of his swim trunks.

She looked down at him. "Good Lord, Russell."

He said, "The weight has got to go."

She was a little beside herself. This had never happened before. He'd seen her naked before. He *had* to see her naked, to check her gluts, her groin, her lower abdominals and how tightly they all tied in, the leanness, the symmetry, but never this. His own nakedness was new, and it brought something boiling to her heart that was a kind of terror.

"I could go to the sauna," she said. "I could swim laps."

"But then they'd see you, wouldn't they," he said. "I want'm to get loose in the bowels when you slip out of your robe to warm up backstage before the contest. Psych, little girl, psych."

Russell never let anyone see the woman he was entering from his gym until backstage just before show time. He himself had done it that way when he was competing and he did it now with those he trained. He thought it gave him an edge.

He stepped close to her and took her face in his hands, hands so huge they held her head like an orange.

The room was getting hotter and hotter and the squeals and shouts of laughter from the pool below their window grew with the heat. Or so it seemed to Shereel, her head caught in Russell's hands. He rocked it gently, tenderly.

Russell said, "Just think of it as another workout. A friend of mine, Duffy Deeter, told me that and I've come to believe it. Fucking is just another workout."

"Russell, I . . ."

He shook her, not roughly, but not tenderly either. "Don't talk. Listen. You've got to put your heart in this. Your *heart*. You've got to *work*. You want that water? You want a nice cool piece of ice to suck on? Here's where you earn it. Earn it here or you don't get it."

And so, there in the steaming Blue Flamingo Hotel room in the middle of Miami Beach, there started a bizarre dance, pointed toward four ounces of water, a twisting and bending and violent thrusting that made Shereel's head ring like a bell tower. Russell handled her as easily as if she had been a child, all the while exhorting her to "*Work*, goddammit, *work*!"

But try as she would, all she could think of was that her mamma and daddy, along with her two brothers and sister and former fiancé—maybe still her fiancé—were all driving down from south Georgia to watch the show this weekend. They had never seen her compete, didn't understand it, but they had seen pictures she had sent them of herself in other competitions and they were curious and they loved her.

Gradually though, the splashing of the pool turned into four ounces of cold water in her head and the tiny glass of water washed away the images of her family and of what she was doing here on the bed which Russell's severe thrusting and rooting had already broken. He was washed down in sweat when she went clearly and completely out of her head and her body showed the first faint moisture.

They broke most of the furniture in the room with Russell snorting and screaming like a madman. "You're a goddamn champion! Work! Get lean! Lean!"

Because her fluid intake had been so carefully monitored, she never would have thought she could have sweated as she was sweating, but when they finally ended on the floor among what was left of the splintered coffee table, she was wetter than Russell. And it had been he who had quit, gasping for air. He was bleeding from long thin scratches across his back and along his legs. Welts were rising in his heavily muscled shoulders, welts that would turn into ugly bruises later. But Shereel was totally unmarked, her fine skin as smooth and unblemished as ever. Because through all the twisting and jamming, hunching and thrusting, Russell had been very careful not to leave any sign of struggle on her. It would not do to mar the flesh he had brought here to win the world.

"Enough," he said in a hoarse, breathless whisper. "We're where we needed to go."

And they were. When she got on the scale she was a hundred and twenty-three pounds. Only when she saw the weight did it occur to her that during the entire time he had thrashed her—

turning her over and over, standing her on her head, on her feet, on her back, on her belly—it was only then that she realized that he had never kissed her. Not that she wanted him to. But she had never been fucked and not kissed. (Her brother, to bedevil her: "Know why you don't kiss a cow when you fuck it? Too far to walk. Har, har, har.")

Russell said, "You can have five ounces of water."

She turned on him, her face tight, her teeth bared. "I only want *two* goddamn ounces! And leave the heat on."

"All *right*," shouted Russell. "You've finally got your game face on."

It was then that he kissed her, a long kiss which he did not notice she permitted but did not return.

T W O

They were sitting in lounge chairs by the pool, Russell in nothing but his trunks, Shereel in a terry-cloth robe that covered her entirely. Only her tiny golden feet were exposed. A straw sun hat shadowed her face, itself half-covered by aviator sunglasses.

All about them, in the pool, in chaise longues, were enormously muscled men, their bodies veined and hairless—and women without body fat, their skin diaphanous, their movements languid and deliberate, abdominal walls ridged with rows of muscle so sharply defined as to seem unreal, the mad imaginings of a mad artist.

Everybody seemed perfect of his kind, teeth incredibly white, hair thick and wildly beautiful, eyes clear and shining with a kind of mindless confidence, as though the world would never die, could never die. Age and death seemed defeated here. They all conspicuously ignored one another as they moved in the contained monuments they had made of themselves. Their skins circumscribed their worlds, worlds they inhabited with obvious joy, contentment, and pride.

Without turning her head, Shereel said, "What about the room?"

"What about it?" said Russell.

"You wrecked it. Everything is smashed," she said.

"Fuck the room. We've got a contest to win. I'll take care of it when the time comes." He paused and squinted up at the sun. "I admire your discipline with the water."

She did not answer.

"I've always admired you," he said.

She looked at him curiously. He had never said that before, and he could see on her face what she was thinking.

"You always knew it," he said.

"It's hard to know somebody admires you when they're screaming at you," she said.

"The screaming was necessary. It was all necessary," he said.

She affected a yawn and pulled her hat lower.

"Just keep your game face," he said. "We've come this far."

"Yeah," she said. "We've come this far."

He turned in his chair and took her shoulder. "Keep reminding yourself of what this is. The top of the world. The best is here. Beat'm and there's nobody left to beat. So many endorsements will come, you'll have to hire somebody to count'm. The gym will grow like a flower. Franchises. Money." He regarded his thick, perfectly shaped hands. "I'll take care of you."

"Don't let it get too thick, Russell."

"Only the truth," he said.

She was about to answer when a black man, who must have been two hundred and sixty pounds and was taller than Russell, walked up. He was wearing a T-shirt over his swimsuit. Across the front of his shirt was the legend:

BLACK MAGIC GYMNASIUM

DETROIT, MICHIGAN

HOME OF MARVELLA WASHINGTON, CHAMPION

Shereel knew who he was. He had been a famous and fierce competitor in his day.

"What's happening, Russell?" He showed a mouthful of perfect teeth.

"I thought you'd tell me, Wall."

Shereel had seen copies of old strength magazines when he had been blowing everybody off the stage. Wallace the Wall he'd been called. "Just called Wallace now. The wall's gone."

Russell smiled. "Yeah, I can see."

"Watch your mouth, white boy," Wallace said. But it was said in a good-natured, bantering voice.

"You're not going to start niggering me, are you, Wall?"

"I didn't come all the way from Detroit to nigger you, Russell Muscle."

"You know I don't like to be called that," said Russell.

"I know," Wallace said.

"So tell me anyway," said Russell. "What *are* you doing here?"

"Didn't you hear, man? The Ms. and Mr. Cosmos is being held here." He paused and looked long across the pool where a young black girl, a single shining muscle of a girl, and a white ropey boy were going through their posing routines in tandem. "Fuck the Mr. Cosmos," he said, "I brought the Ms. Cosmos. Hell, I ain't greedy. Ms. Cosmos is enough, and I brought her all the way from Dee-troit City."

"Sure you did, Wall," said Russell, confidently. He *was* confident. "Sure you did."

Wallace rolled his eyes and sighed. Then he turned to Shereel. "It's good to see you, Miss Dupont—even if I can't *see* you."

"It's good to see you, Wallace," she said from under her hat.

Russell said, "Her tan's peaked. *She's* peaked. Class of the field."

Wallace ignored him. "You looked awful good in Los Angeles."

"Good enough to win," said Russell.

Wallace looked at him now. "You bring anybody for the men's division?"

"We're here for one championship, same as you. Ms. Cosmos. Shereel's wanted it bad enough. Nothing here can touch her. If I was you I'd save myself some expenses and pack up and go back home now."

"It's always a pleasure talking to a gentleman, Russell Muscle." He turned to go but stopped long enough to say, "Ah,

Miss Dupont, Marvella is looking for you. And I wouldn't doubt before it's over she finds you. You might check over your shoulder now and then."

When he was gone, Russell said, "Asshole."

"He's not a bad guy," said Shereel.

Russell glowered and growled and rattled in his throat. "Everybody here's an asshole. Babykillers! Fatherfucking fags and faglets! Don't you goddamn forget it!" Then hissing: "It's those scumbags against us. I want to see some hate cook in you. Hate, goddammit."

"Russell," said Shereel calmly, "you're a madman."

"I'll show you what madness is before this is over," he said. "I'll show you crazy."

An announcement came over the public address system above the pool. "Will Miss Dorothy Turnipseed please pick up the house phone for a message at the desk?"

Shereel's head jerked upward.

Russell said, "Don't move. Don't move an inch."

"That'll be my family," she said. "It couldn't be anybody else."

"Don't they know your goddamn name's not Turnipseed anymore? Don't they know you're Shereel Dupont?"

"They know that's my stage name."

"Your stage name." It was a statement.

"That was what was stamped on the contest photos I sent them. I had to tell'm something. They wouldn't understand anything like *changing* my name."

Russell had forgotten all about her family coming to the competition. "Jesus Christ," he said, "if this gets out it could lose it for us. Nobody named Dorothy Turnipseed could ever be Ms. Cosmos."

The voice on the PA system asked if Miss Turnipseed was in the hotel.

"You stay put," said Russell. "I'll pick up the phone and handle this."

He got out of his chair and strode toward the phone at the side of the pool. Shereel watched him go and the thought occurred to her that if her name wasn't Turnipseed, she probably wouldn't be sitting here beside the Blue Flamingo Hotel pool now.

She had walked into Morgan's Emporium of Pain, answering an advertisement for a secretary for general office duty in a strength gymnasium. She did not even know what a strength gymnasium was, but she had taken the eight-week secretarial course at the school for WOMEN WITH BUSINESS ASPIRATIONS in Waycross, Georgia. She was there for almost a week before she found out what the word "aspirations" meant, but she did find out finally and she did graduate. And as soon as she graduated she left home for Jacksonville, Florida, to look for work. She didn't exactly know why she left, but she had known since she was a little girl that she didn't want to live out her life in Waycross. She knew she didn't want to be just another Turnipseed in south Georgia.

So one day she walked into the gym and handed Russell her one-page résumé (they had spent a good bit of time on a unit of study called THE RÉSUMÉ at WWBA, as the school was called by almost everybody, and Shereel was proud of the one she had managed to produce).

Russell had been distracted, training as he was a short man doing squats under a bar weighted so heavily that it bent slightly each time he went down. The snorts and groans from the squatter frightened Shereel but she was almost out of money and she needed work badly.

Russell glowered at the résumé when she handed it to him and then screamed at the short squatter: "Get up! Push, you goddamn wimp!"

Then without looking at her he said, "I think I already found the girl I want. Goodbye."

"But you haven't even looked at the résumé," she said.

Russell screamed at the squatter and then glanced at the paper in his hand. He was about to scream again but didn't. He looked hard at the résumé.

"Dorothy *Turnipseed*?" he said.

"Yes." She was looking past Russell at the short man stuck
at the bottom of his squat. His eyes bulged. Tendons stood out
in his neck. She thought he might die down there caught under
the weight.

"Your real name?" he said.

"There are many Turnipseeds in Georgia," she said.

The squatter let the weight drop behind him and then he
himself collapsed onto his back. He did not move where he lay
but Russell did not seem to notice.

He regarded her for a moment. "Can you count?"

The question angered her but she needed work. "Yes."

"Do you know the ABCs?"

"You want me to say'm?"

"I want you to answer my questions, do what I say, and
otherwise keep your mouth shut. I'm the only one allowed to
be funny in here—and I'm never funny."

Then for reasons he never revealed, he hired her on the spot.
When she walked away the short man was still lying faceup.
He might have been dead except that his right foot twitched at
irregular intervals.

But the next day when she came to work, the same man was
straining under the same enormous weight, and Russell was still
screaming at him.

She went to work in the tiny, nearly airless office and she did
her job well, answering the phone, responding to Russell's
mail—most of it asking if he would come and give a seminar at
some gymnasium, or if he would consider being a guest poser
at some competition halfway across the country. And she
straightened out his chaotic filing system, keeping track of the
membership, who was behind in dues or who had canceled.

Russell hardly spoke to her that first week. She was fascinated
by the women in the gym—sleek and beautiful—sweating and
grunting right along with the men. But she never once considered working out herself until Russell walked into the office and
did not so much ask as demand that she bring a leotard the next
day for a workout. Since she wanted to keep her job, she ap-

peared in the leotard the next day, a brief, powder blue, skintight thing that made her feel naked when she stepped out of the women's dressing room. Russell came to stand in front of her and she did not know what to say or do as he examined her. That's the way she thought of it, an examination. He took her by the shoulder and turned her. He felt the alignment of her spine, he stared hard and long at her legs, her arms, the way her pelvis tilted. It took only two or three minutes, but felt like an hour, and she blushed the entire time although that seemed to be the only thing about her that Russell did not notice.

"Just as I thought," he said. "I knew it when I saw you. You've got great bones."

"*Bones?*" she said.

"Bones."

Back home she'd had boys make remarks about her ass or her hips or her breasts, but this was the first time anybody had ever mentioned her *bones*.

"You fell into a great gene pool," he said.

She didn't have the faintest notion of what he was talking about. Gene pools had not been covered at the secretarial school in Waycross.

"You can do anything with *anything* in a weight gymnasium. Except bones. Bone configuration is something that can't be touched. You've either got bones or you don't. You've got'm. Bones like yours come along every decade or so. Do you want to be a worldbeater, a champion?"

"A champion what?"

He snorted. "Stop with the goddamn questions. I'll get another girl for the office. Tomorrow you start training. You're going to live, eat, sleep, and dream of being the best. Everything in the fucking world is wrong with you but that incredible bone structure. But I'll fix the rest of it. I'll fix everything."

And he had. He'd made her somebody, made her hear thundering applause and shouts of approval, even love. He'd given her a cause in the world, a cause such as she had not known existed for anybody. And for that, she had done everything he had asked of her. And she was glad to do it, even to having her name changed. Actually he had named her Sheree Dupont, but in her first contest (which she won) the first name had been misspelled in the program and she had been Shereel ever since.

Russell came storming back along the edge of the pool toward her, his face flushed and a vein forking out above his nose and across his forehead, a vein nearly as big as a pencil. He dropped onto the chaise longue beside her. From the way he was breathing, he could have just finished a two-mile run.

For some reason, it pleased Shereel. She said, "I thought you'd gone to shit and the hogs had eat you."

"That Georgia humor wears thin quick," he said.

"What the hell ails you?"

"There's a whole goddamn army of Turnipseeds at the registration desk."

"What did they say?"

"I only talked to one of them. Some grump son of a bitch that wouldn't listen to anything. I told him for them to register and go on up to their rooms. He didn't say who was with him but it sounded like he'd brought half the county. There was a monkey zoo of Grit voices babbling down there."

"Where did you say I was?"

"Out."

"Out?"

"Right."

"What did he say?"

"He told me to go to hell. He said that you may be out but that by God he was in. He said he hadn't come all the way to Florida to sit in a goddamn hotel room."

"That was Daddy."

"I can understand a lot more now. You know what the old bastard said they were going to do?"

"Don't call Daddy a bastard, Russell."

"All the Turnipseeds are coming down here to the pool. He said they all meant to go in a bathing. It took a while for me to find out what he meant. *In a bathing*—that's not even English."

"It is in Waycross, Georgia."

"We're not in Waycross, Georgia."

"We'll see. But I wouldn't talk too sharp to Daddy. He's killed two men aready."

Russell groaned and said, "This whole goddamn contest may be down the drain. Come on, let's get the hell out of here before they show up right here in front of everybody."

He took her hand and pulled her off the chaise longue.

Alphonse—called Fonse by everybody but his wife—
Turnipseed, dressed in a J. C. Penney suit that was green and
too tight, stood directly behind his son Motor, who had both
his elbows on the registration desk, one on either side of the
form he was filling out. From time to time, he briefly touched
the point of the ballpoint pen to the tip of his tongue as he
wrote.

Motor was wearing a suit identical to his father's—green and
tight, dangerously binding at the crotch, and too short in the
leg. Just before they had left to come south, the J. C. Penney's
back in Waycross had had a STAYING IN BUSINESS SALE with many
fine bargains. But the one that caught their eye was MEN'S SUITS
$99—ANY TWO SUITS FOR $110.95.

Standing on the sidewalk in front of the store, their huge red
hands alternately hustling their balls and mining wax out of
their ears with kitchen matches, Motor had said, "Hell, Daddy,
one of us is fixing to git a suit of clothes for ten dollars and
ninety-five cent."

Alphonse had regarded Motor for a long slow time, sending
stringy globs of tobacco spit into the street as he did, his eyes
inward-looking and abstracted before he finally said, "Eleven
dollars and niney-five cent." And then as he walked into the
store, over his shoulder: "Plus tax."

"You 'bout got her done, Motor?" This was Turner, Alphonse's younger son, who had been given his mother's maiden
name.

Motor, touching the pen to the tip of his tongue again, said,

"Yeah, I 'bout got her, but these little squares you got to write in ain't as big as they might be."

"They gone take our money, Motor. I don't know as I'd bother much with what I wrote down," said Harry Barnes, called Nail Head or usually just Nail or sometimes Head, who was Dorothy's fiancé and a much decorated veteran of the Vietnam War and who did not look just right out of his eyes although he had before he had gone to Vietnam.

Nail did not have much patience and he was wearing the same brown suit Turner had on, bought from the same J. C. Penney sale. It had been Alphonse's wife, Earnestine's idea to match the clothes they were wearing. She and her daughter, Earline, were wearing J. C. Penney's MARKED DOWN DRESS UPS—red imitation silk skirts and blouses with enormous pleated bows in back. They had spent a week rebuilding the garments to accommodate their girth, being as they were what Earnestine always referred to as "Naturally stout women."

Earnestine maintained it was a good idea to wear sets of matched clothing so they couldn't get lost off from each other in the crazy crowds of Miami.

"I heard all about the crowds," she said. "A tourist is crazy enough to eat its young."

She stood with her daughter now, sharing a bag of pork skins, both of them patiently chewing and shifting from foot to foot, causing the shiny red bows to undulate over their massive hips.

Motor looked up, ran his ink-stained tongue over his lips, and slapped the pen down on the marble-topped desk. "That's it. She's done."

Behind the counter, the slender young man, clipped, combed, and coiffured, slowly turned the card with his long tanned fingers, the nails of which were buffed to a high gloss, and dropped his startled eyes to examine it. His eyes had been wide since these people had appeared before him to register. He could not quite believe them, and he had made a great effort not to stare in an unseemly way. It was the precise reaction he had had to the Mr. and Ms. Cosmos competitors when they started arriving two days earlier. He couldn't believe them either, but he had found he did not have to worry about staring at them in an unseemly way. They liked it, unseemly staring, even loved it. It seemed to be the point of their lives.

"And how will you be paying for this, sir?" asked the clerk, whose name was Julian Lipschitz.

"How's 'at?" said Alphonse.

"Wants to know how you gone pay for it," screamed Turner into his father's good ear, the left one. The good ear was only half deaf.

Alphonse took off his black felt hat—all four men were wearing black felt hats—and turned it slowly in his hands as though examining it for an answer. He took out a package of unfiltered Camels and lit one with a kitchen match, using the thick yellow nail of his thumb to pop it into fire. He let the cigarette dangle from his lips, his flat gray eyes squinting through the smoke.

Julian made a point of waving his hand through the smoke. He hated people who used tobacco. He, himself, practically lived on natural yogurt and jogging. Jogging and natural yogurt made him feel spiritual. For that reason if no other he felt an immediate oneness with the bodybuilders. He had also taken a course in philosophy at Miami–Dade Junior College, while studying hotel management. And so that was the phrase in which he thought of it: *immediate oneness*. But these horrible people in their horrible clothes!

Waving at twin pillars of smoke issuing from Alphonse's nostrils, Julian said, "If you could . . ."

"Wait," said Nail.

"What?" Julian blinked, trying to see through the smoke which of the men had spoken. It was the one who did not look right out of his eyes.

Nail said, "I said *wait*. Fonse is thinking."

"Sir, I do need to—"

"What you need to do is to shut the fuck up," Nail said. "Fonse don't like to be asked too many questions."

Alphonse put his hat back on his head, squaring it carefully and with great deliberation. Then he said so quietly that Julian unconsciously leaned toward him, "I thought to use money."

"He thought to use money," said Motor as though using money had never occurred to him before.

"That will be fine, sir," said Julian, thinking, My God, these people not only dress like barbarians, and act like barbarians, they *are* barbarians, dangerous, violent barbarians. "Yes, fine. I'll just need some identification."

"Identification?" said Earline, stopping with a pork rind poised at her mouth.

"Anything will do," Julian said, "driver's license, credit card, just about anything."

Earline shouldered past her brother and deposited her enormous breasts on the desk to confront Julian. "This," she said, popping the pork rind into her mouth, "is the United States of America. You thinking of summers else. You don't need papers to travel in the United States of America."

Earline knew her rights. She had herself graduated from the Waycross Junior College. When she left with her two-year degree in Problems of Living, she made up her mind never to take any guff from ignorant people again.

Julian had a response for just such a statement and had been waiting for—hoping for, really—the chance to use it. It had been thought up by Dexter Friedkin, the hotel manager, a job to which Julian aspired. It was designed to get rid of just such guests as these.

Julian pointed toward the glass doors of the lobby, beyond which were a beautifully manicured dying hedge and two tall palms that died on a regular basis every two months and had to be replaced.

"That," said Julian, "that out there is the United States of America. In here is the Blue Flamingo Hotel. And we require identification."

Fonse had cupped his left ear with his hand and listened to this, looking first at his daughter and then at Julian. Never taking the Camel cigarette from his lips, pillars of smoke still pouring from his nostrils, he cut his pale gray eyes toward Nail and made the slightest nod of his head.

"Yessir," said Nail to Alphonse. He reached out and gently moved Motor out of the way so he could put his own elbows on the desk and fix Julian with a look unlike any look Julian had ever seen before. For the longest time he only looked and then slowly and deliberately he took off his own felt hat and examined it carefully. He was still looking at the hat when he spoke, his voice very quiet and even and deadly. "I volunteered to fight for this goddamn country in a time of war. Got a bad foot to this day from stepping on a stick dipped in Veet Nam shit. Now you think you want some of me, son, but you really don't. Neither you or you old mama neither one wants none of me." He carefully put his hat back on his head and raised his eyes to Julian, who had quietly closed his when Nail got to the part about stepping on a stick dipped in Veet Nam shit. "Now you shove them goddamn room keys across to me or I'm gone come over the desk, and take you by the ears and bite you nose off."

Without ever opening his eyes, Julian's long-fingered hand—gone pale now under the tan—pushed two keys across the desk, and with the same hand slapped the nipple of a little bell and called in a voice like the call for help from a drowning man: "Front."

A young Cuban with a velvet-covered dolly appeared as if by magic. He looked at Nail Head, who seemed to be in charge. "May I take your bags, sir?"

"Won't be necessary, son. Totem ourself," Nail said, looking at the keys in his hand. "Whereabouts is 1520 and 1521?"

"The elevator is just there to the left across the lobby, sir."

Nail watched the young Cuban, who was smiling for all he was worth, and then turned to look at Turner.

"Place strike you as strange, Turner?"

"Hell," said Turner, "driving in ever tree I seen had a light in it and a stick propping it up. Strange is just something I think we gone have to get used to hereabouts."

Fonse, his good ear still cupped, nothing moving but his

eyes, listened to all this, the ashes from the Camel that never
left his lips falling to the carpet, where his son Motor thoughtfully stepped on them with his steel-toed boot. The Cuban
bellhop watched him grind the ashes into the carpet and never
stopped smiling. His job did not include taking care of the
carpet. And from staying alive for twenty-two years on the
streets of Little Havana in Miami, his blood had already told
him that these were people he needed to get away from and
stay away from.

Fonse nodded at the Cuban and said, "He ain't our kind of
people is he?"

"No sir," said Motor, "I don't believe he is."

Nail said, "Cain't say as he hears real good neither. Any of
you all hear me ask him where the goddamn elevator was?"

Earnestine pushed forward and took the keys from Nail
Head's hand and looked at them, then said to the bellhop,
"Honey, don't you worry about a thing. These are all my
men—nasty at times to them they don't know real good, and
all of'm sometimes mean as snakes—but they mine everone.
And I'm gone see they behave." She held up the keys and
spoke too slowly, too loudly, as though speaking to an idiot,
which she thought she was. "How do you get to where we
stayin' at?"

The bellhop somehow spoke without altering his smile. "The
fifteenth floor. Take the elevator if you wish." He waved vaguely
in the direction of the elevator. "When you get off on fifteen,
turn right."

She smiled at her men, who were still watching the Cuban.
"Like I told everone of you, you can ketch more flies with honey
than you can with vinegar."

"Ain't none of us wantin' to catch flies, Ma," said Motor.
"What we wantin' is a place to set down."

"Sugar dumplin', you just tired," she said. "That was a right
long ride and some tight in the cab of that truck."

They had made the trip from Waycross to Miami in two pick-
ups, Nail's and Fonse's, both Chevys.

FOUR

"What are we going to do with them?" said Russell.

"What do you mean, what are we going to do with them?" Shereel said.

"What the fuck did I say?"

"And what the fuck did I say?"

Russell took two deep breaths and glanced toward the window and composed what he hoped was a reasonable face before answering.

"All right, I'm going to allow that. The hate's cooking in you. You're beginning to grind your teeth and hope for somebody's death. That's game blood, game thinking, game *face*." He took another deep breath. "But try to remember who you're talking to. This is Russell Morgan. Your trainer. Your life."

They were back in Shereel's room amongst the broken, ruined furniture. The air conditioning had been turned back on. Russell sat on the dresser, the only thing still in one piece. Shereel, still wearing her terry-cloth robe and sunglasses, was lying flat on her back on the carpet, thinking of water. She thought it was time for another four ounces. She *knew* it was time for another four ounces. But she told herself she'd die in hell with her back broke before she'd ask for it, although her tongue felt thick and covered with fur.

"You're not my life, Russell."

What he wanted to do was slap the shit out of her. She wasn't thinking straight, and slapping the shit out of her could only help, but it wouldn't do to mark her with a bruise.

"I'll let that pass, too. But I do wish you'd say something about how we're going to handle your family. You're not going to let them ruin this for the contest."

"Nothing's going to ruin the contest. I've suffered like Christ on the cross for this competition and I mean to take it . . ." She tried to moisten her lips but her tongue passed over them dry and rough. "My family never messes with anybody don't mess with them first. Specially Nail."

"Nail?"

"Harry is actually his name but nobody calls him that but his blood kin. Everybody else calls him Nail Head or just Nail."

"Nail? Nail, for Christ's sake? I thought your brothers' names were Turner and Motor. Motor's bad enough but you didn't say anything about one named Nail Head."

"Nail's not my brother. He's . . . I've known him a long time."

"And?"

"We were close."

"How close?"

"Russell, let's concentrate on the contest, okay?"

"I am concentrating on it. How close?"

"Well, I guess we were engaged."

"Why didn't you tell me before?"

"You never asked."

Russell raised his arms and looked at the ceiling and said, "God, why are you doing this to me?" Then to Shereel, "You can't *guess* you're engaged. You either are or you aren't."

"Nothing is either one way or the other with Nail. I haven't even talked to him in a while. He won't talk on the telephone and he won't write letters. And he won't read letters written to him. Nail's, well, Nail's different."

"Different?"

"And dangerous."

"Sweet baby Jesus, can this get any worse?"

"Probably. Nail likes to beat the shit out of people. He says he finds it relaxing. Releases his stress, he says."

"Shereel, you've allowed a certifiable lunatic to come fuck up your chances of winning the world."

"You don't *allow* Nail to do anything. He goes where he wants to. Runs on his own time. But he's really a nice guy, a sweet guy."

"Who likes to beat the shit out of people."

"You don't understand," she said.

"You may be on to something there," he said.

"He doesn't do it willy-nilly, just any old way, beat up just anybody."

"Well, why didn't you say so. That just makes everything fine."

"No, he likes to find people that need the shit beaten out of them. Actually, he tries to find three or four at one time, you know, in a group, a whole group of assholes. He says beating the shit out of three or four at one time helps relieve his stress better. You've got to understand he's about as nice a guy as you'd want to meet. Unless you happen to be an asshole."

"Comforting," Russell said. "That sets my heart right at ease."

"But he wasn't always like that until he went to Vietnam. He had a very bad job over there and it made him fond of strangling people."

"Strangling . . . Shereel, I think I've heard all of this I want to."

"Maybe. But you haven't heard all you *need* to. You need to know all of this. He is, after all, *here*. And it's better to know. In Vietnam he was in something called the rat patrol. What they did was go down into the tunnels looking for, as Nail calls them, those little slant-eyed fuckers. They had tunnels dug all over the country and Nail went down in them to shoot'm or kill'm with his knife. But once he strangled the first one, he got to like it—that's what he says, says it's something about strangling a man that's, well, satisfying—so anyhow he got to like it and never got over it."

"I was right to start with, I didn't need to know the rest of this and I sure as hell don't understand."

"Nail says his dream is to find three or four assholes down in a tunnel and strangle them all. Says he thinks he might get over his stress forever and just be his regular sweet self again if he could find four assholes in a tunnel right here in the U. S. of A. But I don't think we have to worry about a thing because there are no tunnels here at the Cosmos or anywhere close by, I wouldn't imagine."

Russell had moved to stand by the window looking down on the pool. His back was to Shereel and she saw every muscle in it, from his hamstrings to his neck, suddenly leap and lock as though a massive spasm had struck him. "It's them. My God, they've appeared. And where could they have possibly found what they're wearing?"

Shereel came to the window and looked down. They were all dressed in electric blue, another of Earnestine's solutions to getting lost off from one another amongst the savage tourists she had read so much about. Earline and her mother were wearing one-pieces with a modest little skirt sewn around the bottom and the men had on boxer-type swimsuits, the eye-blinding blue of which only served to emphasize their skins, which were whiter than any skins Russell had ever seen—lighter than milk—except for their sunburned wrists and hands and necks and the lower part of their faces, since they lived in hats that covered their foreheads. Alphonse was still living in his. Of the four men he was the only one still wearing his black felt hat.

"What the hell's he wearing that ridiculous hat for?"

"Daddy keeps his hat on the bedpost. It's the first thing he puts on in the morning and the last thing he takes off at night."

"Quaint," said Russell.

"None of us are perfect," she said. "And if I was you I wouldn't mention I thought it was ridiculous. Daddy's funny about that hat. Had it a long time and he's funny about it."

"Those women," said Russell, "could use the Morgan Dachau treatment for weight reduction."

"That's my mama and sister you're talking about, Russell. They're just naturally stout, fine, healthy women."

"One, they're not healthy, and two, what they are is fat."

"I'd keep that to myself, too, if I was you. Saying something like that about the women of the family is what Nail calls being an asshole."

"I guess he's the one with the tattoos."

"That's Nail, all right."

"Illustrated like a goddamn comic book."

"Saying something like that would qualify as being an asshole, too. I shiver to think of Nail hearing such a thing."

"This whole thing makes me shiver," Russell said. "Why does your daddy keep looking up like that?"

"If I had to guess, I'd say he was checking the time."

"Checking the time?"

"By the sun. Daddy doesn't wear a watch. Doesn't need one. He can get the time, give or take a minute, by checking the sun."

But she was wrong; Alphonse was trying to make out the window of the room he lived in. But he was having trouble discovering which was the fifteenth floor. He kept losing track. He was not a good counter, and besides his eyes were going bad on him and he refused to wear glasses. But he thought he'd found it.

"I believe it'as that'n four from the corner yonder." The others were looking up with him. "Yeah," he said, "I make it to be the one four from the corner."

"May be, Daddy," said Motor.

"Hell of a thing living on the fifteenth floor of a hotel, the fifteenth floor of *anything*. It ain't many white men and no niggers at all that'd want to live that high in the air. Ain't natural."

They continued to look up at the window they thought was theirs.

"Hell," Nail said, "one time on R and R to Tokyo I lived on the thirtieth floor of one such as this. Thirty floors up. Course I don't remember a hell of a lot about it. I stayed on the outside of a quart of Jack Daniels ever day the whole time I was there. It was a rule you had to stay drunk the whole time on R and R. Don't know who made it up. But all of us—I mean *everbody*— stuck right to that rule.'' He laughed and at the same time reached down and hustled his balls, an adjustment he and the other men made every few minutes. ''The only fun I ever had over there was drinking that Jack Daniels and strangling them little slopes that all looked like they come out of the same mama.''

''Now, son, you don't start that talking about drinking. You know how you get.''

''Best I remember,'' said Nail, ''I get major league drunk.''

They were all very large men—better than six-three—with substantial bellies, except for Alphonse, who was about the size of a retired jockey who might have been a bit consumptive. But their bellies were hard whiskey bellies and their arms and legs were roped with heavy, ill-defined muscle. But the one who stood out among them was not Nail, whose skin was filled with sinking ships and bloody-taloned jaguars and many bold, multicolored legends that said things like DEATH BEFORE DISHONOR and IF YOU LOVE SOMETHING/ TURN IT LOOSE/ IF IT LOVES YOU/ IT WILL COME BACK/ IF IT DOESN'T COME BACK/ HUNT IT DOWN AND KILL IT, and a perforated line in the shape of a heart in the center of his chest, with the line above it reading CUT HERE and the line under it reading IF YOU CAN, and many other wondrous designs including Mount Everest with the Marine Corps emblem balanced atop it.

But it was not Nail, despite his elaborate coloration, that caused people to stare, it was Motor, who was entirely covered with not very light, not very fine hair. When he shaved every morning, he started at his collarbones, and the hair that tufted out of his shirt at the back of his neck made him look like he was wearing the tail of a fox. His mother, Earnestine, was convinced he was marked with hair because when she was carrying him she dreamed more than once that she was going to give birth to a hairball, which while she had never seen it done, she'd heard of just such a thing happening many times in the county.

By the time Motor was twelve years old he was pretty much as hairy as he was ever going to get, and many times—totally against her will and causing her much pain—she would look at him when he was working about the farm without a shirt and the thought would come, completely formed and completely irresistible: It walks and talks and bleeds like a boy but if it ain't a hairball, it'll do until one comes along. Therefore, because of the thought she could not resist, she showed him more love, care, and concern than Turner or Earline or, for that matter, even Alphonse. Motor was her favorite, hair and all. She had told him so relentlessly how beautiful the hair was that even Motor loved his hair, all of it, even that on his feet. The only thing was, his mother could not stand to touch him. He reminded her of a dog. But, good mother that she was, she kept it her secret, and her secret alone.

When they finally lowered their eyes from the fifteenth floor, they found that all movement in and around the pool had stopped. Every man and woman was staring at them. Alphonse and his family returned the stare.

Finally Motor said, "What you reckon ails them?"

Alphonse took off his hat and studied it. When he did take off his hat there was a fresh package of Camel cigarettes resting on top of his head, along with several kitchen matches stuck in the cellophane of the package. He opened the package, fired up one of the kitchen matches with a thumbnail, put the package back on the top of his head, and covered it with his hat. Immediately and regularly as a clock ticking, streams of smoke issued from his nostrils. The cigarette hung at the corner of his mouth and jerked slightly every time he breathed.

"I don't think," said Alphonse, "they our kind of people and it looks to me like they might've come down with something bad."

"Well, it is two blue-gummed pulpwood niggers over there," said Nail, "and a prime nigger wench, but the rest of'm seem white to me even if they are a tad deformed. But you cain't tell, foreigners'll fool you at times. Won't know till we speak to one of'm. But even then it's foreigners I've heard that talk just like normal people."

Turner said, "Don't know as I'd want to get close enough to speak. Like Daddy says, ever last one of'm looks to be come down with something, and whatever it is, they all got it. Might be catching for all I know. Way things are this day and time whatever they got might make you dick commence to fall off."

"Turner," said Earnestine, "you a grown man but that don't mean you can talk any old way—specially here in front of me and you sister. You want me to take a stick to you? Is that what you want?"

"No ma'am," he said. "Forgot myself."

"All right then," his mama said. "You know I won't have talk such as that."

"They all some knotty, ain't they," said Turner. "What do you think made them grow them knots. Look at that one feller yonder. Looks like sompin' big as a grapefruit growing right where the calves of his legs ought to be."

"I known this'd happen when we left home to come off here amongst strangers."

"We come to see Dorothy, Ma," said Earline.

"Well, we ain't see her, have we?" said Earnestine, anger and frustration edging her voice.

"She'll turn up. She ain't forgot us. She's just gitting ready to do whatever it is she's gone do."

Nail turned and spoke into Alphonse's good ear. "I wouldn't mind coming down with that nigger wench. With the size of her, she's got the look of one that might could make my ears pop off."

Alphonse said, "What you reckon happened to her ass and titties?"

"I expect it's all under there somewhere. A man'd just have to search her good. And I don't misdoubt I'll do it before it's all over."

"I know the feeling, son. But try to keep a lid on you pot and behave yourself. Dorothy's here sommers."

Just then an enormous, hairless, veined man diagonally across the pool from them dropped to one knee, placed his fists on his hips, and went into a lat spread pose. Slowly, great thick wings of muscle emerged from his hips to his armpits, and kept on emerging until it looked as though his upper body would explode. His eyes seemed glazed, distant, focused on something only he could see. First veins rose and stood in his forehead, then his neck, and finally in his shoulders and arms, the veins working like worms suddenly come alive. He did not appear to be breathing. The others turned from Alphonse and his family to watch him. They stood stock still, the breath seeming to have gone out of them, too.

Earnestine looked at the swelling man with some alarm. "I believe that one's having a fit."

Earline pulled at her swimming suit, the bottom of which the cheeks of her ass were vigorously chewing, and said, "You reckon we ought to get help? Or do something? If worst comes to worst, I been trained in CPR."

Nail said, "I been trained not to give a shit."

"What do you reckon he's doing?" Alphonse said.

"I know what he's doing. He's having a fit is what he's doing. I seen it in movies when I was getting my degree in Problems of Living."

"He don't start breathing pretty soon," Turner said, "it's gone turn into a problem of dying real shortly now."

"I was thinking the same thing myself," said Earline, "and I was not trained to stand by and watch somebody die. They don't call what I studied at the junior college Problems of Living for nothing."

"This is not going to work," said Russell, standing with She-reel at the window looking down on the pool.

"What's not going to work? Russell?"

He pointed down at the pool. "That."

"I suppose that's something else nasty you're saying about my family."

"Your family's fine, Shereel. In Waycross, Georgia. Not here. Them here at the Cosmos with you in a dogfight to win the world is a mistake. I can smell disaster. I can smell disaster coming off them from all the way up here."

"You worry too much, Russell. They're my family and I know how they are. They're no trouble at all unless trouble comes looking for them. Everybody here is so eat up with the desire to win that they won't even notice Pa and them."

"But Pa and them, as you call them, will sure as hell notice the competitors, get in their way, generally fuck with them. And I know and you know that every last man and woman here is running on a very tight wire. Starved down and trained to the point of death, they're nothing but nerves and muscle. Every fuse down there by that pool is so short that you can't even get a match up to it before the bomb goes off. I wish there was something we could do, something we could think of."

They had been looking down on the pool while they talked. Shereel said, "If it comes to that, I'll...Jesus, would you look at that?"

Russell knew immediately who she meant, the guy down on one knee doing a lat spread.

"Look at that fucking back," she said.

"You've seen it before, Shereel."

"I know I've seen it before. But the mass, the symmetry, the cuts. I could see it every day for a year and never get over it. It's impossible to believe a back that big with that kind of definition. Has anybody ever had that thickness and also been cut up like that?"

"Not that I know of. Better bodies through better chemistry. He's pumped so full of anabolic steroids he may actually live to be thirty years old."

"How long is he going to hold that pose? I can see him starting to tremble from here with the tension."

"He'll hold it until he's intimidated everybody out there. It's one way to do it. His way. Been doing that as long as he's been competing. I don't approve the method or the approach, and I

also don't give a rat's ass. I always thought you ought to wait
and let'm see what you're holding when it counts. And the only
time it counts is in front of the judges."

"Can he win?"

"Oh, sure, that back will win his class, but he won't win the
overall. He'll never be Mr. Cosmos. He's holding no calves at
all and you can't win without calves. Only thing that ever kept
Wall from winning the Cosmos, no calves. A nigger can be
incredible from the knee to the hip, but there's never been more
than three or four in the history of the sport that could develop
calves."

"Why do you suppose that is?"

Russell turned his mean smile on Shereel. "God's little joke
on the nigger."

"Wall's your friend, Russell, you shouldn't use that word."

"Wall is not my friend, and he wouldn't give a shit one way
or the other anyway. Besides friendship is for another place.
Don't even think the word. You don't have any friends here."
He glanced at the pool again. "Not even me."

"Not even you, Russell?"

"I'm here to see you win. To *make* you win. Desire and guts
is the name of this game. And it'll make everything a hell of a
lot better if you'll remember it. War, Champ, fucking *war*."

Earline adjusted the suit that was binding her badly about the
buttocks and said, "I cain't stand to watch this."

Their attention was focused on the bodybuilder holding the
lat pose; the veins, starting to appear now in the abdominal
wall, were as big as pencils. Everybody else at poolside was
watching him too, a few of them shifting nervously from foot
to foot, and in an involuntary reaction starting to flex their own
lats, even the women.

"He needs help," said Earline. "He may be gone cataronic."

"Cataronic," said Nail. "Don't believe I know much about
that."

"You ain't got a degree in Problems of Living, either."

Nail said, "It's always something to be grateful for."

"Try not to git on my nerves, Nail, at a time like this," she said. "I believe we may be in a crisis here."

"I ain't in no crisis," said Motor. "I ain't even been in the water yet."

Earline said, "In your basic cataronic state you cain't or sometimes just *won't* move. And you can see he's starting to tremble. And if he's breathing, I shore cain't tell it. He may need mouth-to-mouth is what he may need. I got training. If I need you, you all gone help?"

"I ain't fooling with the feller myself," Turner said. "Don't even know him. For all I know he may like to be cataronic. May fall into it everday about this time. People is a whole lot funnier than you think."

"Nobody *likes* to be cataronic," said Earline. "It's a serious affliction. It ain't something you fall into or out of just to be doing. Look how red his face is. And it ain't nobody making a move to help. Probably ain't had no training like I have. Can I count on you all for help or am I just gone have to go it alone? Nobody that knows what I know just stands by and does nothing. That's for them that's ignorant. When push comes to shove, even a health professional like me sometimes needs help. One thing's for shore, he cain't last much longer like he is."

Her mother, Earnestine, adjusted her own suit and bent slightly at the hips, her huge thighs quivering as though she meant to break into a sprint. "Do what you have to do, honey. We behind you. These men don't do what you say do, it'll be a while before they forget it." She raised her voice into a mild scream that turned every head at poolside: "That goes for you too, Alphonse."

But Fonse had his good ear cupped with his hand the whole time they were talking and had followed everything they said. He adjusted his balls and said, "I never let a youngun of mine down yet."

"If we save the sumbitch," said Nail, "can we go in a bathing then? Cause you know, Earline, I don't ever do nothing without everbody's approval."

"I'm *asking* you for help, Nail. I ain't told you you had to do nothing."

"Well, in that case," said Nail, "les jump that sucker and save his ass in the name of love and feeling for our fellow man."

"Oh shit," said Russell, tearing away the blind from the window. "They've gone crazy down there."

Shereel, who had stretched back out on the floor and was deep in a kind of fugue state dreaming of cold water, leapt to her feet and went to the window. As thirsty as she was, what she saw startled all thought of water out of her head.

The entire Turnipseed family was racing down the edge of the pool in a kind of flying wedge, with Nail in the lead, followed by Motor and Turner, and then the two women. Earnestine and Earline moved surprisingly fast and light on their feet for women so heavy. Fonse, the Camel still hanging from his lips and one hand holding his hat to keep it from flying off, brought up the rear. Shereel noticed for the first time that her father still wore his heavy work shoes and black socks.

"What the hell are they doing?" demanded Russell.

"I wouldn't want to guess," said Shereel, "but I have the feeling we'll know soon enough."

And they did. It was not in the least subtle. The five of them simultaneously hit the bodybuilder still on his knee in the lat spread. So concentrated on his pose was he, so focused on his pumped and swelling body, Shereel knew that he probably never saw them coming. Nail and the Turnipseed brothers were all bigger than the bodybuilder and probably stronger, too, Shereel knew, because like everybody else counting down the days to contest time he was probably living on a six-ounce can of tunafish with a fresh lemon squeezed on it, three stalks of celery, and a vitamin packet a day, ripping the fat from the striated layers of muscle covering his body, getting cut up like a skinned squirrel. And that's about how much strength he would have, that of a dead and skinned squirrel.

So the Turnipseeds and Nail handled him like a baby. Nail sat on his chest, Motor and Turner on each of his legs. Earnestine had him by the hair of the head and Earline had the heel of her hand on his chin trying to force his mouth open. Fonse stood above them, waving his arms, his mouth working around the Camel, apparently shouting instructions.

All the other bodybuilders—men and women—had rushed to the other end of the pool and stood packed closely together, craning their necks in an effort to see what was being done to one of their very own by these strange creatures who had appeared among them, and who were not—it was sickeningly apparent—one of them, but rather only normal, malnourished men and women who could have been selected at random from any segment of the regular old pathetic American populace. None of the Cosmos contestants made any move to help their fellow athlete pinned to his back at the far end of the pool, because after all they had their own perfect bodies to protect. A single scratch or abrasion on their uniformly tanned bodies could lose the Cosmos for them. Nobody with a scratch on his skin could possibly win any more than anybody with a tattoo could win. Perfection was the name of this game and they were not about to take any risk for anybody.

"What the hell is she doing to him?" said Russell.

"That's my sister Earline."

"I didn't ask who it was, I asked what she's doing. My God, is she kissing him? Goddammit, she is, she's kissing him."

"That's what it looks like."

"I'm surprised they can hold him down that way, *whatever* they're doing."

"My brothers go two and a quarter apiece. Nail's more like two-fifty. The guy they have pinned on his back doesn't have much of a chance no matter what they want to do to him."

"It looks like they're killing him. That's what it looks like they mean to do. Should we call somebody? Police? Some goddamn body? This won't do."

"Whatever's going on, you can be sure they mean him no harm."

"Then why is Nail choking him?"

"Nail's not . . . Well, it *does* look like he might be strangling him a little."

"Goddammit, Shereel, you can't strangle somebody a little. He's choking the shit out of him."

"Way he's thrashing around, Nail's probably just trying to calm him down."

"We've got to do something. You can't calm a man down by strangling him."

"With Nail it's probably only force of habit. He'll stop in a minute."

"In a minute he'll be dead."

Down below, they saw Earline pinch the bodybuilder's nose shut with her thumb and forefinger and clamp her mouth firmly on his.

"Oh, I see now," said Shereel. "She's just giving him CPR."

"CPR, for Christ's sake?"

"The kiss of life," said Shereel. "When she was going to school studying the Problems of Living, she told me all about it. One of the courses she had to pass. Even practiced on me."

"That man's in better shape than all those Turnipseeds put together. He doesn't need the kiss of life."

"Apparently, Earline thinks he does. And when you see somebody might need it, that's no time to stand around and think."

"I can look at her and tell she's never had a thought in her head, standing around or otherwise."

"There'll be trouble if you can't learn to keep a civil tongue about my family."

"The hell with my tongue. I can see what they're doing to him."

"You ever had a course in CPR, Russell?"

"What kind of question is that?"

"The kind you ought to answer. I know you haven't or you wouldn't be going on like this. She's closer to him down there than we are up here. She saw something we didn't see."

Russell said, "What I saw was a great bodybuilder—a world-beater—doing a lat pose and intimidating everybody around him."

"That's not what Earline saw, not from the looks of things."

Russell turned and took her shoulders and shook her roughly, the way an angry parent might shake a child. "Do you understand the shit, the heat, that could come down behind this?"

Shereel watched him, her face calm but her eyes blazing, and then said in a low deadly voice, "Russell, if you don't take your hands off me and keep'm off, I'll snatch your balls right off your body."

Russell took his hands away and smiled in astonished and genuine pleasure. "Little girl, I love your goddamn attitude. Your attitude is peaking, peaking right along with everything else. Your game face is in place and solid. Hell, you can't be responsible for what your family does."

"I never thought I could," she said. "Only a fool would think he could control the Turnipseeds."

F I V E

r. Dexter Friedkin's office—more elaborate than Julian thought any hotel manager's office ought to be and also the very kind he planned to have someday himself—was large and heavily carpeted and so was Mr. Friedkin. The hair he wore was long and wavy and stylishly gray, and when Mr. Friedkin was nervous he adjusted it like a hat, which was an unconscious gesture that still astonished Julian, even though he had been seeing it done at irregular intervals for the last four years. That was how long he had been at the Blue Flamingo Hotel, during which time his duties had changed very little and his salary not at all, but he had been given—nearly six months ago—the title of assistant manager. Julian had always thought toupees were glued or at least taped down and maybe most were but not Mr. Dexter Friedkin's. He could slide it forward or tilt it back or even cock it a little to one side depending upon his degree of nervousness.

At the moment he had slid it dangerously low on his brow, dangerous because Julian couldn't very well ignore it if the wavy mass of gray hair suddenly slipped entirely off Mr. Friedkin's head and fell onto the desk where Mr. Friedkin was sitting and in front of which Julian was shifting nervously from foot to foot because he had brought Mr. Friedkin what he liked least: news of trouble. Without ever having been told, Julian knew that any mention—or even recognition—that Mr. Friedkin wore a toupee would mean instant dismissal. And apparently every other member of the hotel staff, right down to the busboys, knew the same thing because, although only a blind man could miss the phony, often mobile, hair, it was never mentioned, even amongst themselves.

"Trouble?" said Mr. Friedkin, taking his hands off his toupee and tenting his fingers in front of his tanned face.

"Yessir."

"I do believe we've discussed this before, Julian."

"Yessir."

"And at some length, as I recall."

"Yessir."

"Then you remember the discussion?"

"Yessir."

"And you do, do you not, expect that someday all of this will be yours?" He untented his fingers and waved his hands to include the large office, the walls of which were filled with shelves of bodybuilding trophies.

"Yessir."

"Then you must surely remember that the assistant manager's job is not to bring the manager news of trouble but to take care of it himself."

"Yessir."

"Then how does it come to pass that you find yourself in front of my desk telling me that there has been trouble in the hotel?"

"I thought you'd best know about it, sir. It's serious."

"Serious, is it?"

"Yessir."

"Does it not occur to you that dealing with serious trouble is just the experience of the sort that will someday qualify you for the desk at which I now sit?"

Julian felt he'd best go ahead and blurt it out or it would never get said.

"One of the guests—actually a whole family of guests—assaulted one of the contestants."

Mr. Friedkin simultaneously shot to his feet and readjusted his toupee with both hands. "What? Assaulted? Assaulted you say?"

"At poolside, sir."

"You mean to say that an ordinary, regular American family assaulted a potential world-champion bodybuilder, a possible Mr. Cosmos?" Stunned, he dropped back into his seat. "But how can that be possible?"

"The men of this particular family—actually the women, too—are quite large, in fact very large, and . . . strange."

"Strange? Julian, did you say *strange*?"

"Yessir."

"And what are strange tourists doing as guests in the finest hotel on Miami Beach?"

"If you'll pardon my saying so, sir, you haven't worked the desk in many years, and some strange ones *do* come in from time to time."

"I'll not pardon anything. And if you let anything happen to ruin this show, you'll be parking cars. Forever. I'll fix it so no hotel this side of Baghdad will hire you. Understood?"

"Yessir."

"All right. Now let's get clear on what happened."

"I didn't see it, but I've talked to witnesses. It was a family of Turnipseeds and apparently they are related to Ms. Dupont. I'd already had trouble with them at the desk, and one of—"

"Turnipseeds. What kind of name is Turnipseed?"

"—and one of them might be a lunatic."

Mr. Friedkin lifted his hair entirely off his head and replaced it, something Julian had never seen him do before. "How can Ms. Dupont be related to something called a Turnipseed? She's going to win the Cosmos, everybody knows that. And 'lunatic'? Is that what you said?"

Julian felt he'd better back off a bit. "Maybe not a lunatic, but he certainly doesn't . . . He has strange eyes." He had, after all, let the family into the hotel without a credit card on file *or* a cash deposit, which was enough to get him fired on the spot.

"He has strange eyes," said Mr. Friedkin, making it a statement, not a question. "Julian, you're starting to babble. Do you know you are babbling?"

"No sir."

"Well you are. Strange eyes, indeed. That hardly makes for a lunatic. Now—and goddammit stop shifting about and stand still, you look like you've got Saint Vitus' dance—now, who exactly was assaulted?"

"Mr. Bill Bateman."

"Bill 'the Bat' Bateman?"

"I didn't know he was called the Bat, sir. But it's the contestant named Bill Bateman."

"You must have seen his back. It's the only back like it in the world. He doesn't have latissimus dorsi, he has wings, spreads just like a goddamn bat. One of the most beautiful things I've ever seen."

"I'm sure it is, sir."

"You're not sure of anything or we wouldn't be having this conversation."

"Well, since I was told the Turnipseeds were Ms. Dupont's immediate family, I didn't call the police or—"

"Don't you dare call the police about anything concerning the Cosmos competition. And they can't be her immediate family. Her name is Dupont. But we'll not settle that question. We won't even *think* about that. We *shall*, Julian, devote our attention and energies to questions that matter. Now, just what did the Turnipseeds in question do to the Bat?"

"They gave him CPR, sir."

"Cardiopulmonary resuscitation?"

"Yessir."

"My God, those fucking steroids. Did he have a heart attack?"

"No sir."

"Well, for whatever reason, CPR is hardly assault."

"He didn't want it, sir."

"Didn't want *what*, Julian," said Mr. Friedkin. "You're beginning to exasperate beyond what even I can stand."

"CPR."

"He didn't *want* it?"

"Or need it, sir."

"Then why did they give it?"

"That's not entirely clear."

"Is there anything in any of this that *is* entirely clear?"

"Apparently not, sir. That's why I thought you had best know about it. They—the Turnipseeds, that is—just threw him—the Bat, I mean—onto his back, gave him mouth-to-mouth, pounded his chest, and at least one of them seems to have strangled him."

"One of them *strangled* Bill 'the Bat' Bateman?"

"At poolside, sir."

"You said that, goddammit. What difference does it make where they did it, anyway."

"Half the other competitors saw it, and they're, well . . . frightened."

"Frightened? Frightened here in the finest hotel on Miami Beach?"

"Yessir."

"What are they frightened of?"

"Apparently of being thrown onto their backs, given mouth-to-mouth, having their chests pounded, and being strangled. The Turnipseeds really do have them going."

"*Going?* Not leaving the hotel surely?"

"It was only a manner of speaking, sir. Nobody has left that I know of . . . not yet anyway."

"Nobody is going anywhere. Except maybe the Turnipseeds. *Turnipseeds*, indeed. Nothing, *nothing*, Julian, is going to spoil what I've worked so hard to put together here. These competitors are members of the tribe to which I myself belong." He swept a hand to include the shelved walls of the office. "To whom do these trophies belong, Julian?"

"To you, sir." Julian's eyes swept over the fake gold-plated statuettes of little men striking muscular poses, with dates engraved on them, and under the dates, titles like "King of Crystal River" and under that "Dexter Friedkin." He also suspected Dexter Friedkin of having had them all made himself and of never having been nearer competition than sitting in the audience.

"Not world-class triumphs," said Mr. Friedkin, "but nobody can deny that I am indeed a member of the body-sculpting tribe. Are we agreed of that, Julian?"

"Totally, sir."

Mr. Friedkin tented his fingers again and swiveled slowly in two complete circles in his expensive executive chair before he stopped and fixed Julian with what he thought of as his Dale Carnegie stare, not belligerent, not threatening, but the look of a winner, confident, self-possessed, one designed—the Dale Carnegie people had assured him—to bring out the best in underlings. All captains of industry had it, and Mr. Friedkin spent every morning practicing it while he shaved.

"You and I, Julian, will *keep* together what I have *put* together. Do you have any idea how many vice-presidents of this corporation I had to convince to bring the Cosmos competition to the Blue Flamingo? Do you know how many other hotels, how many other *cities*, wanted this competition? Do you have any notion at all of the intense negotiations that brought the ABC network here to film for a segment for their *Wide World of Sports?*"

Julian knew Mr. Friedkin was in his rhetorical question mode—a mode he fell into easily and one which was never to be interrupted, and so Julian concentrated on the Miami skyline that shined white as bone under a blazing sun through the window behind Mr. Friedkin.

"Can you conceive, Julian, of the logistics of bringing these men and women—*perfect* men and women, I might add—from the four corners of the world to compete here? And do you have the vision to comprehend the publicity, not just nationally, but around the globe, that will accrue to the Blue Flamingo? And did you take the time to notice the civic leaders cooperating in this venture, behind us all the way, civic leaders from the governor right down to the police chief, whose names appear on our Cosmos letterhead stationery? And who is responsible for that? You are standing before the man responsible for that. The work, the organization, the vision, the . . . the . . . *genius* is not too strong a word, were all mine. It all came from this desk." His eyes, which had wandered to his trophies, snapped back to Julian's. "Well, what do you have to say?"

Julian knew the answer immediately. "I was awaiting instructions, sir."

Mr. Friedkin made a noise in his throat which he thought made him sound lost in thought but which in fact made him sound lost in doubt. Julian had heard it many times before and knew what was coming.

"Julian, I pose a hypothetical and highly speculative question: If the Cosmos show—that is, the rewards that accrue to me for bringing it to the Blue Flamingo—should take me out of this chair and into the higher echelons of management, and further, Julian, you should then come to occupy this chair—this very chair—and such a problem as this were brought to you, what would you do?"

Julian had seen the question coming and was ready. "I'd make every effort to calm the Bat with some small gratuity such as covering his expenses at the hotel for the duration of the show and I'd try to get the Turnipseeds to accept better accommodations at another hotel on the beach at our expense."

"Better accommodations?" said Mr. Friedkin. "There are no better accommodations than the Blue Flamingo."

"I was thinking of suites rather than rooms such as they have now."

"And at our expense?"

"Spend money to make money," said Julian, quoting a favorite Friedkin axiom.

Mr. Friedkin made the sound in his throat again. Then: "Spend money to make money."

"Losing the show may be the price of keeping the Turnipseeds in the hotel."

"Very well, Julian, here is what you do. Make every effort to calm the Bat with some small gratuity such as covering his expenses at the hotel for the duration of the show and try to get the Turnipseeds to accept accommodations at another hotel on the beach at our expense . . .''

"But, sir," said Julian.

"I know, Julian, there are no better accommodations than the Blue Flamingo on the beach. I was thinking of suites rather than rooms such as they have now. What do you think of that course of action?"

"I think it brilliant, sir."

"And that is precisely why I occupy this chair and you stand dancing about in front of it, Julian," Mr. Friedkin said. "Now get out, and get the job done."

"Yessir."

Julian was nearly to the door when Mr. Friedkin said, "And send Miss Beverly in on your way out."

"Yessir."

Julian had hardly closed the door when a tall, slender young lady, wearing too much makeup and carrying a notepad, came in and crossed to Mr. Friedkin's desk in smooth long-legged strides.

"Miss Beverly, I need to draft some ordinary and rather boring correspondence."

"Of course, sir," she said, placing her pad and pen before Mr. Friedkin and carefully hiking her skirt daintily just an inch or two so that she might kneel more easily and crawl under Mr. Friedkin's desk and unzip his fly.

Mr. Friedkin picked up the pen and adjusted the pad to a more comfortable angle. Presently a beatific look came upon his face and Mr. Friedkin asked softly, "This certainly takes some of the tedium out of the necessary chore of boring correspondence, don't you agree, Miss Beverly?"

A wet and not very intelligible sound came from under the desk. It was the answer Mr. Friedkin always got to the question he always asked, and one which he invariably interpreted in the affirmative.

S I X

As Shereel was drinking the last of four ounces of La Croix Artesian water—guaranteed pure, no salt—and running her sharp pink tongue around the rim of the glass to get the last few drops hanging there, the phone rang.

Russell picked it up. "Who?" he demanded. It was the only way he ever answered the phone. He watched the La Croix bottle in front of Shereel. He didn't want her sneaking another sip. You couldn't even trust a goddamn champion in this world. Especially one dying of thirst.

"Wall, what are you doing on my goddamn telephone?" he barked. And then: "Not good enough," he said, about to hang up but didn't. "Why? I'll tell you why: You *couldn't* know anything I'd want to know or need to know." He watched Shereel while he listened. "I don't know a goddamn Julian," he said finally. He had faked his own game face earlier, but now that Shereel had on a real one, it had made his own blood high. He felt like *he* was about to compete. That made his face as genuine as hers, and that put him in no mood for bullshit of any kind. He felt dangerous. He knew he *was* dangerous. "What did you say to me, Dickhead?" he spat into the phone, his face going a shade darker. Then: "Oh, Julian *Lipschitz*. Well, tell the fucker he has my sympathy, but that's not enough reason to talk to him." Again he started to put the phone back on the hook but ended by pressing it harder against his ear, listening for a long time, glancing at Shereel as he did. She had her eyes fixed on the beaded bottle of mineral water.

"Tell'm I don't think we can help him with that," he said.

"Tell'm we've got the world to win. Let him run the hotel and we'll win the world. Tell'm that, Wall. And while you're at it, tell'm he ought to do something about his name. That's the first thing he needs to do because 'Lipschitz' won't do for a name." As he listened he reached over and moved the La Croix bottle out of Shereel's reach. She followed the bottle with her eyes. "Name, Wall? What about her name? Turnipseed, you say? How should I know? Ask Lipschitz, he's got the same problem. No. We don't have a comment on that. And I think, Wallace, I think you better get out of my life. You're already in over your head." He picked up the mineral water bottle and drank the rest of it, listening, while Shereel watched him. "He said that, did he? Ask Lipschitz if he ever coughed with broken ribs. Threat? Me? Wall, you know I don't make threats."

"Who *is* that? Is it Wall?" asked Shereel, moving her tongue on her mouth, which was already dry again. She wondered if she could spit.

Russell ignored her and glanced over the broken room. "No, tell'm he can't come up here. Conference room? Which conference room would that be?" He was silent a moment, looking at the ceiling. "Okay then, as soon as we can make it. And stop thanking me, goddammit, just stay out of my life. Take care of your own girl and leave mine to me. Dupont, goddammit. *Ms.* Shereel Dupont." He dropped the phone into the cradle and stared off through the window.

"Was that Wall?" she said.

"Yes."

"And what was that about Lipschitz?"

"It's a guy's name."

"A name?"

"That's what *I* said. Anyway, whatever his name, I guess he runs the hotel."

"What'd he want? Did a maid tell him about this room and what you did to it?"

"*We* did to it. But it's not the room. It's the Turnipseeds. Lipschitz had Wall call us. He said they've run amok."

"Amok?"

"It's what he said but I didn't even comment on it. Crazy's what he meant."

"Craziness does not run in my family."

"To hell it doesn't. Wall was down there. He saw the whole thing when your family attacked the Bat."

"They didn't attack him. They gave him CPR. I could see that from all the way up here."

"They threw him on his back, pounded the shit out of him, and strangled him is what they did. But that's not the point or the problem. The problem is Wall talked to your daddy and your brothers, to Nail Head too for all I know."

"That wouldn't have been possible. Forgive me for saying so but Wall's a strange nigger and none of them—specially Nail— goes around talking to strange niggers."

"Wall can Tom with the best of 'm when he wants to or needs to. Probably called'm boss. Oh, yeah, I can hear'm. Yassah, white boss, yassah."

"Now, *that* could have worked. They could have had a good long talk if he'd done that."

"Apparently he did and they did. And that's the problem."

"I don't get it."

"Wall sure as hell did. He thinks your name is Dorothy Turnipseed."

"My name *is* Dorothy Turnipseed," she flared back at him.

He came over, palmed her head, and pulled her face within inches of his, and when he spoke his voice was like compressed steam escaping: "Your name is not *now* and *never* has been Dorothy Turnipseed. You goddamn get that down cold and believe it in your blood. You are *Shereel Dupont.*"

"*I* can get it however I get it, but by God my daddy and brothers will kill over Turnipseed blood."

"And I," he said, his voice still hissing, "will kill over Ms. Cosmos."

"God," she said, "I believe you would."

"Believe it."

"I do, Jesus as my witness."

"Leave Jesus the fuck out of this. I'm the only witness you need."

"What'd Wall want us to do?"

"It wasn't what *he* wanted. It was what Lipschitz wanted."

"And?"

"To see us in the conference room downstairs."

"What for?" she said, the memory of months of pain and denial suddenly making her remember who she was, what she had suffered for.

"If we knew that we wouldn't have to go, would we?"

"Take care of it, Russell. I'm too dry for a Lipschitz."

"You're not dry. I'll tell you when you're dry."

"There is no way I can go down there without another drink of water."

"You can go. I'm here to see that you get to the place I've been pointing you since the day we met. And stop thinking about water. Just pretend it doesn't exist. Because, for you, it doesn't. Okay?"

"You rotten son of a bitch."

He patted her affectionately on her rock-hard shoulder. "That's the girl I love."

"You never loved anything but yourself."

He paused on his way to the door and, without looking at her, said in a quiet, bemused voice: "Almost right. What it is . . . I never loved anything but winning." And then in an even quieter voice: "And that means beating somebody else. That's the world: the beater and the beaten. I didn't cause my mama to suffer my bloody birth to come out here in the world and get beaten."

"And you said the Turnipseeds were crazy."

"Get your sunglasses back on," he said. "Button that robe to the chin and come on. Lipschitz is waiting."

"Let him wait. I don't hurry for anybody named Lipschitz."

"How about hurrying for Russell Morgan then?"

"How about kissing my ass?"

He showed his humorless grin. "Shereel, half the men in the world would cut off their lips to kiss your ass."

"Let's go see Lipschitz," she said. "He can't be any worse than this conversation."

SEVEN

The conference room was long and paneled in dark oak. There was a table down the center of it with twenty leather-covered chairs on either side.

The first thing Russell saw when he came through the door followed by Shereel was Nail's eyes. Once his eyes were locked on Nail's, he didn't feel he could look away first. This was no time to be intimidated. And Russell knew immediately why he was called Nail Head. It had to be because of his eyes, flat and without light and solid black. There was nothing to mark the iris from the pupil. And his face was as empty of expression as his eyes.

He was not at the table but off in the farthest corner tilted onto the back legs of one of the chairs doing what looked to Russell to be cleaning his nails with the biggest knife Russell had ever seen. He thought it was a switchblade but Russell had never seen or even heard of a switchblade that long.

"How come it is you got on that housecoat, Sister Woman?" asked Nail in a voice as flat as his eyes. "You cold or just what?"

He was speaking to Shereel but his eyes never left Russell's and his lips seemed not to move at all.

"It's too long to explain," said Russell, his voice as full of rage as he could make it because he knew this one was trouble and Russell wanted him to understand right from the start that if it was trouble he wanted, he could have it. "It's all part of pre-competition psych. *That's* why she's wearing the robe."

Nail's eyes moved for the first time, cutting to Shereel.

"This him, Sister Woman?" asked Nail. He moved his shoul-

ders as he spoke and the unbuttoned shirt that he was wearing
over his swimsuit fell open and Russell found his gaze locked
now on the perforated heart in the middle of Nail's chest and
he silently read the instructions printed there: CUT HERE and
under that IF YOU CAN.

"Nobody's called me Sister Woman since I left home, Harry."

Russell looked at her and she was smiling, a wonderful open
smile that Russell had never seen before.

"And I ain't been called Harry by nobody but my old ma since
I got back from strangling slopes for Lyndon Johnson, democ-
racy, and the love of God his own fucking self."

"Same old Nail," said Shereel.

"Yeah, looks that way, don't it." He pointed his knife at Russell. "This him?"

"Is this who?" demanded Russell.

"Yes," said Shereel.

Nail said, "Looks like somebody taken a air hose and blowed
him up, don't it? But if you say he's a Russell Muscle, I believe
it. Hell, everybody's got to be something."

"My name's Russell Morgan." He looked at Shereel.

"It was just something I wrote home," she said. "Goddammit,
Russell, stop looking at me like that. It was *only* a letter."

"With you calling me Russell Muscle in it."

"Don't feel bad, bud," said Nail Head. "Hell, nothing wrong
with a nickname. I'm called Nail myself. Nail Head."

He touched the point of the enormous blade to the tip of his
tongue in a way that made Russell feel like an ice cube had
slipped down his spine. He wanted this over with and he wanted
it over quickly.

Russell said, "I got a call from a Mr. Julian Lipschitz."

Nail was doing something with the knife that suggested he
was debating whether to split his own tongue down the middle
or not. He took the knife away and said, "Yeah, Julian Lipschitz.
Ain't that a God's wonder? He come up to the room to talk to
Fonse, but Fonse and the rest of'm had gone off in search of a

Colonel Sanders, thought to bring back a couple of buckets of that fried chicken. It ain't nothing here in the hotel fittin' to eat."

"So?" said Russell.

Nail said, "He talked to me instead. I wouldn't look for'm to show up if I was you."

"Nail Head Barnes," said Shereel. "What *ever* did you do?"

"Me?" said Nail. "I ain't done a thing."

"Then why isn't he coming?" she asked.

"Decided against it," Nail said.

"But he was the one wanted the meeting in the first place," Russell said.

"Yeah," said Nail, "so he told me. But I pointed out to him it weren't necessary."

"You didn't happen to point it out to him with that knife, did you?" said Russell.

"Me and this knife go back a long way," said Nail. "Somehow I'd think you'd have better sense than to say anything about this knife right here, Muscle."

"My name's Russell Morgan."

Nail stood up, looked at his blade, then out the window beside him, and finally back to Russell. "Your goddamn name is anything me and my knife say it is. Can you follow that, you blowed-up sumbitch?"

"I don't have to follow anything," said Russell. "There's laws for people like you."

Nail smiled, and his red thin lips reminded Russell of a cut throat.

Nail said, "There ain't a goddamn thing for people like me. Ain't nobody ever made a law that had anybody like me in mind." Nail paused. "What we got us is a little problem with names. Now, Muscle, you and me already got it straight about ours." Russell opened his mouth to speak but Nail held up his thick hand, palm out, and Russell's mouth clamped shut on a half-spoken word. "But ours is just nicknames so they don't count. But other names now, real goddamn names, is caught hard to blood. Fuck with a name like that, you fucking with blood. People where I come from don't take kindly to such as that."

Shereel said in a tiny voice, "Nail, it's only a stage name, just something to put on a card to use on the stage."

She was scared enough to sound like she was telling the truth but Russell had made her change it legally.

As Shereel spoke, Nail came across the room toward her. He stopped within inches of her. Russell, as totally pissed as he was—and more than a little frightened, which he would have admitted to no one else but which he freely admitted to himself—could not help admire the smooth grace with which Nail moved across the carpet. No question, there was real strength there. Unfortunately, he knew there was unpredictable lunacy there, too.

Nail's hand, the one holding the blade, raised and with a quick delicate flick that even a surgeon could have admired cut the top button from the robe Shereel was wearing. Russell did not even realize what he had done until he saw the button bounce off the near wall.

"Nail, don't," said Shereel. It was not a game voice at all, thought Russell, but that of a little girl. A scared little girl.

The blade flashed, caught the light, and another button popped against the wall. When the third button came off, her taut naked breasts stood high and tight, topped with dimpled nipples the color of strawberries. Shereel never moved. She did not appear to be breathing. Russell was stunned into silence, not by Shereel's nakedness, but by the quick incredible accuracy of the knife. A man with that kind of skill could take your foreskin off without ever touching the head of your dick. And as the buttons popped from the robe, Russell could feel his balls ascending straight out of his scrotum. And with his disappearing balls came the sudden knowledge that there were only two things to do with a man like Nail: Kill him or get him on your side and keep him on your side.

Nail briefly flicked his blade one last time and Shereel stood before him naked but for the briefest of yellow string panties, and the framing backdrop of her robe.

Nail stared directly and for what seemed forever at Shereel and at her panties, from which blond hair curled on three sides. She was also acutely aware that she was still full of Russell's come. "Yeller," Nail finally said. "Now I like that, damned if yeller weren't always my favorite thing in the world, right up there with pussy its very own self."

"There's no need to talk that way, Nail," Russell said.

Never taking his eyes off the tiny triangle where Shereel's thighs met her belly, Nail said, "Need, you say? What the fuck's need got to do with anything? Me and my knife done give up on need a long time ago. I ain't here to talk about need. I'm here to talk about names. Names and blood."

He reached out and looked as though he was about to take one of Shereel's breasts in his hand but he only let his palm slide slowly down her rib cage over the deeply ridged abdomen, stopping just short of her panties.

"Now this right here," said Nail, "is a Turnipseed. Got Turnipseed blood wrote all over her." He turned to look at Russell. "It is some hereabouts thinks she's a Dupont, whatever the hell that is."

Shereel stepped away from his hand. "Nail, it was in the letters I wrote, more than once, and Shereel Dupont was stamped on the pictures I sent home."

"Hell," Nail said, "I known all that before we ever left to come off down here. Earline read them letters out loud to everbody she could corner about forty times but we ain't talkin' letters and pictures here. We talkin' blood. Your mama and daddy ain't named you no Shereel Dupont."

Russell said, "I named her and there was good reason for—"

Nail cut him off. "You must be from either New York City or else from California."

"California, actually," Russell said.

"Figures," said Nail. "Now if I was you and I was standing in front of a man holding a ten-inch blade I'd shut the fuck up while he was trying to talk about blood."

This was all more important to Russell than blood—even his own—and if he had to risk bleeding, then so be it.

"We're not talking about blood here, Nail, we're talking about money."

Nail turned back to look at him. "Money?"

"Money," said Russell.

Nail said, "Mr. Muscle, I got me a brand-new, paid-for Chevy pickup out there in the parking lot and five hundred dollars in cash money on my hip. I ain't studying money and—as it turns out—don't seem like it's a sumbitch in this whole goddamn place can hear when you talk to'm. Sooner or later, it's gone come to my goddamn knife. And I ain't met the sumbitch yet that didn't understand my knife when it speaks."

Russell pushed on, as scared as he was, his eyes locked on the blade of Nail's knife. "Let's see if we can't work this out. Give me five minutes. You don't buy what I'm selling, then it's all over, but what I need to tell you is this is all for Shereel. For Dorothy's good. This is all for Dorothy. Even the name she's taken is to get her where she needs to go. Answer me this, Nail. Do you love her?"

"Say what?"

"Do you love her?"

"Love's a word I never got much mileage out of."

"Then do you like her, like her a lot?"

"I'm here six hundred miles from home ain't I? And yeah, I like her, not that it's any of you goddamn business. It's even talk she's my fee*and*say. You don't git to be a fee*and*say without a hell of a lot of liking going on, and your five fucking minutes is about up."

"There's a Ms. Cosmos contest taking place in this hotel to-morrow and—"

"You ain't talkin' to a fool. I can read. I known it was a contest."

"If Dorothy—using the name Shereel Dupont because that's how the contest people know her—if she wins, and she will if you or somebody else don't cause something to stop it, if she wins, Nail, she'll end up with more money than both of you could count in a lifetime."

"Shit, it ain't that much money in the world."

"Shereel, tell him."

"It could mean a million dollars—not all at once, but it could in time."

"You tellin' me she could make her a million dollars?"

"Just exactly that, Nail. Shereel, take off the robe."

"You keep that goddamn thing on," said Nail.

"It's all right," she said. "It's business. Only business."

She let the robe drop to her ankles and slowly turned in front of Nail.

"Is them panties held on by suction?" asked Nail.

Shereel fixed him with her fiery little eyes: "They're held on by the finest body in the world. That's what it's all about, that's why we're here."

Russell asked, "Does she look like the girl you knew back home in Waycross?"

"What happened to her tits? What went with *them?*"

"Tits don't count in this contest, Nail," Shereel said.

"They better not because I seen bigger tits than them on master sergeants in the Marine Corp."

"What about the rest of her, Nail?" asked Russell.

Nail looked at her hard and long, then dropped his eyes to examine his knife. He pressed a button and snapped it shut. It was in fact, Russell saw, a switchblade. Nail fitted the knife snugly into a little black leather case attached to his belt.

"Well?" said Russell.

"I ain't never seen nothin' like her," Nail said in a voice quite unlike any Russell had heard him use.

"Never?" said Russell.

"Not even close," Nail said.

"Now," said Russell, "you've got everything right. There's not another one like that in the world. And she wins it all tomorrow, wins it unless somebody—anybody—causes trouble for her."

Naked but for the bikini panties Shereel moved forward and fitted herself into Nail. Russell saw Nail's eyes close and heard a great exhalation of breath.

Shereel had her arms around Nail, her hands buried in the thick hair that covered the nape of his neck.

"Help me, Nail," she whispered. "Please say you'll help me. I've beat myself like a dog to get here, now say you'll help me take it home. I didn't know what pain and suffering was until I put myself through this."

Russell saw Nail's huge, red hands slip under the yellow panties to cup the sculpted globes of Shereel's ass and at the same time felt his balls descend hotly and beat like a pulse in the distended sack of his scrotum. It was victory and defeat in the same instant. Russell didn't know whether to laugh or cry, bolt from the room or attack Nail.

Nail solved it all for him. "I don't understand a goddamn thing about all this, Sister Woman, but the Nail is stuck to the bone and will stay the distance. Anybody fucks with you has got to come by the Nail to do it." Then without taking his face from the place where he had buried it where Shereel's neck met her shoulder, he said, "Mr. Morgan, I believe you needed somewhere else."

"Right, Nail. I'm on my way." And he headed for the door, his balls no longer beating like a pulse but pounding now like the biggest drum God ever imagined.

E I G H T

Mr. Friedkin never looked into the mirror without his hairpiece in place, not even to shave. The toupee was the first thing he put on in the morning and the last thing he took off at night. Because he couldn't be sure it would stay attached during the night, he had not slept with a woman since he was thirty, over twenty years ago. But he managed quite nicely because he had Miss Beverly. There had been a whole string of Miss Beverlys over the years, but the one he had now was the best of the whole crop, the very best. He'd had to give her four raises in the last year alone to keep her, but what the hell, it was the price of doing business and he would charge it off to the hotel anyway. He could remember nothing of the string of Beverlys over the years except their mouths and their enthusiasm or the lack of it. Because right at the head of the list of the things he would not—could not—tolerate was an unenthusiastic suck. All of them—all the girls—that had come and gone had been named Miss Beverly. He, himself, had named them. Whatever their real names were he not only did not care, he actually did not want to know. It was all handled through personnel. The people in personnel knew their job and they took care of it without question. All of the people in his hotel did as they were told without question or else they did not have a job very long.

Over the years, he had managed to put together a loyal, blindly obedient group of subjects—that was the way he thought of those who worked for him: subjects. Mr. Friedkin was not an uneducated man. He knew his Machiavelli. Some of his subjects loved him, some hated him. But they all feared him. He could smell the fear on them when they were in his presence, a damp, cloying odor, an odor he prized and loved best of all others in the world.

Miss Beverly had been in twice more since Julian had left that morning to help him get through the boring, but necessary, chore of business correspondence and he was feeling right at the top of his game. He was about to go into the executive washroom and examine his features when the call light came on his phone.

He picked up the phone. "Mr. Lipschitz is here to see you, sir," said Miss Spaulding, a gray-skinned mousy young woman who actually ran the office and whose mouth would give even sucking a bad name.

"Miss Spaulding, I thought—no, I remember distinctly telling you—to hold my calls. Tell Mr. Lipschitz that he has his instructions and that I mean for him to carry them out."

"He's hysterical, Mr. Friedkin—"

"Hysterical? Did you say hysterical? You know as well as I do that hysteria is not allowed in the Blue Flamingo Hotel."

"—and hurt," said Miss Spaulding.

"Hurt? He can't be. I forbid it."

"He's coming in anyway. I can't stop him."

"Well, then . . ."

But the door opened and Julian burst into the room, his eyes crazy and shot with blood and wearing a bandage over the bottom of his nose so that he had to breathe through his mouth.

"I'm cut," said Julian in a wild, strange, gasping voice.

"Cut?" said Mr. Friedkin, reaching for his hairpiece.

"Cut," said Julian, "cut, goddammit."

Forcing himself to be calm and to turn loose of his toupee Mr. Friedkin said, "That's impossible. You know as well as I that nobody is allowed to be cut in the Blue Flamingo Hotel."

"Then what the hell is this?" demanded Julian in a voice cold and belligerent that Mr. Friedkin would never have recognized as Julian's had he not been watching Julian say it and at the same time rip the bandage from his nose.

Blood was crusted at the bottom of his nostrils where each of them had been split in what seemed to Mr. Friedkin to be quarter-inch gashes on each side.

"My God, Julian," said Mr. Friedkin, pressing his stomach hard against the edge of his desk. The few times he had ever seen blood on anybody, including himself, he had puked. And it didn't take much, far less blood than was turning black below Julian's nose and on his upper lip.

"Is that all you've got to fucking say? 'My God, Julian'?"

Mr. Friedkin's gorge settled from his throat and the inclination to puke left him. Was this Julian, *his* Julian, speaking to him this way? Still, his nose *had* begun to leak fresh blood, bright rivulets of it, again.

"Exactly how did this happen, son?" He had never called Julian 'son' before. But then nothing of this sort had ever happened before.

"I went to see the Turnipseeds and something called a Nail Head cut me."

"What did he say to you?"

"Not a goddamn word. He just cut me. So fast, I didn't even know I was cut till I tasted blood running into my mouth."

"Well, did he say something then: why he'd cut you?"

"Indeed, he said something then," said Julian, assuming his registration-desk voice out of force of habit.

"Well?" said Mr. Friedkin, wishing to God Julian would press the bandage back to his nose to stop, or at least hide, the little trickles of blood.

"He said, 'That was for nothing, motherfucker. Now, do something and see where I cut you.'"

"And what did you say?" asked Mr. Friedkin, feeling they were finally getting somewhere.

"What is this," Julian said, the color rising in his face, and a vein starting to pulse in his temple, "twenty questions, you silly asshole?"

The last time Mr. Friedkin had seen the color rise like that and a temple begin to pulse, the man had not had a split nose, he'd had a stroke. Of course it was more or less expected. He was eighty-six years old and sitting in the hotel dining room having a breakfast of prunes sprinkled liberally with orange-flavored Metamucil.

Mr. Friedkin said, "Calling your immediate superior in the Blue Flamingo Corporation a silly asshole can have serious consequences."

"What the hell is this?" demanded Julian, jamming a forefinger up one of his bleeding nostrils. "Inconsequential?" He pulled his finger out of his nostril and, in his passion to make his point, reached across the desk and nearly stuck it up Mr. Friedkin's nostril, which brought the bile boiling again into Mr. Friedkin's throat.

"Sit down, Julian. Anything can be worked out amongst civilized men, men of goodwill."

Julian sat and pressed the bandage back to his nose. "The one in 1520 calling himself Nail is neither civilized nor has he ever heard of goodwill."

"But if Shereel Dupont is in fact a Turnipseed and Mr. Nail is a relative, then maybe . . ."

"He's not a Turnipseed. Nail Head is a nickname and his last name is Barnes. And to top everything else he says he might be her fee*and*say."

"Her what?"

"Fiancé to you. Fee*and*say to him. I think it's why he may have cut me. I had trouble figuring out what he was saying. I could say he lost patience with me, but that would be wrong. He doesn't have any patience to lose. None. He's the one I told you I thought was a lunatic. I no longer think he's a lunatic. I *know* he's a lunatic."

"What in the name of God are we going to do?" said Mr. Friedkin, adjusting his toupee by wiggling his ears and shifting his scalp, another trick Julian had never seen before. But his mind was not on Mr. Friedkin's hairpiece at the moment; it was on his own nose.

Julian said, "The first thing we're going to do is to get me to an emergency room and have my nose looked at."

"And the first thing they'll know is that you've been cut,"
Mr. Friedkin said, getting up from his desk. "And the second
thing they'll do, because they have to by law, is call the police.
And there we are, in shit up to our necks going down the toilet
with the Cosmos show."

"Easy enough for you," said Julian, whose nose hurt too badly
for him to give thought to losing his job. "But it's *my* goddamn
nose."

"I'm here to take care of you, just as you will someday sit
behind this desk and take care of people. Here, let me take a
good long look at that nose."

Mr. Friedkin did not move from behind his desk as he desperately swallowed against his rising gorge at the thought of
actually having to touch Julian's swollen nose, pulpy now with
half-dried blood. For Julian, the thought of sitting behind Mr.
Friedkin's desk reduced the pain in his nose like a shot of novo-
caine. He no longer tasted the blood draining into his mouth
but sat where he was.

And so there they remained for quite a long time, neither
seeming to notice that nothing was being done for the nose,
nothing being done for anything at all really.

A button on his phone lit up, and Mr. Friedkin snatched up
the receiver and shouted: "For God's sake, Miss Spaulding,
whoever or whatever it is, no. Goddammit, no."

But he did not replace the receiver and finally said, "Well,
thank God, send him in." He looked at Julian and smiled, the
threat of puking having left him. "It's Russell Morgan. He'll get
all of this fixed right away. Russell and I go back a long way."
Which was a total lie unless you counted sitting in the audience
watching Russell win countless bodybuilding competitions or
sitting on the toilet in his parents' bathroom jerking off to the
pictures of Russell Morgan in muscle magazines.

Wallace "the Wall" Wilson had the best girl and the biggest girl. There was nobody—including Russell Morgan, his chief competition—who would dispute that. But could she win? Wallace simply did not know. Nobody did. Not even Russell. Maybe especially Russell. Their girls stood at the opposite ends of the spectrum of where female bodybuilding was going. Or maybe was *not* going.

Nobody knew or could agree on what women wanted or needed to be. Not even women themselves. With men it was easy. Men needed to be as big, as thick, and as defined—their musculature cut, each muscle standing separate and distinct from every other muscle—as could possibly be accomplished.

A good big man would beat a good little man every time. It was true that a great bodybuilder, Frank Zane, who was by every standard of the sport small had won the world, but it was also true that when he did he was not competing against Arnold Schwarzenegger. When Arnold came along, neither Frank Zane nor anybody else had a chance. Arnold was not only more massive than anybody else but he was taller, too, with maybe the exception of Lou Ferrigno. And above all else, he was good. Good as God.

And every year he had competed he had won the world until he retired. He had won it seven times before he retired, married rich, and put what no movie audience had ever seen on the screen. He could not act, but who the hell cared? All he had to do was take off his shirt to be worth ten million dollars because every man's dick in the audience got hard and every woman got wet to the knees. When Arnold shucked down to posing briefs, it was magic, mystery, and fantasy time. Mainly fantasy. And the fantasy never dealt with but two things: mounting and being mounted.

Now that Arnold had retired to sell popcorn and dreams—that the dreams were wet, wild, and totally unattainable mattered not at all, that's why they were dreams—but now that Arnold was out of competition there was a new champion, Lee Haney, black and massive in a way that even Arnold had not been, massive beyond belief and perhaps even dreams. He had won the world six times in a row and everybody knew he would beat Arnold's record of seven world wins. Lee Haney would win as many times as he wanted to win. There was nobody on the horizon who could touch him. The competition every year was for second place behind Haney.

But where did that leave women bodybuilders? Again, nobody knew. Everybody thought he knew when Rachel McLish won the world. She was muscular, and also perfectly symmetrical and coordinated, but most of all she could be put in a dress and taken home to mother. But in a short period of time following Rachael McLish's reign as world champion, if you put a world-class female bodybuilder in a dress, she could not be taken home to mother or many other places because they looked like men tricked out in women's clothing. Out of posing briefs and off the stage, they were monsters to behold. The judges and the fans that followed the sport as well as the competitors themselves could not decide what the ideal woman ought to look like.

It was a dogfight. One year a woman in one of the lighter divisions would take the overall; the next year a woman bigger than most men could ever hope to be, one that only looked human as long as she was under posing lights, would take it. Up close and dressed in anything feminine, female bodybuilders started looking like something God had made suffering from a divine hangover and caught in delusional terrors beyond human imagination.

Wall's woman, Marvella, would win her division. And Russell's Shereel would win hers. But which one would win the overall, the best in show? Which one would in fact and in name win the world? Nobody knew. The world of bodybuilding was as neatly divided in opinion about women in the sport as if the division had been made with calipers and a scale.

This Cosmos here at the Blue Flamingo Hotel on Miami Beach was being billed as the Future of Female Bodybuilding, billed as the way it would go. And Wall had bet his reputation not just on the side of Olympian proportions, but on the side of unthinkable size. He had decided it was the American way. Where was the American who owned anything that he did not wish was bigger? Wall's waking hours were haunted by Donald Trump, and his dreams were shot through with whole populations of Donald Trumps, amassing, gathering, piling, higher and higher, adding numbers without end, because as everybody knew, numbers had no end.

Russell Morgan had, on the other hand, bet his reputation on everything that was in contradistinction to Wallace's. He reasoned—though it could hardly be called reason because it was only dimly conscious on his part and certainly he could never have put it into words nor would he have wanted to—but he knew in his blood that bigness was finished. We had long since pushed west to the Pacific Ocean and there was nowhere else to go. What good were a million or so megaton nuclear bombs when we could not even kick the ass of a raghead named Khaddafi living in a tent in the middle of the fucking desert? And hadn't a puny country of malformed, slant-eyed slopes sent our best fighting men back to us humiliated or dead or permanently deranged?

No, bigness was dead or as dead as it could ever be. Which meant it could never be entirely dead because men had balls. If God had left balls off the human race, we would probably—Russell again knew in his blood—still be peacefully munching fruit on some African savanna. But men had balls and consequently their arms or their dicks could never be big enough.

Nor anything else. Except maybe their women. Their women could be kept small, small and perfect in a way men could never be because men could never accept being small—whether perfect or not—and still stay sane.

And that was why Wallace had gone straight to anabolic steroids for his girls and Russell had not. Shereel was clean. She had never had a spike loaded with a syringe full of male growth hormones thrust into the hard, sculpted cheek of her ass, while Marvella's cheeks—just as hard and just as beautifully sculpted, but massive in their monstrous size and power—were on a regular basis nakedly proposed to Wallace's expert ministrations with needle and syringe.

And that was where he was now, the needle lying on his thick and callused palm, ready to give her an injection of the magic juice, the breakfast, lunch, and dinner of the modern champion. Marvella was going through her posing routine to taped music under lights and in front of a ceiling-to-floor mirror he had installed in her room. The routine was only ninety seconds long but she had been at it now—the routine, over and over again—for just more than an hour, a routine that was a fluid kind of dance in which she struck and held poses that lasted only seconds at a time, poses that made parts of her body leap into configurations as though cut from black marble: double biceps, abdominals, hamstring and calf like inverted diamonds, split and striated quadriceps, and flared latissimus dorsi.

The floor under her feet was awash with her sweat. Veins—called vascularity in the parlance of the trade—worked alive over her entire body. Two veins big as pencils even traced down her tightly muscled stomach and disappeared into the tiny white triangle of cloth covering the prominent ridge of bone under her pubic hair.

She had worked tirelessly and without complaint, locked into her own private trance that had room for but a single dream, the top of the world, not only beating but humiliating every woman who dared come against her.

Whether she was training or posing or competing, something

another champion, Smokin' Joe Frazier, had said always blazed
in a place only she could see: "I don't want to knock my op-
ponent out. I want to hit him, step away, and watch him hurt.
I want his heart." Like the great fighter, Marvella wanted her
competitor's heart. Winning wasn't good enough. Only total
destruction satisfied. That was the steroids cooking in her blood.
Pure chemical hostility and brutality. And Wallace knew it. That
was why he held the syringe so lovingly and with such tenderness.

"Marvella," Wallace said softly as the music to her posing
routine ended.

The music started again, but she had stopped, standing utterly
still in front of the mirror, watching the sweat run on her black
unblemished skin, her eyes clear and wide and watching not
Wall but her reflected image in the mirror as her massive rib
cage rose and fell in a slow, powerful, and unhurried rhythm.

Even though Wall had created her—building her over the
years in slow, agonizing increments of size and power and stam-
ina—she remained to him a magnificent mystery and an intimidation, an intimidation that he fought daily, sometimes literally
hour to hour, even minute to minute, a battle never to let her
see. No trainer could show intimidation in the face of the athlete
he trained. That way led not only to madness, but also to certain
defeat, which was worse.

But God she was beautiful, beautiful beyond anything he had
ever seen or thought to see, five feet ten inches tall, a hundred
and fifty-five pounds of rock-solid muscle cut to ribbons and
perfectly symmetrical: sixteen-and-a-half-inch neck, sixteen-
and-a-half-inch upper arms, sixteen-and-a-half-inch calves, tiny,
almost delicate wrists, knees, and ankles, and a twenty-four-
inch waist that had an abdominal wall unlike any he had ever
seen on any athlete, man or woman, showing as it did six distinct
layered rows of muscle under skin utterly without subcutaneous
fat, the finely toned rows of muscle starting in her solar plexus
and ending where her richly furred pubic hair grew at the base
of her belly.

He wanted her, wanted her in a desperate way he had never wanted another woman, and he meant to have her. But not until she won the world. Nothing could get in the way of that. And he could wait.

Patience and perseverance is the price of mastery. That was the logo on his BLACK MAGIC GYMNASIUM stationery. It was even tattooed on the bottoms of both his feet, the only place a body-builder could confidently hide a tattoo. His own trainer had the words indelibly stitched onto the bottoms of his feet when he himself was hardly more than a boy, long before he even understood what the words meant. But he had come to understand finally and he lived by them.

His trainer, the legendary maker of myths, Jonathan "Greatness or Death" Goldstein, Jewish and long dead now, made sure he understood, understood in such a way and so profoundly that the tattooed legend ultimately left his feet and came to live stitched into his beating heart. Wall had never told that to a living soul, but he knew it to be true. Marvella had the same line on the bottoms of both her feet.

She had stood without moving since he had spoken her name, her eyes locked on her mirrored image, her face with high, flat cheekbones and wide smooth brow showing nothing at all, no sign of exhaustion or any trace of the extended torture of an hour of nonstop posing. An hour of posing was worse by far than three hours under heavy weight in the gym. Wall had never known another athlete—and that included himself—who could go the way Marvella could go. And he owned her, this marvelous Marvella, just as he owned her younger sisters, all back home in the Detroit gym now, Starvella, Shavella, Jabella, and Vanella (the lightest by far of the five sisters, the color of richly creamed coffee, and the most beautiful), owned them the way Jesus had owned the disciples. He did not know when that way of thinking about them had come to him, but when it had, it stuck. And he knew it was true. He owned them just as "Greatness or Death" had owned him.

"Come get it, Champ," said Wall.

Marvella turned and showed him her brilliant teeth in a smile open and deeply affectionate as any lover's. But the smile was not for him. It was for the spike he held out toward her in his open hand.

She did not so much walk toward him as she floated, floated the way dancers float, her toes slightly turned outward, the balls and heels of her feet meeting the floor simultaneously with each step she took. Her eyes never left the needle, or the loving smile her face.

She reached and touched the syringe, letting her long, slender fingers, fingers covered with little pads of yellow callus, trail softly over its length. When she touched the steel of the needle itself, her lips parted in a quick little intake of breath and Wallace saw the wet tip of her tongue.

He turned her and with his free hand gently pulled down the bottoms of her posing briefs, pulled them all the way down, marveling as he always did at the deep, darker, lovely furrow between her high, thickly muscled cheeks.

"Bend," he said, his voice gone hoarse, and the breathing ragged in his throat.

She bent, put her hands on her knees, and proposed herself to him. None of this was necessary and surely she must have known it, but if she did she had never objected. The injection could just as well have been given low on her hip. But this was the way it had always been done, over a period of seven years now, since the time she was fifteen years old.

"Give it to me," she said, her own voice husky now. "Give it *all* to me."

He buried the shining steel needle in her, buried it deep, and held it there a long beat before depressing the plunger on the syringe.

TEN

Russell had Julian's head caught in his huge hand and he felt a mad desire to tear it right off his shoulders. But instead he pushed it far back on the thin stem of his neck so that light from the window behind Dexter Friedkin's desk fell deep into his blood-encrusted nostrils.

"What do you think?" said Dexter Friedkin.

"I've been permanently disfigured," moaned Julian, unable to move under Russell's hand. Russell's brutal, impersonal fingers felt like iron clamps and a curious looseness had flooded first Julian's bowels and then his loins. God, it hurt, hurt in a way that made him wish it would never stop.

"Permanently disfigured, my ass," said Russell. "Shut up and let me take a look."

"Precisely," said Dexter Friedkin, looking at a spot just over Julian's head to avoid looking at what Russell might be doing. "Do try to be a man, Julian, for heaven's sake."

Russell used the thumb of the hand that wasn't holding Julian's head to tear away the bloody scabs from his nose in one vicious swipe, and Julian farted briefly. He even thought he might shit himself in a spasm of joy under Russell's rough handling. The thought frightened him terribly and in a focused effort of will he clamped the cheeks of his ass shut. It was not the thought that he might besoil himself that frightened him so, it was that he might do it in a spasm of joy. No such feeling or thought had ever come to him, and Julian felt basely and wonderfully violated, which shamed him beyond saying. What he was feeling cut back across—and canceled—all his yogurt and jogging and avoidance of tobacco, his buffed nails, tanned skin, and his sense of oneness with the bodybuilders.

He farted again, this time not briefly and not quietly. Dexter Friedkin heard the fart and was furious. Employees of the Blue Flamingo Hotel were not allowed to fart, at least not during working hours. They were all warned—right down to the dishwashers—to avoid offensive foods, foods that caused flatulence. Cabbage, peanuts, and by far the worst, beans. Guests of the finest and most expensive hotel on Miami Beach had the right not to suffer farts, unless, of course, they were the farts of the guests themselves.

From where he sat behind his desk, still careful not to see Russell's examination of Julian's bloody nose, Mr. Friedkin said softly but sternly, "That will be quite enough out of you, Julian."

"Sorry, sir," Julian said.

"You pussy," said Russell.

Julian clamped himself tighter and said in the smallest of voices, "What?"

Mr. Friedkin said, "Shut up, Julian."

Russell shook Julian's head roughly. "You're not cut, you're scratched, you little asshole. If Nail wanted to cut you, you wouldn't have a nose now. All you need is a couple of butterfly Band-Aids."

Julian squirmed under his hand, whether from pleasure or from pain he had no notion, and said, "But the blood . . ."

"All head wounds bleed like this, dipshit. Your nose is as full of blood vessels as your scalp. Don't worry about the blood."

"I think I need a doctor."

"And I think," said Russell, turning his head loose and clamping Julian's nose between his thick fingers, "that you need to keep your nose out of my business before I rip it off your face."

"Mr. Morgan, I'd really rather you not do that," Dexter Friedkin said. But he was lying and only wished that he himself could give Julian's nose a good twisting. He was quite put out with him for coming into his office with a wounded nose.

As for Julian, he had gone instantly and completely rigid but he did not make a sound except the one he could not help: a sudden, rapid clapping of his cheeks against the chair where he sat.

Russell turned his attention full upon Dexter Friedkin but held fast to Julian's nose, even giving it a little twist now and again, first to the left and then to the right, to emphasize his words as he spoke.

"*We*—all of us—the *Cosmos* itself, you, *me*, everybody's going down the *shitter*."

Julian's nose hurt all the way to his navel. He felt himself sinking toward a delicious faint.

"Why don't you turn Julian loose and sit down, Mr. Morgan," Dexter Friedkin said. He thought Julian had probably been hurt enough to teach him a lesson, although he was not yet at all sure what the lesson was. But more than that, the threat to his show made Julian's nose, even Julian's life, irrelevant.

Russell had forgotten he even had Julian by the nose, but he gave it one final vicious turn before taking his hand away and cleaning his fingers of blood and snot on Julian's shirt. He looked back at Dexter Friedkin just in time to see him adjust his hair with both hands. Jesus, the son of a bitch was moving his hair around on his head like a baseball cap. Had he been doing that all along and Russell simply had not noticed? Probably so. It occurred to Russell Morgan that this entire hotel was rotten with weirdness, a raging epidemic of behavior that was not acceptable, that was without discipline. This was not the first time he had been shaken badly at a bodybuilding competition by the realization that he was probably the only normal person there. But he had always been careful because if he knew anything he knew that weirdness was more contagious than swine flu. A prudent man took precautions not to catch it.

Russell put his hands on Dexter Friedkin's desk and leaned toward him. "You've got problems, Dex. Everything is turning very sour."

Dexter Friedkin reached for his hair, caught himself, and instead tented his fingers, a habitual gesture to keep him from moving his toupee. "I know all about what happened down by the pool. The Bat will be taken care of."

"I could give a shit about the Bat," Russell said. "I'm talking Turnipseeds." He turned to look at Julian, then back to Dexter Friedkin. "You have a hotel doctor?"

"Of course we've got a hotel doctor," said Dexter Friedkin. "And nurse, and physical therapist, and..."

Russell held up his thick square-fingered hand and Dexter Friedkin swallowed the rest of whatever he was going to say.

"Julian, go see the doctor. If I take hold of you again I won't be so gentle."

A little shameful jolt of pleasure leapt out of Julian's lap at the thought of what Russell Morgan might have in mind for him, but Julian sat without moving, looking at Mr. Friedkin.

"Go let Dr. Gonzales take care of your nose, Julian," Dexter Friedkin said.

"Yes sir," Julian said.

When he was gone, Dexter Friedkin, unable to contain himself, moved his ears, causing his scalp to shake his hairpiece as though a breeze had moved through it. "I admire you," he said to Russell, who had straightened from the desk. Had this fucker's hair actually moved?

"I have always admired you, Russell Morgan," Dexter Friedkin said.

"What?"

"You have no more loyal fan than I."

"That's good," Russell said. "But I'm not the point here. What do you know about the Turnipseeds?"

"I know everything that concerns the Blue Flamingo Hotel. I make it my business to know. The Turnipseeds are a minor inconvenience, just another family of tourists."

"I wish to God they were, but 'minor' and 'inconvenience' and 'tourist' won't cover the Turnipseeds."

"They'll be leaving us shortly, I assure you."

"You can't assure me anything about the Turnipseeds, and they won't be leaving."

"Of course they will. This is my hotel."

"It's your ass too if you fuck with them."

"I beg your pardon."

"We're talking certified lunatics here. Killers."

Mr. Friedkin shot out of his chair and did a nervous little dance around his desk to where Russell stood. "Lunatics? Killers? I'll not have it. Do you hear me? I simply will not have it. Besides, I've already decided to get them better accommodations—that is to say, suites at another hotel on the beach. They'll go and be glad to do it."

"No, they won't."

"They're living like Orientals up there right now," Dexter Friedkin said, pointing to the ceiling. "The men packed in one room. The mother and daughter in the other. I'm getting them suites, goddammit. *Each* of them a suite, just to get them out of here and make sure we cut our losses."

"They still won't go."

"If it comes to that, they'll have to. I'll have them thrown out. I'm not without friends in high places in this town. I don't want to do it because it'll be messy but I will."

"You just don't know how messy. It can't be done. Shereel Dupont is a Turnipseed."

An ugly pallor spread under Dexter Friedkin's tan. "A Turnipseed?"

"A Turnipseed."

"But how can that be?"

"What you've got upstairs is her mama and daddy, two brothers, a sister, and . . . and . . . well, she says her fiancé. The fiancé is the craziest of the bunch. They're all semi-nuts, but the one called Nail Head is the most dangerous."

Dexter Friedkin stumbled around the desk and collapsed into his executive's chair. "God," he said, breathing the word softly in a long exhalation of breath. Then: "How could this happen? Her name is Shereel Dupont."

"But before it was Shereel Dupont, it was Dorothy Turnipseed."

Dexter Friedkin said, "But how could a contender"—he glanced quickly up from where he had been holding his face in his hands—"a winner of Ms. Cosmos be named Dorothy *Turnipseed*?"

"She couldn't. That's why I made her change it. I knew long ago what she could be but not with that name. The judges would never pick a Turnipseed to represent the female bodybuilders of the world. Never. So we've got to make sure the word never gets out that she's a Turnipseed. That would be very, very bad for her, the Cosmos, the hotel . . . and for you, Dexter."

"What on earth am I to do?"

"Exactly what I tell you."

"Thank God for Russell Morgan. I've always admired—"

"Yeah, you said. But I don't want or need to hear that now. You can stroke me later. In the meantime, make the Turnipseeds happy. You got that, Dex? *Happy*."

"If that's what it takes. But—"

"No buts. That's what it takes. Get'm into different rooms, the best you've got. The suites you talked about. Tell'm it's all on the hotel, the suites and anything else they want. You got that? *Anything* they want. They'll be pissed about the name change, but they're country. Shove'm enough grits and they'll be happy."

"Grits?"

"A manner of speaking, goddammit. Get with the program. And while you're at it, put a shorter leash on that young fucker that was just in here."

"Julian?"

"Yeah, Julian. Keep him out of my way. And be sure he knows the Turnipseeds've got a free ride."

"I don't like what it'll cost, but if that'll fix everything . . ."

"It won't fix everything. But it's a start."

"My God, you mean there's more?"

"Let me just run this down for you, Dex, so you'll know where you are. Wall, that liver-lipped motherfucker, saw what the Turnipseeds did by the pool, talked to them, and found out that Shereel Dupont was really Dorothy Turnipseed—*their* Dorothy Turnipseed from Waycross, Georgia. Wall went to Julian and Julian had him call me for a meeting. Then the young asshole—you really ought to try to get better help, Dex—went up to the Turnipseeds' room—I guess to bring them to the meeting—met Nail Head instead, and got his nose bloodied for his trouble. But, Shereel will handle Nail, and Nail will—I hope—handle the Turnipseeds. That only leaves Wallace Wilson for me to deal with."

"I know you're equal to the task, Mr. Morgan," Dexter Friedkin said. "I've always admired you. Do you know I remember watching you when you were only a lad of nineteen?"

"Which contest?"

"The big one."

"The Teenage Mr. America?"

"That's the one," said Dexter Friedkin, his hands grabbing each other to keep from grabbing his hair.

"You were there?"

"In the front row. And I never missed one of your shows after that. You've been a lifelong hobby of mine and an inspiration. Do you know when I was born?"

Russell Morgan did not answer. This kind of shit made him nervous. Besides, Dexter Friedkin's ears were fanning the sides of his head and his hair was fairly dancing.

"You old Gemini," Dexter Friedkin said. "I'm a Gemini too."

"No shit," said Russell, without the slightest notion of what he was talking about. He had no time for astrological signs and readings, because he did not believe in luck—either good or bad—he believed in strength and discipline.

"You and I go back a long way," Dexter Friedkin said. "Maybe we could have a little workout together before the contest. I'm proud to say that I'm a member of the body-sculpting tribe too. I'm sure you noticed the trophies." He waved his hand to indicate the shelved walls filled with little plaques and little metal men in flexed poses.

Russell ignored the trophies and came around the desk, sat on it, and sat staring down at Dexter Friedkin for a long moment during which Dexter Friedkin unaccountably blushed.

"Dex," said Russell, "do you want this Cosmos competition to be a success?"

"More than anything in the world."

"Give me the line that advertises it, the slogan that's taped right now on the wall of every weight gymnasium in the world, the question that will make this the biggest and richest contest in the history of the sport. Can you do that, Dex?"

"Of course I can. If I may boast a bit, it was I who thought of it."

Grimly, Russell said, "You may boast a bit. Say it!"

"'How big is the perfect woman?'"

"And you know that the fight is between Shereel and Marvella."

"Everybody knows that, and I think—"

"Never mind what you think, Dex. Why aren't you on the phone to your people making the Turnipseeds happy? *Very* happy, so we can make sure of having a fucking contest. And that includes Harry Barnes. Make him the happiest of the bunch."

"I will, Russell. I'll do it right now."

"Good," said Russell Morgan, getting up and walking toward the door. Without looking back, he suddenly stopped and said, "And while you're at it, get some people up to Miss Dupont's room and install a floor-to-ceiling posing mirror for her and replace all the broken furniture. Somebody trashed the fucking place."

Behind him Mr. Friedkin fairly screamed: "Trashed? What do you mean trashed?"

Russell turned slowly to face him and in a quiet, matter-of-fact voice said, "I mean, Dex, somebody broke everything in the room."

"But that is vandalism! And vandalism is not allowed in the Blue—"

"Stop with the not-allowed bullshit," Russell said. "Just do it. I think that'd be a better use of your time than wiggling your ears to move your rug around."

Mr. Friedkin gasped and both hands flew to his head. And that is the way Russell left him, holding tightly to his hair.

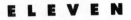

arline was lying naked on the king-sized bed shaped like a heart, which she very nearly filled, and staring at herself in the heart-shaped mirror above her. Her breasts, each slightly bigger than her head, had collapsed on either side of her and now lay snugly in her armpits. She was in a mild state of shock. Her whole family was and had been since a small army of bellboys had appeared with velvet pushcarts to move each of them into suites.

Her daddy, Alphonse, had very nearly cut one of them with his pocketknife before they finally made him understand that the Turnipseeds were now guests of the hotel in honor of Ms. Shereel Dupont and that their lodging would cost nothing, neither would their food, telephone calls, laundry, or anything else they might require.

"Would you care for anything while your things are being moved?" asked a huge black man wearing white gloves who was directing the bellboys, all of whom were Cuban.

"That's mighty white of you," said Alphonse. They had just finished several buckets of Colonel Sanders fried chicken, and Alphonse was sucking his teeth and digging in his mouth with a long nicotine-stained finger. "I guess you could step out and git some toothpicks and a carton of Camel cigarettes, if you a mind to."

The man in the white gloves silently snapped his fingers and a wiry little bellboy who was about sixty years old with a thin gray mustache flew out the door without a word.

Alphonse cackled and slapped his thigh with his felt hat and said, "Ain't no flies gone light on that feller even if he ain't our kind of people."

"Wisht you'd thought to tell him to bring back a little chocolate ice cream to go behind that Colonel Sanders," said Motor, who still wore only his bathing suit and was absently wiping his fingers on the long silky hair covering his belly.

Without the big man even snapping his white-gloved fingers, another Cuban flew after the one that had just left.

Earnestine, who had come with her daughter there to the room where the men were staying to share the Colonel Sanders fried chicken, was impressed. "Any wonder why these skinny little spicks from Cuber taken over Miami? They fast. They *real* fast."

And the Cubans were fast. Before Alphonse had finished picking his teeth and they had got through the biggest tub of ice cream any of them had ever seen, Earnestine and Fonse had been moved into a suite together and the others into a suite of their own. Earline had to take the bridal bower, rooms ordinarily reserved exclusively for honeymooners but the only suite still available because of the unexpected and sudden demand.

The enormous bed had a mirror attached to the canopy that covered it, and Earline watched now as her hand slid into her purse lying beside her. She withdrew a Colonel Sanders drumstick wrapped in a napkin which she had put there to eat later instead of throwing it away because little children were starving in Ethiopia. Earline stuck the drumstick in her mouth and stripped the meat off of it slowly as she carefully examined herself in the mirror above the bed. God, there was a lot of her. With her feet nearly a yard apart her thighs still met all the way to her knees.

But her skin was pretty. Nobody could deny her that, she thought. Pretty and soft and whiter than milk and without blemish. With her free hand she lifted one of her breasts and set it on her sternum, but then she took a deep breath and it slid off and tumbled into her armpit again. Her navel was as deep as a teacup and when she sighed, the broad lake of her stomach trembled.

She stared a long time at the slightly reddish triangle of hair where it grew thick and curling at the base of her belly. How lovely and silky it was. She could not remember when she had seen it last. The mirror was the only reason she was seeing it now, and—she realized—the mirror was what made it too embarrassing to touch. But she wanted to touch it. She did. Its silkiness made her want to feel it on the ends of her fingers. It made her feel pretty.

And she did not often feel pretty. The slightly reddish hair seemed to glow not with reflected light but with a light of its own and it made her feel pretty even if both her breasts were under her arms and her dimpled thighs cleaved one to the other all the way to her knees. Her sister had never had a problem with her weight but fat had plagued Earline for as long as she could remember. Despite her mother's assurance to the contrary, Earline was convinced that men were not attracted to women with a weight problem.

"Weight problem?" her mother had said the night she had been graduated from Waycross Junior College. "Now that you old enough to talk about such as this, lemme explain a little something to you. Ever man says he wants to stand in front of the preacher with a little bony thing like Jane Fonder—you know, that sweaty little hipless and titless wonder who jumps around on the TV—but if a man does marry one like that he wishes ever night of his life he could put about sixty pound on her before they git between the sheets. It ain't saying a thing agin menfolk but they do like to have something to root around in, something big and soft that wears easy."

Earline felt the blood come up out of her breast and neck and flood her face.

Her mother took Earline's face in her hands: "Well, now ain't you a precious thing. By the good Lord's grace, I can be proud I raised a girl who can still blush when she's twenty year old. I can be proud of that if nothing else. Ain't many left any more that can blush oncet they git past ten. Don't you worry about a thing, you gone make some man a good wife."

Earline raised her hand and touched her lips, lips covered
with a slippery film of grease from the Colonel Sanders drumstick. She moved her fingers over her lips and little jolts of
pleasure radiated out from her mouth and took her whole body,
all the way to her feet, making her toes wiggle, because she was
not feeling her fingertips on her lips but rather Bill Bateman's
lips when he had been pinned underneath her and squirming.

She closed her eyes so that she could not see her hand as she
buried her fingers in the silky triangle of her pubic hair and gave
it a long, not very gentle jerk, first this way and then that, all
the while feeling Bill Bateman's monstrously hard chest swelling
against her, each muscle individually leaping there, finally buried deeply in her breasts that had suddenly come alive from the
heat of him.

And all the while her singing nerve endings were sending
splattered indecipherable messages to her brain, she kept telling
herself over and over that she was a professionally trained therapist in Problems of Living. And the first problem of living—it
had been endlessly drummed into her—was breathing. She had
been stamped, certified, and approved as one qualified to keep
the lungs breathing, to keep the beating heart beating. Then
why had Mr. Bill Bateman, universally called the Bat she had
learned later at the same time she learned his name, why had
the Bat turned into a single devouring pair of lips? She knew
then and knew now it was his tongue, first erratically thrashing
and then stroking rhythmically inside her own mouth, that had
taken her mind off her professional obligations.

She took her hand out of the hair between her legs and opened
her eyes and saw in the mirror above her that her breasts, still
snugly caught under her arms, had turned a bright red and that
her nipples had hardened in an unseemly way. What did it all
mean? The single thing she knew was that whatever it was had
not been covered at Waycross Junior College in the course of
study for Problems of Living.

She sat up on the side of the bed, with her hands caught
under her stomach, which sat now squarely in her lap. She

breathed deeply and slowly. This simply would not do. She had
to get hold of herself because she believed deeply in common
sense. And yet everything in the rooms she now occupied
worked against control, common sense, and what her head told
her was possible.

From where she sat everything she could see was heart-
shaped and bright red, done in velour or velvet or maybe both.
She was not sure. She was sure of very little in this place. She
was glad to have been given it to live in, but it was unlike
anything she had ever seen or imagined. And while it made her
feel good, it frightened her more than a little. This was a place
for people who had just been married, but not only had she not
just been married, she had never even been close to being married. And to her mind marriage was more than a little like these
rooms, beautiful and strangely wonderful, but at the same time
scary, too.

Not only were the bed and the mirror above it heart-shaped,
but so were the lamps and nightstands on either side of the bed.
The long, thickly padded bench at the foot of the bed had been
bent into a heart, too. The heavy drapes that hung at the win-
dows fell in loops of hearts, and even the ankle-deep, blood-
red carpet that covered the floor had the designs of swirling and
looping hearts in it. She turned her head and saw that the pillow
beside her was not only formed like a heart, but had little hearts
sewn into it, which themselves formed still larger hearts. It made
her head swim and she got off the bed.

She padded naked across the bedroom to the door that led
into the sitting room where every single piece of furniture was
shaped in varying and wondrously convoluted forms of hearts.
Without thinking about it or even realizing she was doing it,
her soft, thick, but curiously small hand lifted and pressed her
chest where she could feel her own heart thumping along in a
maddened little frenzy as though she had been climbing flights
of stairs or perhaps running.

The thought came to her that no woman belonged in such
rooms without a man, and that thought was scariest of all be-

cause she had had so little intimate contact with men in her life. Her size had kept her from such contact and she did not even resent it. It seemed to her just and right. She knew she was a pretty girl, but large, very large. And so a male hand, a hand she had dreamed of in the night and thought of in the day, had never come to examine with delicious and caring tenderness her various creases and declivities and—she freely admitted, because she prided herself on a certain common sense and acceptance of the inevitable rightness of the world—her monstrous roundnesses, monstrous even if they were covered with what she knew to be her best asset, her very beautiful, unblemished, and naturally soft skin. Yes, she did have wonderful skin, but *God* such a lot of it.

She turned away from the sitting room to the door that led into the bathroom. She moved on the balls of her feet as though she were stealing through a place where she did not belong and, consequently, might at any minute be discovered, found out, and confronted. Such a feeling was not new to her. She had known it off and on all her life, that feeling of being found out and confronted, a feeling of being found guilty, although she had no idea what it was she might be found guilty of.

One look into the bathroom made her face hot with shame and something larger and of greater consequence than even of shame, which she only dimly recognized as desire, the desire of blood pounding against blood. Because she knew all about matters sexual, all the wet nocturnal spasms that happened between men and women. But she only knew them secondhand, by hearsay. She knew things that she felt deeply and darkly at the center of herself that she could not for the life of her have told anyone, even herself, maybe especially herself, *how* she had come to know them. But the knowledge was there anyway, rooted in her as solid as bone.

The bathroom was enormous, but it was not its size that brought the rush of rising blood in her. The heart-shaped design of everything in the apartment had been strange enough, had brought thoughts rushing into her that she could not have even named, but the shape of the heart had followed her right on into the bathroom and it was overwhelming. The sunken heart of the bathtub was not only big enough for two people—*a man and a woman*, the thought screamed inside her head—but it was big enough for a whole family of people or maybe just big enough for two people—*Man, Woman*—to participate in ingenious, inventive, unsayable flounderings. And even the little steps leading down into the tub were hearts too.

She cut her eyes from the tub in an involuntary rush of embarrassment and desire only to have her gaze fall on two toilets. *Two!* And not only were they shaped like hearts, they were close enough for two people sitting on them to hold hands. The possibility of two people doing such a thing made her feel faint.

She moved closer, still creeping quietly on the balls of her feet, to better see the two dainty little thrones, but before she even got close enough to verify what she already knew, it was obvious that one of them could only be a bidet. She knew what it was for and even knew the word, even though she had no notion where she had ever learned the word *bidet*, and certainly she had never seen one. She crept closer and peered into it and entirely against her will she not only imagined sitting on it but also imagined Bill "the Bat" Bateman sitting beside her. More than that, they were holding hands naturally and without shame. She clearly felt his thick, callused hand in hers and felt too his hot and wonderful eyes locked on hers. She stood for a long time, not moving, not even thinking, rather only lost in the wonderful moment, a moment she wished for with all her heart.

When she finally did hear the bell on the door of the bridal bower chiming out "Here Comes the Bride," she had no notion at all how long it had been ringing. She did not know which one of her family it might be but she was glad for the relentless chiming that interrupted her thoughts and took her away from her contemplation of the little thrones. She turned on her heels and charged out of the bathroom, moving with surprising swiftness and lightness because in spite of her size she had a gait that was smooth as glass. She charged back into the bedroom where her one-piece bathing suit was still on the floor where she had dropped it at the foot of the bed. She'd still been wearing it when the Cuban bellboys had moved her to the bridal suite.

"Minute," she called, "I'm coming just in a sec."

She thought briefly of pulling herself back into the bathing suit but decided against it because it was a tad tight, being as it was two sizes too small—she bought everything two sizes too small—and it would take too long to pack herself back into it. And all the while the wedding march kept chiming despite the fact that she never quit trying to make whoever was on the other side of the door understand that she would be right there in a sec.

Over by the door lay her open suitcase, a blue, packing-crate-size thing that she and her mother had once found on a trip to Jacksonville. Earline bent, her cheeks flaring open like a vast flower, and pulled out her blue print housecoat, the first thing that came to hand in the suitcase.

She was still belting it about her middle as she opened the door, saying, "You old honey, I kept on hollering I'd be just a sec," and found herself face-to-face not with a member of her family but looking rather dead into the face of Mr. Bill "the Bat" Bateman, who was wearing wraparound, aviator sunglasses and the same posing briefs he had been wearing down by the pool when she had thrown him on his back and given him CPR against his will.

Bill Bateman stood still as stone regarding her with his finger on the doorbell. But at least he had stopped ringing it even if he had not taken his finger off it. She was startled not just by the fact that it was the Bat, but by how short he was: hardly a half-head taller than she. He had seemed like a giant when she had him on his back down by the pool, her mouth searching for his as he thrashed about under her, the thick, striated lobes of his heaving chest pressing up into her breasts.

They stood regarding each other until finally Bill Bateman slowly dropped his hand from the bell and said, "Well, hi there again."

Earline's eyes followed his hand as he dropped it to his side and her eyes came to rest on the tiny red bikini briefs he was wearing, or more precisely on the ingenious way he had arranged his cock and balls behind the thin triangle of fabric, drawing his cock up and turning it in such a way that the head of it proposed itself to her like a tiny doorknob, a doorknob that for one totally insane instant she felt she might actually reach out and take into her hand. She was suddenly, intensely aware of the pendulous globes of her breasts swinging loose under her thin housecoat and she gathered it tightly at her throat with both hands and said: "I thought you was Motor or Turner or maybe Nail Head." She spoke without raising her eyes, directly addressing the knob of his cock.

Bill Bateman's expression did not change and his voice was light and quick as a young boy's. "Motor or Turner or maybe Nail Head, you say?"

The accent was Southern and Earline was glad for that, for the familiarity of it, realizing also that in her confusion she was very nearly strangling herself, so tightly did she squeeze the housecoat at her throat. She released her grip a bit and said, "Or maybe even my mama and daddy name Alphonse and Earnestine." She knew she was babbling but could not help it. At least, though, she had managed to raise her eyes from the posing briefs to the sunglasses he was wearing, which she thought was just the cutest thing.

"Nosirree," he said, "I'm Bill Bateman, called the Bat by near 'bouts everbody since I been eighteen year old." As he spoke, his chest had been gradually swelling, the thick wings of muscle underneath his arms flaring, until Earline imagined he might be about to drop to one knee right there in the doorway and commence doing what he had done earlier down by the pool that had confused her into thinking he might be at death's door. But then as quickly and easily as he swelled up, he deflated, his famed wings disappearing somewhere into his back. "And I just come by up here to say I was sorry about down there by the pool. I didn't understand exactly, you see, how—"

"Mercy me," said Earline, "I ought to be the one doing the apologizing 'cause if anybody misunderstood ittas me and me alone, not even my fambly. They just went along with it 'cause I got the degree in Problems of Living, and I just told'm—"

"No need for nobody to apologize for nothing," said the Bat. "And that's how come I come by, to say that."

Which was a lie. He had come by to admire her fat. Bill Bateman was a secret connoisseur of fat, especially of fat women, and most especially if they seemed to enjoy their fat, which this one seemed to.

"I know your name," said Earline, "and I ain't even innerduced myself." She liked this one, even if he was a short thick one. Normally Earline admired tall thin ones. But she liked this Bill Bateman even if he was called the Bat, and a short thick one at that.

"Oh I know all about you," said the Bat, "and you family too. I was told all about you when they taken and given me a free ride on account of what happened. Wudn't for you and the rest of them that jumped me—well, I don't mean jumped me. I understand now—but anyhow on account of you-all I got me the nicest place you ever seen and a free ride to boot." He leaned and stuck his blunt head through the door and quickly scanned the room. "Course, I ain't got nothing quite this fancy I don't believe but it'll do me just fine."

"This here is the bridal bower," said Earline, "is how come it looks like it do."

The Bat snatched his head back into the hall and away from her ballooning breasts toward which he had been inclining. "Don't git me wrong," he said. "I didn't know you was in no bridal bower."

Earline saw right off what he was driving at, what he was thinking. She blushed deeply but was enormously pleased nonetheless. "Now, Mr. Bat, you ole thing, it ain't nobody in here but me. I ain't got no use for a bridal bower. I thought to have me a career before I went ahead on and got myself married. A course it is real hard this day and time for a girl like me to stay single very long."

Bill Bateman immediately leaned in toward her, his head specifically inclining toward her breasts, between which he thought, if given the opportunity, he could make his head disappear. "Now I know that is right for a dead solid fact, a pretty girl like you."

Earline thought she might swoon. "Ittas just the only one of these big ole places they had left after they taken and given one to Daddy and Mama and Nail Head and Motor and Turner, all of'm one apiece, so here I am in the bridal bower right by myself, but it is real nice even if I do say so myself." She stopped and took a long deep breath because in her nervous state standing there in front of the Bat in nothing but a thin print housecoat and keenly aware of her nakedness underneath and aware too of the Bat's knoblike cock pointing toward her from under his little panties, standing there like that had caused her to speak without breathing in one long stringing gush of words. "But I ain't showing the manners my mama raised me to have," she said, when she had her breath back. "Why don't you step in and visit a minute? We don't have to talk right here in the doorway this-away. That is, Mr. Bat, if you a mind to and got the time."

"I ain't got a thing if I ain't got time," said Bill Bateman.

And so quickly did he spring into the room that he would have surely run directly into her if she had not been light on her feet, sidestepping his charge, turning and bouncing back into the room, the unrestrained flesh of her hips undulating in wonderful waves under her robe.

"But you don't Mr. Bat me," he said in a little gasp that he had meant to be a sort of witty chuckle. "You just call me the Bat, or Billy Bat or Bill the Bat or Batey Batman just like everybody else."

He had kept coming straight for her as he spoke and she

moved and twisted and turned before him in a kind of dance around the room. Her robe fluttered and her flesh flounced and she had unaccountably fallen into a soft, giggling little laugh that she couldn't stop and that she thought would surely make Billy Bat think her afflicted.

But the Bat had not even heard the little sounds of laughter bubbling in her throat because he was concentrating on getting close enough to smell her. He knew the heavy fragrance of her body would come into his nostrils and even onto his tongue as deep apple pies hot from the oven and burgers dripping cheese and grease and all manner of candies and fudge brownies. He longed to heft a slab of her in his two callused hands and lick her deep sweet flesh and taste the marvelous freedom of her life that could only be expressed in such fat as she carried.

It was his deepest, fondest wish—but a wish that he usually managed to keep secret even from himself—to be drowning in a lapping sea of fat just as this Earline was who would not be cornered there in the bridal bower but rather danced and maneuvered before him as a matador might dance and maneuver before a charging bull. He finally stopped short, snorted once through his nose, and made several quick little gestures with his feet as though he might be pawing the rug.

Earline stopped too and watched him, her soft inexplicable laughter turned gaspy in her throat from the exertion of out-maneuvering Billy Bat, by which name he was now firmly fixed in her mind. Billy Bat had a nice sound, one which she immediately realized reminded her of bonbons. She loved the sound of bonbons and she loved the sound of Billy Bat and already the two were linked and singing in her head: Billy Bonbon Bat Bon Billy Bat Bat Bon. This happened to her quite a lot, a sound linking up with bonbon and becoming a little song in her head because bonbons were at the center of her life. Turner or Motor or sometimes even Alphonse would joke in front of company that she could eat a long ton of bonbons on any given day or night, and they would all laugh and she would laugh right along with them. But it was not a laughing matter and she knew it.

On her very own, in the middle of the second semester of her pursuit of the degree in Problems of Living, she had diagnosed bonbons as one of her Problems of Living. She couldn't eat a long ton of the sweet wonderful little things, but she knew that she could eat a number-two washtub full, although she had never done it. Not at one sitting anyhow. But she was never far from her bonbons, and she wasn't now. She had a five-pound box that was about half full in her open suitcase. And as Billy Bat snorted and pawed in front of her, she cut her eyes toward the suitcase and knew that in spite of herself she was going to have to have a few.

Any crisis brought this rage for bonbons on her. And Billy Bat was definitely a crisis, he and the cute little way he had contrived to arrange his cock and balls so that she kept thinking of a doorknob that needed taking hold of and twisting, opening into . . . into what? She knew and she did not know. She knew in theory well enough, but not in practice. And if the course of study in Problems of Living taught anything, it taught the necessary virtue of practice. And the excruciatingly terrible wonder of the moment was that she was alone in the bridal bower with Billy Bat where the practice of *anything* was possible.

"You light on you feet, Miss Earline," said Billy Bat, "light as the wind a blowin'."

"Why that's the sweetest thing," she said, and meant it. "That's potry, 'light as the wind a blowin'' is."

"Nothing but the truth, Miss Earline."

"Now you just call me Earline. You don't have to 'Miss' me."

Billy Bat's quick savage little feet pawed the rug. "I hope I don't have to miss you, Miss Earline. I don't want to miss you."

"Now Gadamighty, that's more potry," she said, "and I told you to leave off Miss Earlining me. Earline is good enough."

"Don't know as I can do that, sweet girl like you. My ole mama raised me to have manners and to respect sweet young girls like youself. And I do respect you. Maybe that's how come I come up here, to tell you that. Never mind what-all went on down there by the pool, I respect you and I want you to know it, sweet young girl like you."

She felt the hot swoon grab at her heart again and the blood seemed to leave her brain and she was light-headed with the last *sweet young girl* ringing and singing somewhere just behind her hot and throbbing pelvis. Billy Bat had called her a sweet young girl more times in four minutes than she had heard out of everybody else's mouth put together the whole rest of her life.

And when her eyes cut this time to the suitcase where she could clearly see the bulge of the box of bonbons under the top layer of clothes, when her eyes cut there this time, they stayed. Sweet baby Jesus, her whole body was a ringing and a singing and a throbbing and a pounding and if she didn't have a good big handful of bonbons to quiet her blood right soon, she couldn't be responsible for her actions, and she knew it, knew she was more than capable of flinging herself on Billy Bat and eating him like a bonbon if she didn't get a good big handful of the real things.

Billy Bat looked down at his feet, which had begun the raging little strokes against the rug again, and when he looked he saw Earline's one-piece right there where she had dropped it at the foot of the heart-shaped bed. The size of the thing fell like a weight in his blood. And when Earline saw Billy Bat's eyes drop to her bathing suit she spun and catdanced to the open suitcase, bent down with her back to him, and seized the bonbons from under her clothes. She came up with the candy in the very instant he came up with her one-piece hanging from his hands and the two of them stood looking at each other, he over the tentlike bathing suit and she over the bonbons that were in a carton big as a bread box. For a long instant they seemed balanced and suspended in each other's gaze.

"Purtiest thing I ever seen, this here that you had on down by the pool," said Billy Bat.

Earline felt her face would explode with the hot rush of blood.

It was as though she had found him holding a pair of her drawers. "You care for one of these?" she said, holding the box out toward him with both hands. She would have offered him anything, including a cup of her blood that seemed to have gone crazy in her veins, anything to take his eyes and mind off her bathing suit.

But Billy Bat could not now look away from the suit he was holding, taking its measure first with his eyes and then very slowly with his hands. She watched, her breath caught in her throat, as he held the top of the suit with one hand, the fabric pressed right against the front of him as though he might be measuring it for himself, and moved the other hand straight down from the ruffled top and across the ribbed stomach to the little skirted bottom, which he lifted and then took the crotch in his thickly muscled hand and, first gently, then with savage tenderness, squeezed it tightly in his iron grip.

The effect on Earline would not have been more intense if Billy Bat had squeezed her very crotch, her very naked crotch that pounded with engorged blood beneath the thin print robe. In fact she felt his hand there where no male hand had ever been, felt it hot and squeezing there, and it caused something to burn all along the nerves of her body in a way that she did not think she could bear. It was the most wonderful thing in the world. It was the most terrible thing in the world.

"Bonbons Billy Bat!" she croaked in a voice unlike any she had ever heard come out of her throat.

Billy Bat jerked his eyes up to meet hers but he held firmly to the crotch of her suit, to *her* crotch.

"How's 'at?" he said in a startled voice.

"Bonbons," she said.

"Thought that's what you said."

"In the box," she said. "You care for one? They real good."

Billy Bat held firmly to the suit and said, "Wouldn't know about that, you sweet girl, I never eat one of them bonbons."

"They real good," she said, unable to take her eyes off his hand between the legs of her suit.

"Cain't go eating candy and stuff like that," said Billy Bat. "I got the best back in the world."

But Billy Bat had first told a lie and then told the truth. It was the single biggest lie and the single biggest truth in the entire life of his world. And putting them side by side like that made him go loose and weak all along his fantastic muscles. Billy Bat's enormous truth was that he *did* have the best back in the world. But his lie, equally enormous, was that he could and did go eating candy and stuff like that. He could eat ten pounds of bonbons in ten minutes. But he could also bring it back up in ten seconds in a spectacular display of puking. Billy Bat could not hold to the rigid diet of a champion, never had been able to, but he was a secret and accomplished puker. He had started jamming his finger down his throat when he was sixteen years old, but he hadn't had to use his finger since his twenty-first birthday. At twenty-one he had become so good at it that he could simply open his mouth and his fantastic abdominal wall would fire the contents of his stomach out of his mouth in an utterly straight line for a distance of as much as fifteen feet.

It was not that he did not eat a champion's diet. He did. And when he did, he kept it. But at irregular intervals, times when he least expected it, the rage for the worst possible junk in the world would fall upon him like a sickness: Baby Ruth candy bars, dozens of them, or blueberry cobbler with artificial blueberry syrup poured over it, or quarts of chocolate ice cream and pounds of chocolate-chip cookies. And some of the times the rage would come in the form of an extreme need for a salt fix—the need often arriving in the middle of the night—and he would get out of his champion's bed and go down to the all-night convenience store and load his car with taco chips and corn chips and cheese chips, any and every chip that was covered in salt, and every salted nut he could find, and after his car was loaded, he would come back home and graze through it all, through all the cellophane packages and waxed boxes and vacuum-sealed bottles, do it all in a mindless stupor until he was packed to the point of bursting, and then he would step out onto his back porch, open his mouth, and fire it all, every last pasty bile-tasting bit of it, in a single solid stream out into the night. Then he would return to his champion's bed and sleep his champion's sleep and the next morning eat his champion's breakfast—always low fat and sodium free—and then go to the gym and train his heart out.

He did not have the freedom to eat and hold what people like Earline had the freedom to eat and hold. And for that reason their fat-layered bodies had come to represent a kind of ultimate freedom to him, a freedom he would never have. He gazed upon them as a prisoner might gaze through the barred window of his cell upon a parade of free men and women moving in laughter and joy through a sunlit street he himself would never be allowed to walk. And he looked upon Earline in that way now where she stood holding her box of bonbons in both hands while the rolls and piles of her wonderful fat seemed to undulate in the most beautiful and inviting way although she herself was standing utterly still, her eyes fixed upon what he was doing with the most private part of her bathing suit, with the most private part of *her.*

"Go ahead on," he said, "eat you one."

"Don't seem right to eat here in front of you, Billy Bat," she said, keenly aware that it was the first time she had used his cute little name aloud, and aware too of the way it dropped sweetly from her lips. "Not if you cain't eat none you own self."

"You got your life, I got mine," he said. "You go ahead on and eat youself one of them bonbons, you sweet girl."

"Well, I do think I might have one on account of I ain't had nothing much to eat and I need a little snack of something to hold me over."

Without taking her eyes off him while she talked, she had ripped the top off the box, jammed one hand inside causing little empty brown-paper bonbon cups to flutter to the floor, found not one but two bonbons, and popped them into her mouth. She closed her eyes and chewed slowly, feeling the syrupy sugar of the candy flood not only her mouth but her whole being with sweetness.

"Yes, you darling," she heard him say from behind her closed eyes. "Eat it. Eat it, you sweet honey."

She heard him say what he said, knew he said it, and yet she could not believe it. No man had ever spoken to her that way. It was almost as though this whole thing might be some wonderful dream and she dared not open her eyes. She took another bonbon out of the box.

"Yes," she heard Billy Bat say, "yes, you sweet girl, put it in you mouth."

She did.

"Suck on it," groaned Billy Bat, "roll it around on your tongue and suck on it."

She did.

"More," he said in a voice gone strange. "Take more in you mouth."

She did, lost entirely now in the sweetness of the moment and his sweet voice talking to her sweetly. She sucked and chewed, her mouth full, the candy deep in her throat. She let her eyelids open just a bit in order to see him through her lashes, to bring him closer to her and to the moment, and what she saw him doing with his mouth over the same intimate part of her bathing suit did not shock her or even surprise her, so natural did it seem in this close moment, and she shut her eyes again and concentrated on what she was doing with her own mouth.

She heard a soft moan start in Billy Bat's throat and it was some time—whether short or long, she could not tell and did not care—before she realized the same moan was in her own throat, hers answering his; she felt herself suddenly start to rise, rise up and seem to open like a flower, and at the same time she rose she started to spin, turning and turning, until she was spent and dizzy and breathing hard. She opened her eyes and saw that Billy Bat had taken her up in his arms, simply scooped her up with one of his massive arms under her legs and the other under her shoulders, and was turning slowly round and round and round there in the bridal bower. Her face was close to his face, so close she could see herself reflected in his dark aviator glasses. It was the first time she had been off her feet in a man's arms since she had been ten, when her daddy had last lifted her.

"You light as a feather, you sweet girl," said Billy Bat.

And she felt light, lighter than she had ever remembered feeling. She closed her eyes again and Billy Bat turned slowly and slowly turned.

T W E L V E

"This goddamn place is big enough to stable horses," said Nail Head from where he lounged in a huge chair by the window.

"It's nice. And it's free," said Shereel. She was standing in the living room of Nail Head's suite, holding her robe closed tightly about her. "For God's sake, try to enjoy it."

"I ain't enjoying none of this," Nail said, looking out of the window, "and I don't look to enjoy it. Ain't a hell of a lot I do enjoy anymore but whatever little bit it is to enjoy sure as hell ain't here in this place. Just to think that I got a bad foot and night sweats from fightin' in the Nam for just such a goddamn place as this and for just such assholes as I've seen on ever hand since we crossed the border into this fucking state. It do make a man wonder." He took a kitchen match out of his shirt pocket, put it in his mouth, and turned to look at Shereel. His thin lips pulled away from his teeth in what could have been a smile if it had had any humor at all in it, which it didn't. "Sister Woman, you don't have to hold that housecoat closed in here."

She badly wanted to leave, to get back to her room, but she only held the robe more closely about her and watched him. "I wouldn't have to hold it together at all if you had not cut the buttons off it."

"But I did, didn't I," he said. "I cut you buttons off."

She didn't answer him and tried to soften the look on her face, because the last thing she wanted to do was anger him. He had been crazy and wild enough before he went off to fight in Vietnam, but when he came back home from the war, he had gone beyond crazy and wild to something else, something scarier. Shereel wished she could name it but she could not. And maybe that was what made him so scary. Whatever ailed him had no name. When she looked into his eyes, it felt like she was looking into a hole, a dark hole that had no bottom.

"It's just buttons," she said. "I can sew them back on."

"Yeah," he said, "at least what I cut off, you can sew back on. Ain't everbody I touched with my knife can say that."

"Nail, I wish you'd quit saying things like that," she said. "I don't need it now, can't for a fact deal with it. I'm here for one thing. I have to concentrate. I have to win."

Again, the thin humorless smile that was not a smile. "Me?" he said. "I got to fuck."

"Not now," she said. "Not here."

"That's what you said downstairs in the room with the big table and all them chairs after we run Mr. Muscle off. As I recall, you very words: 'not now, not here.'"

"Good," she said. "I'm glad you heard and remember. But I wasn't talking about that *particular* room. I meant not *here* at the contest, not *now* when I have to win."

While she had been talking he had reached into the top of his swimming suit and released his cock, which now stood enormous and purple-veined in his lap. "Sister Woman, I didn't drive six hundred goddamn miles in my pickup truck to jack off."

The head of his cock had a housefly tattooed on it. Shereel could remember the first time she had seen it when she was fourteen years old. She had brushed at it with her hand, thinking to make the fly go away. Well, that was then and this was now. Things had changed.

"Things have changed," she said.

"Say again," he said, absently stroking his cock as though it might have been some exotic pet but never taking his eyes off her.

"I said things have changed."

"Thought that's what you said."

"If you'd think for a minute, you'd see and understand."

"A man that's worth a damn cain't do much of anything when his dick is hard. It was a time when you known that, Sister Woman."

She felt the skin tighten around her eyes and there was something in her head that was threatening to break loose. She could feel it straining to break loose deep inside her head, break loose and roll to God knows where.

"You can stop with the Sister Woman shit, too," she said.

"What you want me to call you than?" he asked, still absently stroking himself as though it was the most natural activity in the world. "Wont me to call you Shereel? 'Fraid I can't do that, Sister Woman."

"As long as nobody else is around, call me Dorothy then," she said. "Somebody else is close enough to hear, Hey You'll do just fine."

He looked down at the housefly for a long minute. Then: "I hate to say this but you talkin' like a asshole. Ole boy in the Nam talked to me that way oncet. We went out on patrol, he didn't come back. But not on account of we run into no slopes. My knife found him in the dark and left him dead on his back."

"You don't need to do that anymore either," she said. "I know as well as anybody and better than most how you are. You don't have to keep reminding me. I know."

"You don't know a goddamn thing," he said, "or you'd git over here and sit on my lap."

"Not here," she said. "Not now."

She was keenly aware she had not bathed since she had been with Russell, and she knew how Nail was. She would end up tasting Russell on Nail's cock. And at the thought of that happening, the vicious little thing in her head that was threatening to break loose jerked and lunged like a madness. And she could hear it snarling and smell the sulfur stink of its breath and heard the question it posed now as it fought to get loose in her head and the question was this: *"Are you a goddamn champion, or a goddamn punchboard?"*

"Not here. Not now," she said again.

"You already said that oncet I believe."

She did not answer him but turned her head slightly and listened to the thing that was very nearly loose. *Champion or punchboard? Who worked and died day in and day out to get here? Was it you? Could it have been you that worked and died? Then why do you have to be a punchboard for every dick that tells you to lie down? Now why is that?*

She turned to look squarely at Nail again just at the moment he was coming out of his chair toward her. He was extremely quick for so big a man, but he need not have hurried. She had no intention of moving. The thing that was trying to break loose had broken loose and was wild and screaming. She listened, standing stock still, as Nail lifted her and carried her to the chair. She only watched as he slipped off her robe and then tore her panties away from her. She was naked and still she only watched and listened as he positioned her over the arm of the huge chair. She moved however he moved her and that seemed to please him.

"Better," he said. "That is *some* better. My, my, now look at this. Sweet baby Jesus, I think I've died and gone to heaven."

She moved and did not know how she moved. It was as though she had thought long and hard about it and planned it, but she had not. Whatever moved her was the thing that was free now in her head and rolling and wild in a snarling cloud of sulfur.

"Well, now," said Nail calmly.

"Yes," she said, her voice as calm as his, as though they might have been talking about the weather.

Her shoulders had turned and her hand had gone to the quick-release case holding his switchblade and her thumb had hit the button and the knife had jerked open in her hand. It was all a blur of speed that she did not think about but when she stopped, she had the silver-blue steel of the switchblade against the base of his cock, her beautiful hand, veined and muscled, holding steady.

Nail Head stood very still, and when he spoke his voice was

calm and abstracted. "Just when I thought I'd died and gone to heaven, too."

"If you go," she said, "you'll go as a gelding."

"You mean to do it?" he said.

"Try me," she said.

"What would you ole daddy think?" he said.

"He probably wouldn't understand. But you would still be minus a cock."

"Them muscles ain't turned you butch has it? How come you so innersted in cuttin' my dick off?"

"How come you can't listen?" she said. "I try to tell you how it is but you won't hear what I say. I have a life too."

The tension was starting to make her hand tremble.

"Shereel," he said.

She looked up at him and away from where she had been concentrating on her hand and the knife and his cock.

"Shereel," he said again, rolling the sound on his tongue. "Ain't got a bad sound to it. So that's what you are, a Shereel now?"

"I'm Shereel now and forever," she said, glancing briefly back at her hand, trying to hold it steady.

"Let me tell you something about that knife, Shereel. I think Dorothy would know it without being told, but a Shereel maybe needs to be told. You ain't ever gone hold nothing sharper in you hand, Shereel. If you don't look out, you gone shake me dickless, tremble us right on into a trick of shit we neither one'll ever git out of. That ain't the sort of knife you can hold and tremble."

"It's something to think about then, isn't it? You thinking, Nail? You thinking about it? Because if I was you, I'd think."

"That's what you would do if you was me, is it?"

"That's what I'd do. I'd rethink the whole thing."

His voice dropped a register and it came to her as the cold and awful voice he had brought back from Vietnam. "You want to cut, you fucking cunt? Then cut."

"You want it?" she said. "Is that what you want?"

"I'd ruther you cut my throat than my dick," he said. "You'd be doing me a favor if you cut my throat." He smiled, not the humorless stretching of his thin lips, but actually smiled. "But then I'd be doing *you* a favor if I cut *your* throat."

Unaccountably, she felt her eyes go hot with tears. "What a shitty thing to say."

Once more he actually smiled. "Look what you got in you hand and where you holding it and say that again."

She did look at what was in her hand and where she was holding it. Jesus, so it had finally come to this. She knew well enough what had brought her here. She had very nearly been able to drive herself crazy is what she had done.

"I don't want to cut you," she said in a voice flat and matter-of-fact.

"Never open a blade on a feller you don't mean to cut, Shereel."

She took her hand away and let the knife fall from her fingers. She got up from where she had been crouched before him and sat in the chair. She looked down at herself and then up at him.

"Go ahead," she said.

"Go ahead with what?"

"Me," she said.

"I don't think so," he said.

"I don't mind," she said.

"I ain't never raped a woman. I had the chance but never did. I'm virgin there and thought to keep it that way."

"It wouldn't be rape. If you want it, take it."

"Maybe sometime down the road we will, or maybe we won't." He turned and picked her robe off the floor. "But not here. Not now."

"Why not?" she said.

"Changed my mind." He held the robe for her. "Here. Git into this and let's go see if we can find you daddy and mama or Earline or some goddamn body."

She slipped into the robe, held it shut around her. "You can be awfully sweet when you want to be."

"I ain't thought about it," he said.

"I have," she said.

She put her arms around his chest and pressed herself into him.

"First you got a knife at my dick," he said, "and now this. Things is stranger and stranger."

"I'm the same girl I've always been," she said.

"No, you ain't," he said. "And you won't ever be again. I kept telling myself in the Nam I was the same man I'd always been, but I come to see that for a lie, come to know I wasn't and wouldn't ever be again. Things sometimes change you down to the bone, and when they do, you change forever."

"I never expected this—any of this—when it all started. If I'd known how things would be, maybe I never would have done it."

"I never expect anything," he said, "so I'd be pleased to say I ain't surprised. But I am. I'm surprised. Me wantin' pussy and you not givin' it up. My own blade in you hand set agin my own dick." He shook his head. "Then you offering pussy and me turnin' it down." He picked his knife up from the floor, folded it shut, and slipped it in the case at his belt. "I should of known the goddamn gears had slipped a cog when Fonse and everbody come up missin'."

"They not missin'," she said. "We know where they all are."

"You remember the room numbers?"

"Suites 1216, 1517, and 911. And they put Earline in the bridal bower."

"I ain't even gone comment on that," he said. "Come on, let's go see if we can find Fonse."

At the door, Nail Head turned and looked back into the suite of rooms for a moment. "You know, I told'm I didn't want this, or their charity neither one, said I could pay for my own bed. But I think I could git to like it." He cocked an eye at her. "And they gone pay for what I eat and do my laundry, too?"

"And telephone calls," she said.

"You know I don't talk on the goddamn telephone," he said.

And he didn't. That was why Shereel had to make the call when they left the conference room and got back to where he had been living in cramped quarters with Fonse and Turner and Motor. They'd found the room empty, cleaned and made up, and a note affixed to the door with a blue ribbon. The note was written in a fine hand on thick watermarked stationery with a gold-leaf border asking that Mr. Harry Barnes—distinguished and official guest of the Blue Flamingo Hotel—call the front desk for important information. Nail had been outraged that anybody had touched his bag, which contained, along with his shaving kit and two changes of clothes, a loaded .357 Magnum wrapped in an oiled cloth and a fragmentation grenade wrapped in nothing.

"Everything's all right," Shereel said. "Just let me make the call."

"If it's Lipschitz on the line, tell'm this time he loses his whole nose."

But it wasn't Lipschitz on the line. It was a careful voice that explained to Shereel when she identified herself that Mr. Barnes and all the Turnipseeds had carte blanche during their stay at the Blue Flamingo Hotel in honor of her—Ms. Dupont—being one of the odds-on favorites to win the Cosmos. A porter would be there directly to show him to his suite. And as Shereel was putting the telephone back into its cradle a discreet knock came at the door. A Cuban with impeccable manners had been waiting for them in the hallway and when he showed them to Nail's suite, there was Nail's bag precisely as he had left it, including the loaded .357 Magnum wrapped in an oiled cloth and the fragmentation grenade naked under his drawers.

"Where 'bouts you going?" asked Nail when Shereel walked right past the elevator.

"I thought we'd take the stairs," she said. "It's only six floors up to where they got Mama and Daddy."

"No way in hell would I walk up six flights of stairs when I got a elevator right here at hand."

"I'm sorry," she said. "I was thinking about myself. I'd explain but it's complicated."

"I don't need nothing complicated just right now," he said. "It's all complicated enough for me already."

"It just has to do with making weight," she said, "and water retention."

"Water what?"

"Retention."

"Thought that's what you said. But I don't think I want to go into that with you. So if it's all the same to you, I'll take the elevator and meet you up there."

"I'll come on the elevator with you," she said. "I just wasn't thinking."

"Take the goddamn stairs if you want to."

She pressed the up button and pulled her sunglasses down on the bridge of her nose and looked over them at him. "Just try to keep yourself under control, Nail."

"I'm by God in control," he said. "Always. It's the fucking world that's out of control."

"Right," she said.

When the elevator door opened, it seemed full already. It was not, in fact, full, but only seemed that way because the four young ladies inside it were very big. All of them were nearly as tall as Nail and wearing the same skintight blue jumpsuits with blue, sequined headbands. Their hands were long-fingered and square and muscular, with nails painted the same color of purple. Their teeth were startlingly white and with the exception of the prettiest and youngest one, who was the color of a creamed coffee, their faces were very black.

"Git on, white boy," said one of them. "Don't worry, we don't bite."

The sight of them had stopped Nail and he stood holding the door open with his hand. "I don't worry 'bout people," he said. "They usually worry 'bout me." But still he did not move.

"Well, how 'bout we worry while we *moving*," said one of them.

Nail still did not know which one had spoken. All four of
them had identical and permanent smiles stamped on their
heavy mouths, red-lipped and wet.

Nail stepped into the elevator and Shereel followed. He
moved to the side opposite the girls, as far away as he could
get, folding his arms across his chest, and looked at the ceiling
to keep from having to look at them. He did not know as he
had ever seen any women before who looked as they looked
and he was confounded by the palpable and awesome power
that seemed to come off them in waves. And Nail did not like
to be confounded and he did not like being in this confined
space with them. Something in their size was threatening and
the fact that they were beautiful angered Nail for reasons he
could not have named and did not know. Plus, he did not
like the way they talked. Nobody talked to him in that tone
of voice. Not women particularly, and especially not black
women.

"Ut-oh, feel the air go rare?" said the lightest and most beautiful girl.

"Vare rare, Vanella."

"We're in with world-class ass, Shavella."

"Vanella, shame your name, girl. Talking nasty. Don't mind
sister, mister."

Nail Head had brought his eyes down to stare at them in
amazement. Why were these creatures talking to him? How did
his life suddenly get joined to theirs, because—unmistakably—
that is what he felt: joined with these four black girls, monstrous
in size and beautiful. Every time they moved the muscles of
their bodies moved too, jerking and quivering in sharp relief
under the thin blue cloth of their tight jumpsuits.

"You talking to me?" asked Nail. "You actually talking to me?"

"Be easy, Nail."

"The frail call him Nail, Starvella."

Shereel stepped around Nail to get between him and the
young women. She knew who they were well enough. And
she was at something of a loss to know how to act toward

them. She knew how Russell would want her to act and if he was along he would have made sure Shereel showed nothing but hostility, or at the very least total indifference. But Russell was not here, and Nail would not understand such behavior from her. He might even think they had done something dreadful to her if she acted that way, and if he thought that it would cause trouble. Besides, she liked them. They were very young, hardly more than very large, incredibly muscular children.

"Good to see you again," said Shereel and smiled.

All four girls in exact and identical movement reached up with their right hands, slipped their dark glasses down onto the flared wings of their nostrils, and glared at Shereel.

Shereel thought they must do such movements on some kind of signal. It had to be something they practiced, because they did it a lot—suddenly the four of them making the same gesture or movement or sometimes speaking the same words at the same time—and it was startling to see. Nail had taken a step back, right into the wall of the elevator, when they did it.

"That was nice," said Shereel, "that was real nice. Good to see you still got your act together."

"Don't come talkin' pretty to us, girl. We can't help you."

"And God knows, Mizz Shereel Dupont, you do need help," said Vanella. She was the lightest and youngest and sassiest and most beautiful of the sisters, and Shereel had always wished she could get to know her. She thought they would be immediate and close friends. But even if it had been possible, Russell would never have allowed it.

"Mercy, the girl need help," said Starvella.

"Now and at the time of her early *de-mise*," said Jabella.

"Because," said Shavella, "because you marked with . . ."

Then all four girls together: "Satan, sin, and death."

Vanella raised her fine beautiful hand in the air, her forefinger extended: "And . . . *and* you will wear ashes and sackcloth."

All of them at once: "*Ashes* and *sackcloth*."

Then as if by long and constant practice, they simultaneously raised their right hands and with their middle fingers pushed their dark glasses high on their noses.

Shereel clapped her hands and, still smiling, said, "That was great. I think your future's in dance."

"Our future's in your *face*," said Vanella.

"Sister Marvella will chew you up and spit you out," Jabella said.

"How it feel to be dead?" said Shavella.

Starvella said, "We ought to put a flower on your head."

"You need flowers *at* your head. You dead!"

"Yes!"

"In front of *us*!"

"At our *feet*!"

"Lordy!"

"Do have mercy!"

"Show a little mercy!"

All together: "*No mercy!*"

The elevator stopped. The four girls turned to face the door as it opened.

"Good to catch your act," said Shereel. "Say hello to Marvella for me. Tell'er I'll show her what a worldbeater looks like."

Neither of the four girls answered. They left the elevator and marched away down the hall, all of them wearing across their broad backs in block letters:

BLACK MAGIC GYMNASIUM

DETROIT, MICHIGAN

HOME OF MARVELLA WASHINGTON, CHAMPION

When the door closed, Nail said, "Don't tell me what that was, I don't want to know." Then before the elevator had gone half a floor: "What *was* that?"

"Four very large girls."

"Don't be a wiseass."

"Starvella, Shavella, Jabella, and Vanella."

"Don't be a wiseass."

"That's their names. Really."

"I ain't got no trouble believing that. They niggers, ain't they? Niggers nowadays all figger to be named like their mamas and daddies lost their goddamn minds. But them that just got out of this elevator was strange. Tell me about the strange of it."

"They're bodybuilders. Like me."

"Oh, Jesus."

"They were only goofing with us, Nail, for heaven's sake. Don't take it so seriously."

"I ain't taking it serious. I ain't taking it. Period. You know many more like that?"

"Well, yes and no. There're not any more like that anywhere. But, yes, if you're talking strange, I know some strange ones. The sport is full of strange people."

"You left home and come off down here and ruint you mind. You know that?"

"My mind is not here to be judged. My body is. Right now body is everything. Got that, Nail? Body."

"Seem like they known you pretty damn good. How'd you come to be so tight with strange niggers?"

"They've seen me compete before. Lots of times. Against their sister, Marvella."

"Marvella?"

"Right."

"Jesus. Now ain't that the niggeringest goddamn thing you ever heard of?"

"Stop with the 'nigger this' and 'nigger that' will you? This is not the place."

Nail Head seemed not to have heard. He had what Shereel thought of as his thousand-yard stare and she knew he was thinking, or trying to think. The elevator stopped and they got off.

"It was one of them in my platoon in the Nam," said Nail Head, looking off down a hallway long as a football field and wide enough to drive a dump truck through. "And his name was Radiator. You believe that? Said he had a brother named Bumper and another one named Wiper. And it just went on and on. Damnedest thing. Said his daddy liked cars."

Shereel had stopped with him there by the elevator. "Nail, I've got a brother named Motor."

"Nickname," he said, "and we know how he got it. Always waist deep in the block of some old wrecked car engine. That don't count. I sometimes wish I could figger niggers, sometimes I do."

"It's nothing to figure about the ones on the elevator with us. They're beautiful young girls who will be champions when they grow older. I won't ever have to worry about them, because by the time they're ready, I'll be on the downhill side of competition bodybuilding. But their sister? That's something else. She's the one I've got to beat."

"You've got to beat a nigger named Marvella?"

"It'll come down to the two of us. Everybody knows it. Only one of us can win the world."

"Well now," said Nail.

"What?"

"Only one you got to git past, you say?"

"It'll only be a matter of how the judging goes. What these particular judges like, whether they like'm big, or whether they like'm . . . well, not so big."

"You think you can beat her?"

"Oh, I know I can," she said. "At least it's possible. I've beat'er before."

"Then you ain't got nothing to worry about."

"Of course I have. She's beaten me too."

"How can that be? She's beat you and you've beat her? What kind of deal is that?"

"Raw."

"Raw?"

"Very raw, but it comes with the sport. We've gone against each other all across the country. Not for the world, of course, but for some major titles. Sometimes it's her and sometimes it's me. I'm down one. She's beaten me three to two."

"I couldn't stand that, not being able to get to the end of it, not being able to settle it. Settle it once and for all, for now and forever. That's what was wrong with the Nam, couldn't settle it. I cain't stand not knowing. I can live with a yes and I can live with a no. I cain't live with a maybe."

They had been walking down the long wide hallway as they talked, walking and checking out the numbers on the doors. "Ah, but that's why we're here at the Cosmos, Nail. To settle it. It *will* be settled here in Miami Beach. She beats me or I beat her. And if I beat her, there's nothing left to win."

He stopped walking and stared at her. "Nothing left to win, you say? Seems to me like that's what Mr. Muscle said."

"That's what he said. This is as far as you can go. The top of the mountain. Of course, you could try to win it again. A lot of people have won the Cosmos more than once. But I could never understand that. Why win again something you've already won, you know?"

"I never thought you was the kind of girl that'd chew her tobacker twicet."

"You always did put things nice, Nail."

"So if you won, you'd hang it up?"

They were walking again and Shereel was watching the numbers on the doors they passed. "I don't know that I'd quit with it altogether but I can't see myself going through this kind of torture again."

"It's them of us who cain't see it the first time."

"I didn't ask you to, Nail. You or anybody else. But I did it. I'm here. And I have to win."

"You'll win," said Nail. "Don't worry, you'll win."

She stopped, put her hand on his chest, and looked up into his face. "You never said that. You never said that before even once."

"If you'd asked me I'da told you. I never had a doubt."

She turned and moved off down the hall, glancing at the door numbers. "I never have a doubt either. Except now and then. Now and then it comes over me like the scariest dream I ever had that I'll lose. Lose after the hell I've had to put myself through." She thought of Russell. "After the things I've done. The things I've *had* to do."

"Put you mind at ease, little girl. The Nail's with you."

"You're sweet," she said. "But you haven't seen Marvella. You don't know big. You haven't even thought of big until you see Marvella. Big and so cut she looks like an anatomy chart. So ripped you can see her liver, or think you can, see it and know right where it is."

"Well," said Nail, "it's big and it's big. And as it turns out, I know right where the liver is. In them that's big or them that's little. Know it and can find it."

She cut her eyes at him. "Nail, you keep that goddamn knife on your belt. You got to promise me that."

"I couldn't . . . and *wouldn't* promise even my old mama anything about my knife . . . Shereel."

"No, I guess I knew that all along," she said. "You do the best you can and that'll be fine. And, Nail, thanks for accepting the new name, for calling me Shereel. I know how you feel about it."

"You don't know a goddamn thing, Shereel. It didn't cost me a nickel."

There was cheering—clapping, whistles, and shouts—coming from behind the door where they had stopped. They could clearly hear Fonse's cigarette-coarse voice—punctuated with fits of coughing—barking "Hot damn!" over and over again.

"This is where they are," Shereel said. "But I don't know what they could be doing in there. Sounds like they're watching a football game."

"Or a lynching," Nail said. "It ain't no way to find out but to find out."

Nail raised his fist and pounded on the door. The noise did not abate, it increased. And the door did not open.

"See if it's locked," she said.

Nail looked at the doorknob but did not touch it. "I wouldn't want to just walk in on Fonse. It ain't no telling what he might be doing in there. Besides, I 'magine Fonse's armed, too."

"What do you mean, armed *too*?" she said.

"Manner of speaking," he said. "Man wouldn't want to come off down here amongst all these people who ain't normal in any way that counts without carrying some ordinance. A Dorothy would've known that. I reckon a Shereel'll just have to learn it the hard way."

"You keep doing that, Nail," she said. "Saying what Dorothy would know and what Shereel would know, and I want you to quit it. Names don't mean a thing. I'm the same girl."

"Names mean everything and you ain't the same girl," he said. "But I guess that's just something else you'll have to learn the hard way."

"Well, it's one thing I don't have to do, and that's stand out here in the hall and listen to my family shouting and carrying on."

She took the knob in her hand, turned it, and swung the door open. But she did not go in. She did not move. Neither did Nail. Shereel opened her mouth to speak and didn't. But her mouth stayed open. Nail's hand unconsciously eased up his side and fingered the leather case his knife was in at his belt.

Nail, who was standing behind Shereel, leaned down until his chin was at her shoulder and his mouth at her ear. "What the hell is it?" he whispered.

"I don't know," she said, whispering too.

Deep in the first room of the suite, which was the largest in the hotel and normally reserved for the highest of high rollers, Shereel's family was sitting in a semicircle of chairs—Earnestine and Motor and Earline and Turner and Fonse—passing a bucket of Colonel Sanders among them, while Billy Bat stood under a floor lamp that had been put on a table and made into a posing light.

"Now I'm gone hit a crab for Most Muscular," said Billy Bat. He exhaled in an explosion of air and then inhaled again, his arms extended in front of him, his fists clenched, and his body hunkered down in a kind of crouch. His muscles from his throat to his ankles swelled, held, then quivered as veins slowly appeared and grew until they were swollen as though they might burst. Still Billy Bat held and swelled. He did not breathe. His eyes glazed and shot with a net of red veins. And still he grew, every part of him standing separate and distinct from every other part of him, expanding as though he were plugged into some secret and outside source of blood by which he was engorged.

"COME ON, BILLY BAT!" Earline suddenly screamed and waved a chicken wing over her head, then popped it into her mouth and ate it bones and all in her excitement.

"Do it, son!" Fonse called as a cloud of cigarette smoke slowly spread about his head.

"Hot damn!" said Motor.

"*God* damn!" said Turner.

"Watch you mouth, Turner," said Earnestine. Then: "Come on, Billy Bat! Come *on!*"

From the doorway, his mouth still close to Shereel's ear, Nail said, "What the hell is it he's doing?"

"I know what he's doing," Shereel said. "I just don't know why he's doing it and why he's doing it where he's doing it."

"His whole body looks like it's got a hard-on," said Nail.

Shereel turned to glare at him briefly. "You can't keep your mind off your dick for two minutes, can you?"

"Someday I'll die," Nail said, "and when I do, I'll have forever to keep my mind off my dick. But that time ain't come yet a while."

Billy Bat had eased out of his flexed pose and was now relaxed under the light, rolling his head on his thick neck as he talked. "Now that right there you just seen is what some of the men contestants do when they asked by the judges for their Most Muscular. A lotta judges don't like to see a woman do a crab though. Some do but a lot don't and the poor women never knows which ones do and which ones don't, so when the females is asked for their Most Muscular, they can crab it, or do somethin' else, so to speak."

"I wonder what I was to look like if I was to crab it," said Motor.

"Why, come on up here, old son, and we'll see," Billy Bat said.

"Billy Bat," said Earline, working on another piece of fried chicken, "you so sweet and kind and gentle. Ain't he, Mama, sweet and kind and gentle?"

Earnestine reached over and patted her daughter's thick shoulder. "It do seem so," she said. "He's a good boy, but then I always did favor Tennessee boys."

"I ain't seen another one like him," said Earline.

Motor had stepped up beside Billy Bat. The light from the lamp over their heads diffused and broke up in the long silky hair covering Motor's body and made him seem to glow.

"Now what you do is," said Billy Bat, "you—"

"Hold on there a sec," said Motor, raising his hand to shade his eyes and look over Fonse's head toward the door. "Well, looka here what Nail Head's gone off and found. Come on in here, girl. Long time no see."

Fonse and Earnestine and Earline and Turner turned to look toward the door where they saw Shereel and Nail still standing with their feet in the hallway but leaning into the room. Fonse popped to his feet and came toward her with his arms out and the Camel cigarette in his mouth carrying a half inch of ash. Earline and her mother squealed and followed.

"I was beginning to think you wasn't never gone show up," said Fonse, throwing his arms about her shoulders. He was exactly as tall as she was. "Take them damn sunshades off so I can see you." And even as she was taking off the dark glasses, he almost kissed her before he realized he still had the Camel in his mouth. He jerked the cigarette away with his hand and kissed her long and hard on the lips. Then speaking over her shoulder to Nail: "Where the hell did you find her, boy?"

"Some more damn complicated," Nail said. "I can flat tell you that. And I don't think you really want to know."

Earnestine and Earline had surrounded them and jerked She-reel away from Fonse and threw themselves upon her with kisses and pats and hugs, all of which Shereel grimly endured, trying even to smile. She loved her family, all of them, dearly. But she did not need this, she told herself. She wished with all her heart they had not come, and she had done everything possible to stop them, to head them off, short of telling them straight out that they could not come. And of course that was impossible. They were, after all, blood. But now, right when she desperately needed all the concentration and focus of will she could find, she had this to deal with. This distraction. This blood. These Turnipseeds.

"Come on here and set," said Fonse. "We got plenty of Colonel Sanders left. Turner, git you sister one of them plastic plates none of us ain't been using. Put some of them baked beans and cold slaw on it, too."

"No, Daddy, thank you," Shereel said, "but I can't eat that."

"Damn," he said, "I forgot. Billy Bat couldn't eat none either."

Shereel looked across the room, nodded her head, and said, "Bat."

"Mizz Dupont," he said.

"Y'all know each other?" said Nail.

"Everbody in bodybuilding knows Shereel Dupont," Billy Bat said.

Shereel looked at Nail and then gestured with her hand toward Billy Bat. "This is Mr. Bill Bateman. Mr. Bateman, Harry Barnes."

Neither man moved to shake hands, but Bill Bateman said, "Just call me Billy Bat."

"Most people call me Nail Head or Nail for short. You can call me that, too, seein' as how it's my name."

"Nail," said Billy Bat, with a slight nod of his head.

"Billy Bat," Nail said, with the same nod.

Fonse, who had just fired another Camel and stuck it in his

mouth, held out his arms to Shereel and said with a sly wink and a smile, "Shereel Dupont."

She went to him and he hugged her against his skinny little body. "Thank you, Daddy. I knew you'd understand," she said.

"Well, cain't say as I did there at first. Howsomever, Billy Bat here come and explained everthing."

"He did?"

"He shore did that," Earnestine said. "About the names and about the bodybuilding and just everthing. Billy Bat is a sweet boy."

"Hell," said Fonse, "he's our kind of people. From Murfreesboro, Tennessee, is where he's from."

"Now ain't that the damnedest thing you ever heard of?" said Nail. "A grown man from Tennessee"—he pointed at the posing briefs Billy Bat had on—"wearing little trick panties in a beauty contest with women and niggers."

Billy Bat smiled. "I ain't even gone take exception to that. You wrong on just about everthing but you cain't help it, you ignorant."

"Say *what?*" Nail said, his hand flinching toward the leather case holding his switchblade.

"You wrong on just about everthing but you cain't help it, you ignorant is what I said." Billy Bat never lost his good-natured smile.

Shereel put her hand on Nail's wrist. "Stand easy, Nail."

"First," said Billy Bat, "it ain't a beauty contest."

"No it ain't, Nail," Fonse said. "He explained all that."

"And," Billy Bat said, "men don't compete against women. Women wouldn't have a chance, if you'll be kind enough to forgive me for saying so, Mizz Dupont."

"I understand," said Shereel, and she did. But she didn't like it. She did not like the idea that anybody in the world could beat her, male or female, on stage under the bright and hot posing lights. This was not the time to think about being beaten by *anybody.*

"And niggers?" said Billy Bat. "Sure, we got niggers. What you probably didn't notice is we got Jews, too. Cain't tell it with most of'm, white as you or me. And, Nail, we got Catholics, too. Bet you hadn't even thought of that. And I know you hadn't thought of this: We got people here that cain't talk a word of English. That's right. Shakes you socks don't it? But they cain't. You know why? I'll tell you why. They from across the water. Krauts and Wops and spicks—you name it, we got it. We got some of everthing from everwhere. But you git used to it. Just part of the price of doing business. If you gone *win* the world, you got to *beat* the world. You may not like it and I may not like it, but the sad truth is that they's Wops and spicks and niggers and Krauts and kikes and Catholics in the world, and a lot of other stuff you wouldn't even want to think about much less talk about."

"But he did," said Fonse. "Billy Bat talked about it all to us, and I don't mind tellin' you, I'm a lot easier in my mind."

"I owe you one, Billy," Shereel said.

"No you don't," Billy Bat said. "It weren't something any white man wouldn't a done if he was in my place."

Turner, who was eating off the plastic plate he'd loaded down with food when his daddy told him to get something for Shereel, said, "He's been showing us different poses and things. It's some they *got* to do."

"Them's the compulsories," Billy Bat said.

"Yeah, them," Turner said, "and then it's some that they can do when they want to. He just got through showing us the crab when you come in. You want to see Billy Bat crab it, Nail?"

"Cain't say as I do, Turner," said Nail. "And I don't mean to pry, but how come you happen to be up here, Billy Bat, talkin' to Fonse and everbody about how this here Cosmos works? Last time I seen you, you was on you back down by the pool with all of us setting on top you and Earline here givin' you mouth-to-mouth."

Earline struggled out of her chair and moved closer to Billy Bat. She looked for a moment as if she would take his hand. "It

was all a mistake because he didn't need none of that mouth-
to-mouth or nothin' else. But I ain't ashamed to say I thank God
for it, mistake or no mistake. Hadn't been for that down by the
pool, I may never of met Mr. Bill Bateman of Murfreesboro,
Tennessee."

"Now don't you go Mr. Bill'n me. I am today and forever Billy
Bat to you, you sweet girl."

Earline felt the blood run up out of her braced and trussed
breasts and flood her face with heat as she blushed. "I guess
we just a mutual admiration society, Billy Bat and me." She
shook herself all over like a dog coming out of water. "So to
answer you question, Nail, Billy Bat was kind enough to walk
me up here to Mama's and Papa's place so I could eat a little
something with'm and he could tell us all about the bodybuilding and how everthin' works so we wouldn't feel left
out."

"And he told us about the name Dorothy taken for the stage,"
said Turner, "and how that's the way more than some do it.
You ain't heard of no movie star with the name his mama given
him, have you?"

"Movie star?" said Nail.

"Movie star is what I said, and it's the same with them that
builds bodies sometimes. That's how come Dorothy's a Shereel Dupont." Turner stopped and cocked his head as though
listening to the sound of his own voice. "Kinda pretty, too,
when you say it real slow. I like it myself. Sherrrreeeeeeel
Duuuuuupooooonnnt. Nice. Real nice. Like surp pouring out
of a jar."

"It ain't nothing but the name of a champion," said Billy Bat.
"It's women in gyms all over the world sweatin' and groanin'
and gittin' it down deep everday—payin' the price—takin'
their bodies apart and puttin'em together a different way, it's
women doin' that all over the world and sayin' Shereel Dupont,
Shereel Dupont, sayin' her name over and over and over while
they do it to keep their courage up and the fire burning in their
blood."

"Godamighty, Billy Bat, you a poet. He's been talkin' like that ever since I met him."

"It's potry and it's potry," Billy Bat said, "and then it's them that looks like Shereel Dupont."

"Me, I ain't never gone strong to potry," Nail said.

Earnestine fisted her hands on her flaring hips and said, "Nail, you just a rank ole boy from the hills of Georgia. You a fine man and we love you, but a drink of whiskey, hound dogs running in the night, and a knife fight'll do you for a good time. This right here is different though." She waved her hand to cover the enormous room throughout which sprays of cut flowers had been arranged in glass vases. "Lookit where they given us to stay. For free too. All on account of Dorothy . . . *Shereel*." She smiled. "Got to learn to say that purty new name whilst we here."

"I guess you found you own place all right, Nail," said Fonse. "I had'm take you stuff on over there and I sent Turner with'm to make sure none of them little Cuburns got to finger'n through you things. They didn't git to finger'n through it did they?"

"No sir," said Nail, "it was just like I left it, only in a different place."

"Your place all right?" said Fonse.

"Like this one," Nail said. "A tad smaller, but you could still keep horses in it."

"Well, the best part about it is it's free," said Turner.

"Yeah," Nail said, "I'd say that's the best part."

"What I want to know," Turner said, turning to his brother, "you gone crab it or not? That's what you'as about to do when they come in."

"Show me one more time, Billy Bat," Motor said.

Billy Bat stepped under the lamp they had contrived to make into a posing light, extended his arms, clenched his fists, went into a hunker, and started to swell, his skin working alive with veins. They were silent, watching. And still he swelled, his eyes starting in a red web, and breathed now and again like an explosive bellows.

"Ain't that the strangest goddamn thing you ever seen?" whispered Fonse behind his cloud of Camel cigarette smoke.

Nail elaborately sucked his teeth and then said, "It's peculiar enough but, no sir, it ain't the strangest thing I ever seen. Matter of fact, it don't even come close."

"Okay," said Motor, "I believe I got it."

Billy Bat relaxed and rolled his head on his neck. When he came out of it, finally turned it loose, it took a minute, as though he were waking from a deep sleep and he had to get his bearings, find out where he was before he moved again.

Motor put his hand on Billy Bat's elbow and gently moved him out from under the lamp. Again, the light fractured in his hair, broke up, and cast his entire body in a kind of halo.

"See if this ain't about what it comes to," Motor said. His arms went out, his hands clenched, and he dropped into his version of Billy Bat's hunker. He held it and turned red in the face. They were all silent, not even moving, until finally the only sound was Motor's erratic, ragged gasps, when he could no longer hold his breath.

"I believe you got the *way* he done it," Turner said. "But it somehow don't look right on you. Cain't put my finger on it, but somethin's wrong."

Nearly simultaneously Shereel and Billy Bat turned their heads and both of them looked out the window.

Earline cleared her throat. "I 'magine Billy Bat had to practice that a long time, Motor, honey, before he got it right. Am I right, Billy Bat?"

"You right about that, you sweet girl," Billy Bat said, still looking out the window.

"I think I know what it is," Turner said. "What I think it is is *hair*."

Shereel and Billy Bat snapped their heads back from the window to stare at him.

Billy Bat thought: Somewhere in that boy Motor, it's a ruint gene.

The thought had come to him the first time he had seen Motor, and it was a thought he had been unable to shake free of. He did not like thinking such a thing, because Motor was, after all, Earline's brother. But he had never seen a pelt like that on another human being, had never even imagined anything like it.

"I believe you might be on to something there, Turner," said Nail.

"You just joking me," Motor said. "You think I don't know you just joking? But you weren't here when Billy Bat was talking about staying shaved slick so you could see the muscles easier. Hell, look at'm. You see any hair on'm? Smooth as a baby's ass is what he is."

They all turned to regard Billy Bat again. Billy Bat looked out the window and unconsciously let the thick palm of his left hand slide over the heavy slabs of muscle on his chest.

"I believe," said Motor, "you could see what I looked like better if I was smoothed down and weren't carryin' this hair."

Now they all, including Billy Bat, turned to regard Motor where he stood glowing under the light.

His mother, Earnestine, a little point of grieving love stabbing her heart, thought: It's enough hair on you to stuff a pillow, son. Ain't none of us will ever know what you look like.

Billy Bat, his hand still tracing the hard sculpted lines of his chest, thought: If I ever seen a ruint gene, I'm lookin' at it right now.

T H I R T E E N

The lobby of the Blue Flamingo was very busy when Russell Morgan, his huge head stuck forward on his thick neck, came stalking in. He was scowling and his eyes, pinched into a squint, glanced fiercely about. Contestants of the Cosmos, men and women, paraded about in skintight, multicolored shorts and shirts, their eyes hungrily bright, tossing their beautifully maned heads like exotic animals in full rut, but all the while studiously indifferent to one another, seemingly indifferent to everything except that which was contained within the limits of their fine, unblemished, and deeply tanned skins.

Beyond the swinging glass doors, cars already had their lights on as they pulled up. And the front desk was crowded with people checking in, three of whom were judges for the Cosmos show. Russell recognized them, powerful men with huge shoulders and tight narrow hips, dressed in conservative business suits. Russell had competed against all of them at one time or another in the long ago time when winning the world seemed not only possible but inevitable. To speak or, for that matter, to even nod to one of them would have been very bad form, but doing such a thing never crossed Russell's mind.

Just seeing them made him want to slap the shit out of somebody. Not only was it unfair, it was totally unjust for men to judge women in competition bodybuilding. As soon as he saw the three men across the lobby, he recognized them as judges. That was all those particular three men ever did, besides running gymnasiums of their own. There would be four other judges, making seven in all, and Russell would have bet a quart of his blood that at best only two of them would be women. Since the high score and low score would be thrown out on the judges' cards and the middle five averaged to determine the winner, that further stacked the deck against the women judges. It was very bad for the future of female bodybuilding and could eventually kill it, or so Russell was convinced.

The winners of female bodybuilding contests ought to have the kinds of bodies that women across the country admired and wanted badly enough to drive them into gymnasiums like Russell's Emporium of Pain, drive them there and make them willing to pay the price, mentally and physically, to get such a body.

But men—especially men who themselves had spent their lives in weight gymnasiums and in competition against other men—could only see size and thickness and mass. Consequently, there had been women bodybuilding champions who were downright scary, women who if you put a sack over their heads, stripped them to the waist, and stuffed their posing briefs so they looked like they had a dick and balls, the result was the ripped and muscled body of a man. Where is the little girl in Peoria, Illinois, who wants to grow up to look like that, goddammit? Where is the mother in Peoria, Illinois, who would suggest to her teenaged daughter that she go down and join a weight gymnasium so that she could build herself a body like that? Those were questions Russell had screamed at promoters of contests all over the country, all over the world, and at every international meeting of sanctioning organizations of bodybuilding contests. And while they could agree with him in theory, the same old shit came down in practice, again, and again, and again.

All of that was about to change. He had the best girl in the world. Shereel Dupont, at one time or another, had beaten every woman of monster size and thickness in the sport. Now all she had to do was beat them here, in this place and time, to crown herself as the ultimate female athletic body, the body that was the standard by which all others would be measured.

So screw the three judges checking in at the main desk there in the lobby. Russell had other fish to fry: namely, to goddammit find Shereel. He had looked everywhere for her, starting with the conference room where he had left her. He had not really expected to find her there—in fact he hoped not to because she would be with Nail, surely, if he had, and he didn't want to run up on Nail again just yet—but he had thought he would check it before he went up to her room. When he did go to her room, workmen were replacing the furniture and installing a posing mirror, but there was no sign of Shereel. Nor was she by the pool where the lights had been turned on against the gathering dusk or anywhere else he could think to look. Jesus, there was no telling how much water she might have drunk (surely, she had not eaten anything!), and by this time tomorrow night she would be on stage winning the world. Or losing it.

Or losing it! That ugly thought kept coming to him, and it was what had driven him into such a nervous, angry, and dangerous state. He wanted to slap everybody in sight, starting with himself. He had lost his goddamn champion! He couldn't fucking believe it.

The three enormous judges had walked away from the desk and revealed Julian—a tiny Band-Aid on the bottom of either nostril—standing there staring at him. A young woman with heavy black hair and blazingly white teeth was talking to him, but Julian obviously was not listening. His eyes were locked on Russell Morgan and they did not waver. Julian's color was bad, his face chalk white except for the area right around his mouth and that was dead gray. Russell started toward the desk and Julian turned and ducked through a door, leaving the young girl still talking.

She stopped in midsentence and looked across the desk at Russell.

"Yes? May I help you, please?" She had the trace of a Cuban accent and was very pretty.

"Get Julian," Russell said.

She looked at him puzzled, as though he might have spoken to her in Arabic.

"Julian Lipschitz," Russell said, pointing to the door behind the desk. "He's in there."

She only smiled harder, more dazzlingly. "Yes?" she said. "Of course. How may I help you?"

"Never mind," Russell said. He walked to the end of the desk counter and came around toward her.

"You can't . . . ," she said.

But he only brushed past her and went through the door. Julian was sitting at a little table with his head in his hands.

The girl had followed Russell in and was at his shoulder. "Julian, I tried to keep him . . ." Her voice trailed off.

"It's all right, Conchonca," Julian said without looking up.

"Get the fuck out of here," Russell said to her.

She said something in very rapid Spanish, her eyes going wider and her face darker as she spoke.

"It's all right, Conchonca," Julian said again.

"I'll be at the desk if you need me," she said.

Russell waited until she was gone. "Where the hell is She-reel?"

To Julian, his voice had an accusing ring, as though Russell thought he might have kidnapped Shereel, and Julian would not have been surprised if that was what he did think. Julian felt as if nothing would ever surprise him again. He felt brain dead.

"I feel brain dead," he said.

"There's worse things than feeling brain dead. *Being* dead, for instance."

"Why do you have to be so nasty?" Julian said, without looking up. His own hands on his head reminded him of Russell's hands, were becoming Russell's hands as he sat there.

"Why do I have to be what? Nasty? Is that what you said? *Nasty?*"

Julian stared between his hands at the flat gray surface of the table. The whole day and everybody in it had turned nasty. The second assistant manager, José, who was Conchonca's brother, was sick and had not come in, and Julian had no alternative but

to pull another shift. And that normally would have been wonderful, because normally that would have been eight hours of
a specific and marvelous kind of bliss beside the beautiful Conchonca, whom he normally loved, but behind the desk with her
tonight all he could think of was having his head squeezed by
Russell's hands, and that was not normal and he knew it. That
was nasty. So he had first come to hate himself and then to hate
Russell. But he still wanted his head squeezed again. By Russell.
And that was not normal. That was nasty.

He moved his face the tiniest bit so he could see Russell's
thickly muscled, blue-veined hands. Something in him could
have kissed them. Something in him could have cut them off
with an axe.

He had told Conchonca about Russell, not about Russell
squeezing his head until he thought he might come, but only
that Russell was not normal. And very big. And nasty. And that
he, Julian, did not want to see him if he showed up at the desk.

Russell stood looking down at Julian and the thought occurred
to him that if this was another time and another place he might
have felt sorry for this little shit, might even have tried to help
him. Julian had been terrorized by Nail and that was enough to
undo anybody. And this kind was definitely undone, broken.

"Your nose was only scratched, right?" said Russell. "The
skin hardly broken?"

The faintest suggestion of concern in Russell's voice made
Julian look up. He touched his nose. "It's not too bad," said
Julian, which is precisely what Dr. Fernando Gonzales had said
when Julian had shown up in his little office in the hotel base-
ment. Dr. Gonzales had been the hotel doctor ever since he got
off the Mariel boatlift and he was very kind and very gentle and
very thorough even when he was in a dreamlike state from
shooting his veins full of Dilaudid, which was most of the time.
"But I had that terrible knife in my face. *Up* my nose. Have you
ever seen that knife?"

"Yeah, I've seen it," said Russell. "Stay away from that guy.
But I don't have time to talk about that right now. Have you

seen Shereel Dupont? You do know her, right?"

"Of course I know her. She's going to win the Cosmos."

"That's the one. I seem to have . . . misplaced her."

"Misplaced her?"

"I can't fucking find her." He put his hand on Julian's shoulder and squeezed. "I don't have time to jack around here like this. I need to find her and I need to find her now."

"Take your hand off my shoulder," said Julian. What he did not say was *and put it on my head*, which is what he thought.

Russell said, "Don't growl if you can't bite, Lipschitz. I'm only trying to get you to help me find Shereel."

Julian was tired and despondent, played-out. It had all been so ugly and tiresome. Finding out about himself. Finding out about the Cosmos competitors. Ugly and tiresome. He felt like leaving and never coming back. But he was, after all, pursuing a degree in hotel management at the junior college, and—like it or not—he had spent entirely too much time thinking about, dreaming of, Mr. Friedkin's desk, office, and title to give it up now. Still, he had felt so close to the bodybuilders, so at *one* with them, and it had all turned out to be so shabby.

"My job is not to keep up with Shereel Dupont," said Julian without looking up from the table. "But I can tell you this . . ." His voice had a little break in it, as though he was about to cry. "I wouldn't be surprised . . . no matter what has happened to her. You Cosmos people are *nuts* and you cause everything and everybody around you to go *nuts*. When I saw all of you coming in, you looked so beautiful and friendly and . . . well, *sane*. But that's not the way it is, is it? You are all mean and selfish and . . . and . . . hostile. Yes, that's it, hostile. You are all insane and hostile bastards."

Julian was breathing rapidly and shallowly like, Russell thought, an overheated Chihuahua. And he looked like he might have a stroke, the skin tightly drawn about his eyes and very red.

Russell considered a moment. "Insane and hostile? Maybe you're not as dumb as your name. Or as dumb as you act. You remember that, Julian: insane and hostile."

Russell went back out to the desk where the young woman stared at him with blazing eyes. "Give me the room numbers of the Turnipseeds."

"I can give you the telephone numbers of any guest in the hotel," she said, and waved toward a bank of white phones on the far wall. "You may use a house telephone. But I am not permitted to give you room numbers."

"And Harry Barnes, too, I guess," Russell said. "Yeah, give me that crazy bastard's room, too."

She said again exactly what she had said before, her eyes hotter and her beautiful teeth showing as though she might growl.

Russell watched her calmly and then said, "Look, Frihole, wipe the fucking grease off your fingers and get me what I asked for."

She said something in rapid Spanish, little flecks of spit spraying across the desk.

Julian had come up behind her. "Give him the room numbers, Conchonca. He's mentally defective. They may *all* be mentally defective."

Russell pointed a finger at him. "You just hurt yourself, Lipschitz. I'll deal with you later. But your time *will* come."

Conchonca punched some keys on a computer terminal and then wrote on a small slip of paper and gave the paper to Russell. Russell walked halfway across the lobby before he looked at the paper. He put it in his pocket. The last thing in the world he wanted to do was go near any of those rooms. Nail Head could be in one of them, and very likely was. It set his teeth on edge to think that he had done something so stupid as to leave her in the conference room with that crazy bastard. But there was that knife. And the crazy look out of his eyes. More than the knife and the crazy eyes, there was the absolute need to have Nail accept her as Shereel Dupont instead of Dorothy Turnipseed. Turnipseed indeed! Jesus, this very moment she might be in the bosom of her family, the Turnipseed bosom. Doing God knows what. Nail Head had mentioned Colonel Sanders fried chicken. Might they be forcing a greasy drumstick on her the very way Shereel's sister had forced CPR on Bill "the Bat" Bateman, forcing her to eat it while Russell stood here in the lobby fingering a little slip of paper in his pocket?

Two of the Cosmos contestants, men and obviously heavyweights, wearing diaphanous, powder-blue tank tops and black, bicycle-racing shorts, walked by Russell. Their voices were light and shot through with indecision like the voices of prepubescent boys.

"We could, but I donno."

"The time weighs heavy. Waiting is an insufferable load."

"Your 'tude is going sour."

"There's nothing wrong with my attitude. I just wish it was tomorrow night."

"Well, it's not. Come on, we might as well go down to the gym and catch a little pump and some heat. Maybe it'll finetune your 'tude. You've lost your fierce, Gerald."

"I *never* lose my fierce."

Russell watched them swagger away, their heavy backs a foot deep in muscle, and shook his head. Fucking two-hundred-andsixty-pound dirt-track specialists. The whole sport had changed up on him. When he started, there had been no women and no she-men, or none that he knew of. Well, there was nothing he could do about it, or that he really wanted to do about it, except now and then it made him feel weird, made him feel lost, the way he might feel if he went home one night and instead of walking into his own house, he made a wrong turn and walked into the house of a neighbor where everything was strange and where he did not belong.

Russell watched the two men where they stood all the way across the lobby waiting for the elevator to take them down to the gym. The thought occurred to Russell that Shereel might be down in the gym. God, she could be down there trying to lose a greasy drumstick or a huge glass of water. If she was working out, she'd better be in oversized sweats to hide her body or he'd kill her. He decided to check it out. At least that way, he wouldn't have to go to the only place left he could think of to go, to the Turnipseeds, where Nail might be waiting with his knife.

Russell hurried across the lobby, caught the door, and got on the elevator. He moved to the back and the two men in identical tank tops turned to stare at him. He could feel the weight of their eyes on him but looked straight ahead, ignoring them.

"You're Ruthell. Ruthell Morgan," said the one called Gerald. He had not had a lisp before, but he had one now.

Russell did not answer.

"Thay, you've been there, and ath one of the great oneth—"

"I haven't been there, I'm *still* there," said Russell, rubbing his bald head with both hands and flexing his heavy chest.

"Well, of courth, of courth," Gerald said, shifting nervously on his feet. "But if you could thay one thing to uth the night before the conteth, what would you thay?"

Russell looked at him and wondered whether or not to answer. Finally: "Stay the fuck out of the gym. You've done all you can do for your body. Now get your mind right." He leaned toward Gerald until their faces were close enough that Russell could smell tuna fish on his breath. "Get your goddamn mind right and never, *never* speak to me again."

Gerald leaned against the side of the elevator, seeming to deflate a bit as he did, and rolled his eyes toward his friend, who rolled his eyes in return and exhaled in a long sigh.

When the elevator opened, Russell got out, but the two men stayed on. Russell walked down a short corridor to two swinging doors over which two blue flamingos preened their feathers. Between the birds was the legend: FLORIDA'S FOUNTAIN OF YOUTH. And then under that in slightly smaller letters: COME FIND IT.

Russell pushed through the doors and stopped. Probably more than half of the Cosmos contestants—in various stages of colorful undress, along with fellow bodybuilders who had come along to cheer them on—were lined out down all four walls—

walls that were mirrored from floor to ceiling. They were every last one using light weight in whatever exercise they were doing, and doing very high repetitions to get the pump, to swell every single muscle to absolute capacity with blood, and at the same time concentrating, focusing themselves on their images in the mirror. Most of them were working with free weights but there was also every machine imaginable in use: back machines and leg extension and leg press and rowing and lat and machines for abdominal crunches.

The floor was heavily carpeted and the solid ceiling of brilliant fluorescent bulbs bounced off the chrome-plated surface of the machines in a thousand points of light. In the far right corner of the gym—the corner farthest away from Russell—there was a rapid-fire banter of voices, one screaming to the other, barking, laughing commands, and cursing encouragement. Without even looking, Russell knew it was the Washington sisters: Jabella, Starvella, Shavella, and Vanella. And he knew also without looking that they would be working with heavy weight—heavy weight and low repetitions—because they were not in the contest tomorrow night and consequently had not been starving for the last three months, trying to rip the last ounce of fat out of their bodies. This was just another workout to them, another joyful, exhilarating opportunity to use the bodies they had built, to unleash again the wild power surging through their hotly lubricated muscles.

Russell saw Marvella standing with Wallace off to the side. Neither of them was smiling—nothing, in fact, showed in either of their faces—and Marvella looked as if she was nearly asleep where she leaned heavy-lidded against the wall wearing very black posing briefs that made her look naked. When she shifted her weight from one foot to the other, her entire body leapt and held in highly muscled definition. Wallace was wearing a white T-shirt with his gym's logo across the front of it and white duck pants. The four sisters, all of them in constant motion around the prone press bench where they were working, wore yellow leotards that clung to them like skin, clearly showing their thickly muscled chests with thimble-sized nipples and perfectly dividing their powerful asses, the yellow cloth of the leotard disappearing in a single crease from the top of their pubic bones, on between their legs, and up between the indented thrusts of their gluts. All four of them held major regional titles in the United States, and God knows what would happen if someday all four of them ever came together to compete in the Cosmos.

Russell watched Marvella, watched her and loved her, as he walked the length of the gym. He had no problem admitting that Marvella was perfect of her kind, beautiful, totally awesome and unbelievable, unbelievable even when you were looking at her. But his was a completely asexual admiration. He would no more have thought of fucking her than he would have thought of fucking a statue of General Lee in a public park. Because Marvella was a monument, a monument of discipline and de-privation and single-minded focus of will and, finally, of pain. She could do anything but win the Cosmos, or so Russell was convinced.

Russell walked past them without even nodding, nor did they make any signs they saw him, but he felt the weight of their collective gaze as their eyes—Marvella's and Wallace's, as well as the four sisters' at the prone press bench—swung to look at him.

There was a door at the back of the gymnasium. Russell went through it into a short hallway. Two small rooms on either side of the hallway had massage tables in them and little metal carts full of various kinds of oil and alcohol and liniment and stacks of folded white towels. But there were no masseurs or masseuses to be seen. At the very end of the hallway there were two doors. The block letters over one said SAUNA and over the other STEAM. Russell stood for a moment listening to the clang of metal plates and the voices of what had to be the Washington sisters, high and urgent like the voices that might surround an automobile wreck, coming from the gymnasium outside. Russell thought Shereel might be taking the heat, sweating it out behind one of the doors he was looking at. But he did not much think so. He could, of course, ask Wallace if he had seen Shereel down here, but that was clearly impossible. He could not very well tell his chief competitor that he had lost his champion.

"You thinking about cooking a little tension, Muscle?"

It was Wall's voice behind him. Russell did not turn to look. "Hadn't thought about it one way or the other," Russell said.

"Damned if I ain't," said Wall. "Thought about that and several other things, up to and including opening a vein."

Russell turned and looked at him. He did not look well. His normally shiny black face looked dull, the color of soot that had been in the chimney too long.

Russell smiled, even though it was the last thing he felt like doing. "Why don't you? Open a vein, I mean. And make it easy on yourself tomorrow night. I don't like to see a friend embarrassed."

"Don't talk shit," Wallace said. "I don't have the mind for it." He looked at the doors marked STEAM and SAUNA at the end of the hall. "If you're not down here to cook a little tension off, what might you be doing?"

"The management touted the gym they had here so heavy in the pre-championship hype," Russell said, "thought I'd check it out."

Wallace looked back down the hall to the door that led out into the gym, then back at Russell. "Place for tired businessmen. See all the chrome out there? And the fucking rugs? Science fiction gym is what it is. Makes me want to spit."

"Then what am I doing talking to you down here?"

"I'm up to my ass in girls. You seen'm out there, nothing but big fucking kids and just as rowdy."

"*Very* big kids."

"They supposed to be back home in Detroit. Marvella don't need that kind of distraction when she's about to win the world, and I damn sure don't need it. But . . ." He smiled. "They free, black, and twenty-one. Well, almost twenty-one. Anyway, they come on their own money and there they are. Thought I'd bring'm down here and see if I could work some starch out of them."

"They didn't look very wilted to me."

"I didn't think to wilt'm. They *never* wilt, my girls don't. But maybe I can knock some of the rough edges off of'm and make'm a little more manageable."

"Try to keep your head up, Wall, and not whine too much. You know I'm always thinking about you, and wishing you nothing in the world but bad luck, all the worst. Just remember, every man comes with his cross to bear."

"Thank God mine's not named Turnipseed," Wall said.

"I been meaning to talk to you about that."

"I *know* you have."

"You don't want to do it, Wall. You don't even want to think it."

"Then how come we talking?"

"None of us need distractions. You don't need those extra girls out there, the ones not competing, just here to get in the way. And I don't need you shucking and jiving about my girl's name."

"It ain't shuck and it ain't jive and you know it."

"Suppose her name was Turnipseed, which it's not, so what? The world's best was named Schwarzenegger. Not exactly the name you run into every day."

Wall smiled and looked at the palms of his callused hands. "A man. You dig? A man. Man can have any damn name he wants. Just like he can have a face ugly as the ass of a baboon. But think about the women who have beat the world, actually won the title. Any of'm ugly? Hell no. All of'm face queens, every last one of them."

Wall was right, and Russell knew it. The name of this game was supposed to be body. *Body*, and nothing else. And so it was for men. But not women. No matter how spectacular the body, a woman needed a pretty face to win. He knew that for a fact. What he did not know for a fact was whether or not a name like

Turnipseed would be enough to shoot a girl down. In his heart, he felt sure it would. In any case he did not want to risk it.

"Her name legally and forever is Shereel Dupont," Russell said, and surprised himself, because in his own ears he sounded like he was begging.

"Legal? Who the fuck gives a shit about legal? That girl was born a Turnipseed, she'll die a Turnipseed. Fack. Dig? Hell, the whole hotel's full of Turnipseeds." Wall exploded with a short barking laugh. "She brought the whole turnip patch with her."

Russell smiled. "She brought more than that. You must have met Nail Head."

Wall did not speak and a certain wildness flickered in his eyes.

"Your color's bad," Russell said.

"Leave color out of this."

"I just mean you don't look black, you look *dirty*. I wouldn't talk nigger, Nigger."

"You stepped over the line that time."

"And you *been* over the line, Wallace. Why can't you go on and pump your girl full of shit so that she dies at thirty of a heart attack and let's just meet on the stage in front of the judges? Why do you have to jack around with names?"

Wallace said, "You don't have to beg, Honky. I already made up my own mind on that. I thought on it. Sure, I'll admit I thought more than some on it. But I ain't touching it. I don't *need* to touch it. I'm leaving the name shit out of this. Maybe I shouldn't but I am. Know why? Using the name would be a cheap shot. And when you holding what I'm holding—Marvella, the best in the world—you don't need no cheap shot. I'm letting it alone."

"Well, you're wonderful," said Russell. "This must mean you still love me."

"I never loved you, motherfucker."

"Did you see Mr. Lipschitz's nose?"

"I seen it."

"Then I guess he told you all about Mr. Nail Head Barnes."

"Said the mother had a knife. What's the deal about that? I

knew he was crazy. Knew that before I heard about the knife. You think you the only one knows crazies? That ain't true, white boy. Only difference is the crazies I know got razors in their shoes. You ever had to look real close at a straight razor, a straight razor in the hand of a crazy?"

"I haven't, as it turns out. But I would bet my nuts Mr. Nail Head Barnes has. And he's still here. No telling where the guy holding the razor is."

The door under the word STEAM opened and Dexter Friedkin stepped out, his hips wrapped in a towel, and stood there in a vaporous cloud, watching them. He had on a fresh toupee. It was the same color and cut but it was not the one he had on earlier in the day. It was a fresh one, and it made him look like a man who had changed hats. He was lean-hipped under the towel and ramrod straight with a flat stomach and high thick chest and deeply tanned. His face broke and held in a mechanical smile as he came toward them.

"Wallace," he said. "Russell. How's the two men who are holding the two best? Tomorrow's the big day. The moment of truth, so to speak."

They did not answer, but only stood regarding him, their eyes moving over him, detached, professional, as though they were butchers and he a side of beef.

"Thought to get a little steam. Settle me down," he said.

As he talked, he moved to give them a side view, turned his shoulder to give them a half-back view, and proposed his right leg for examination. Water from the steam mixed with his own sweat ran on his body, but his fresh hair was bone dry, every false strand in place. He was not at all nervous and Russell thought for a moment he might strip away the towel and display the rest of himself. But he only put his fists on his hips and swelled his chest.

"Long hours and short pay for me, heh, heh, heh. I've got quarters here in the hotel, and I'll be staying on site, so to speak, until the contest is over. Got to be on top of things."

Still neither Russell nor Wallace spoke, and Dexter Friedkin looked down at himself as though to inspect his body, but his gesture made Russell think he was just making sure he was still there.

"If you're thinking about heat, I recommend the steam," said Dexter Friedkin. "Wet heat for me every time. But one man's meat is another man's poison, so take your pick. Me, I've got to go take care of a little boring business correspondence. Good luck to both of you tomorrow."

Dexter marched past them down the hall and turned into one of the rooms marked masseuse and closed the door.

"Don't believe I've seen one just like that before," Wallace said in a bemused voice.

"A walking collection of minor miracles," said Russell in an introspective voice, as though talking to himself. "Impressive, very impressive. For what it was."

"Yes," Wallace said. "Like I said I have never seen one just like that. I heard, but I'd never actually seen one."

"Me either," said Russell. "But now we have."

"Now we have," Wallace said. "How do you read him?"

"That tan didn't come from the sun."

"Or from a lamp."

"Out of a bottle. Non-stain, non-run paint-on called Health Glow. I sell it to middle-age housewives who stumble into my gym."

"And . . ." Wallace paused, considering. "I'd say a tummy tuck."

"Major league liposuction," said Russell.

"Ass tightened and lifted, too."

"Never heard of a breast implant on a man."

"But he had it. Pretty fucking good chest, too."

"Can you do calves like he had with a knife?"

"Beats the shit out of me. But if pecs, why not calves?"

"How many times you think he had his face stretched?"

"Motherfucker had so much skin pulled so high, when he gets tired, his face wants to sit down. You think?"

"Sounds about right to me."

"Mothering meat-molding surgeons some more clever, too. You see stitches? Even one stitch?"

"They hide'm in the skin folds. Like you say, meat-molders are some clever. Give you a constant hard-on if you want to go down and buy you one."

"Naw!"

"Sure they can. I read all about it. You walk around carrying a semi all the time and when you want the genuine, USDA hard-on, they got a little bulb somewhere up your ass and you just squeeze your cheeks together until you pump your dick as big as you want it to get."

Wallace shook his head and blew out his cheeks. "Russell, ain't you goddamn glad you and me involved with something normal and healthy and human and righteous before the Lord?"

"Every day of my life, Wallace, every day of my life."

They had been staring at the door Dexter Friedkin had disappeared behind while they talked. Now they turned to look at each other.

Wallace said, "But that shit don't change anything between you and me."

"Nothing," said Russell. "Nothing at all."

From the gym, they could hear more than one of the girls calling Wallace.

"Shit," said Wallace, looking over his shoulder toward the door. "You wouldn't want to take care of four future worldbeaters for a while, would you?"

"Not hardly," said Russell. "If they in your way why don't you make'm go home or otherwise stay the hell out of the way?"

"Make'm, you say?" said Wallace. "You don't use the carrot and the stick on them. Only the carrot. They too goddamn big for the stick."

"You grew'm," Russell said.

"Yeah," Wallace sighed, "I grew'm." He turned and went back down the hall with Russell following him out into the gym.

Marvella still leaned lazily and heavy-lidded against the wall. Her head turned just barely to look at Wallace. "They want to see me *move* something," she said, her voice as lazy and drowsy as her eyes.

"A little something to dream on tonight," said Vanella.

"Can she do it, Bossman?" said Jabella.

Then the four of them together, their hands coming forward like drawn pistols, their thumbs cocked, their heavy mouths smiling like the end of the world: "Can she *do* it?"

"Do it," said Wallace.

The slightest hint of a smile touched Marvella's beautiful face. Her head nodded almost imperceptibly, and the four sisters moved together to slam two wheels on each end of the bar resting in the iron cradle over the prone press bench. Russell glanced at Wallace. Marvella was standing there cold, and four plates, each of them forty-five pounds, had just been loaded onto an Olympic bar, itself weighing forty-five pounds.

"Jesus," said Russell, "you gonna let her get under two and a quarter without warming up?"

Wallace did not even look at him and he spoke with deliberate indifference. "For Marvella, two and a quarter *is* warming up."

Marvella stepped away from the wall and Russell was instantly reminded of something sleek and catlike and powerfully lethal. She dropped her heavy-lidded eyes to the bar, then glanced up at her sisters, who were beside themselves, doing little synchronized, pulsing movements in their yellow leotards. Marvella windmilled her arms as a baseball pitcher might do to loosen his shoulders, snorted three times through her nose in rapid explosions of breath that sounded through the entire gym, causing the other bodybuilders to stop whatever they were doing and turn to look at her, then dropped flat-back onto the bench. Without hesitation, she took the bar and pumped effortlessly through eight repetitions with her sisters clapping in absolute unison each time the bar went down and each time it rose again.

When Marvella came off the bench, a single leaping shimmer of muscle, Wallace said, "What do you think, Muscle?"

"I think," said Russell, "it's too goddamn bad that tomorrow night is not a power-lifting championship."

"I know you do," said Wallace to Russell's back as he walked away. "I know for a *fack* you do."

When Russell got to the elevator, he took the little slip of paper that the lovely Conchonca had given him out of his pocket and looked at the suite numbers written on it. He had nowhere else to look for Shereel but to knock on the door of one of these suites. With the way his luck was running it would probably be Nail's, and when the door opened, God knows what he might find. But if that's what he had to do, that's what he had to do.

As the elevator door opened, Russell said aloud, "I didn't goddammit come this far to get beat," startling two women competitors of the Cosmos in the heavyweight class who were on their way to the gymnasium for a last pump.

"Insanity time," said one of them.

"If God protects the insane, we're all safe," said the other.

They both laughed as the elevator door closed. Russell studied the numbers on the little slip of paper and with his forefinger touched them as he silently started a rhyme from his childhood: Eenee, meenee . . .

The rhyme put him off on the twelfth floor. He walked slowly down the hallway looking at the room numbers and finally stopped in front of a door. He did not let himself hesitate but knocked loudly. There was no answer and he knocked again, this time still harder.

A muffled male voice came to him from inside the room. "Jess hold by God to what you got, I'm a coming." It was not Nail, for which Russell was profoundly grateful.

The door opened and Russell instantly recalled what the two girls had said minutes earlier as they got off the elevator. He took a quick falling step backward into the hallway as if he had taken a blow to the chest. Nearly filling the door in front of him was Motor, the hairy one, wearing only a towel. Only now he was about half as hairy as he had been before. He was holding a can of Edge shaving cream in one hand and a safety razor in the other. The hair was mostly missing from his chest and stomach and the fronts of his legs. The skin where the hair had been removed was red and angry-looking, and little bits of blood-spotted toilet paper were stuck over it like decorations where Motor had nicked himself. Tufts of shaving cream blossomed on his shoulders and along his arms like twirls of Dairy Queen ice cream.

Motor smiled widely, showing his broken and stained teeth. "Hey, I know you!" Russell did not, could not, speak. "How you doin', biggun?"

Russell stared at the angry skin, the blood-bespecked bits of toilet paper. "I don't believe . . . I don't believe . . ."

"Don't believe what, biggun?"

". . . we've met."

"Hell, it cain't be two like you. Your head's just like I'as told, too, slick as owl shit. Come on in, Mr. Muscle."

"Russell Morgan," said Russell, recovering himself a little.

Motor smiled more broadly still. "That may be what you mama named you, Bud, howsomever you made youself all the way into sompin' else. All the way to a Russell Muscle is what you done. I knowed you quicker'n you could say it, and I ain't never laid eyes on you. Like I said, it cain't be two like you."

"I was just looking for Shereel," Russell said.

"And I was just shaving myself down," said Motor, "so I can crab it better. Goin' straight to Nair after this. Went out and bought myself about a goddamn gallon of the stuff. Whadda you think?"

Russell did not know what he thought. He had been unable to follow what Motor was saying. But he did know one thing: He would have taken Nail Head Barnes over this . . . this . . . whatever this was.

"Shereel Dupont," said Russell, without knowing what was going to come out of his mouth when he opened it. But when the name came out, he said it again. "Shereel Dupont."

"Hell, I rectum sore," said Motor in a great spittle-spray of braying laughter. "Little joke there. Rectum sore. Reckon so. Git it?" He shook himself like a great mange-ridden dog, sending flecks of shaving cream flying into the hallway. "Shereel Du-

pont. I rectum sore. Turnipseeds allas had class. Nothing *but*
class. And now Dorothy's done turned into a Shereel. And me?
I'm shaving down to learn to crab it. Who woulda thought it?
Come on in, you can hep me shave my back." He half turned
and dropped the towel to show Russell the forest of hair still
growing down his back and over the cheeks of his ass. "Hard
for me to git it back there."

"I don't think so," said Russell.

"You don't think so? You ever tried to shave you goddamn
back and you ass before?"

"No."

"Did, you'd know it ain't a easy thing to do."

"That's not what I meant."

"It's what you said," Motor said, taking a pull with the razor
at the little tuft of hair beside his navel. "You don't look none
too good neither. You feeling all right, are you?"

"I need to find Shereel."

"Why didn't you say so? She went on back to her room after
Billy Bat got through crabbin' it and doin' the compulsories and
tellin' us about warmin' up and greasin' down."

"Warming up and greasing down," Russell repeated, light-
headed and giddy.

"That, and first one thing and another," said Motor. "Billy
Bat ain't never met a stranger and damned if he ain't a talker."

"Billy Bat?" said Russell, totally lost now and a little frightened
in the strangeness of it all, as though this might be something
he was dreaming.

"From Murfreesboro. Billy Bat is a Tennessee boy, you know."

Russell Morgan could not respond.

"You gone stay out there in the hall or you gone come on in
here and watch me shave off the rest of this hair?"

Russell knew the answer to that. "I'm staying out here."

F O U R T E E N

Earline broke the surface of the water in the heart-shaped, sunken bathtub of the bridal bower and the rounded hump of her smooth, thick shoulders emerged into the steaming air like a whale beaching, or so Billy Bat thought, himself insubstantial as a ghost where he stood looking down upon her through the heavy, swirling steam that had risen from the heated water, risen and filled the sealed-off bathroom until Billy Bat could hardly see her from two feet away. He hunkered lower and saw that her eyes were nearly closed and she was smiling as she slipped back down deep into the water and rose again, wet-slicked and beautiful, tiny beads of moisture dependent from her long eyelashes. She breathed deeply and exhaled loudly, blowing a spray of water through her pursed heart-shaped lips, only deepening Billy Bat's impression of a whale, a free-swimming, free-living whale of magnificent size and weight, reveling in its freedom to do whalelike things, which included eating constantly and freely whatever it came upon in the vast deep of its world. And he would have liked nothing better than to tell her what she reminded him of. But he could not. She would surely misunderstand. And God knows he had had a hard enough time getting her here in the bathtub of the bridal bower to start with. He was not about to run the risk of a misunderstanding now when the next thing was to get her out of that goddamn one-piece.

Billy Bat smiled down upon her, and Earline, watching him through the wet lashes of her very nearly closed eyelids, smiled back. Earline felt so at peace, so safe, so . . . so *loved*. Yes, loved.

And in the steaming water of the deep tub, she felt light, lighter than she had ever imagined feeling, a lightness of the sort she had only dreamed. And safe, God did she feel safe. Partly because of the trust she had in Billy Bat, but mostly because of the ribbed and buttressed embrace of her bathing suit that she wore as she floated and bounced in the scalding water, submerging and surfacing again as playful as a child.

"Is the water too hot?"

Her eyes had closed without her even being aware of it, and when she opened them to answer, Billy Bat was kneeling by the tub, his face beaded with steam and very close to hers.

"No," she said and surprised herself that her voice was a whisper.

"Your skin," he said.

"Yes."

"Your beautiful skin."

"Thank you."

"Don't thank me," he said. "Never thank me for telling the truth. The beauty of truth is that it does not need a thank you, thank you."

"God, I cain't hardly stand it when you talk potry."

"See the blush on your shoulders. Your entire body is blushing."

She could hardly say it, but she managed to get it out. "My entire body."

"Just as I said it would."

For the first time through the heavy, swirling steam, she saw his hands. Over each of them was draped a thick white washcloth. In each of the corners of each of the washcloths was stitched a blue flamingo standing on one leg, its long slender neck shaped into a question mark. An enormous question mark. An enormous question mark that swelled to fill her eyes, the heart-shaped tub, and finally the steam-filled bathroom.

"Beautiful skin," he said.

Her eyes were closed and she did not answer.

"And beautiful skin is the foundation to it all."

Behind her eyes she remembered that was the answer to the enormous question she felt swelling everywhere about her. Her beautiful skin was the answer to why she was sitting in the tub in her one-piece with Billy Bat kneeling beside her with a heavy washcloth in either hand. He was about to buff her up, and stimulate her largest organ.

The very notion of him stimulating her largest organ made her light-headed to the point of swooning, which is just the way it had made her feel when she first heard it earlier while the two of them sat on the heart-shaped loveseat in the bridal bower.

"My largest organ?" she had said sitting very still, keeping her eyes averted but remembering the way he had looked doing the crab in her parents' suite, remembering the way the little knob of his cock, somehow sweetly melancholy and terribly vulnerable, had looked behind the thin fabric of his posing briefs.

"Didn't know that, did you?"

"What?" she said, lost in the memory of sweet melancholy and vulnerability.

"That you skin is you biggest organ."

"No," she said. "I didn't know that."

"Is though," he said. "And the foundation to everything."

She could still taste the Colonel Sanders in her mouth and remember the quiet, natural way he had taken her hand and held it while he was walking her back to the bridal bower.

"Most people think it's your liver," he said, "but it ain't. You skin is you biggest organ. And you can thank God every day of you life you got the skin you got. Casts off toxins, poisons . . . and dirt," Billy Bat said in a musing voice.

"What?" she said, not really wanting to know, not really listening.

"You biggest organ do," he said. "Along with some other things is how you git rid of what hurts you body, you poisons, and the rest of it."

"Yes," she said, not listening.

And he knew she was not listening, knew she did not care, but that was fine with him. He only wanted to lift her heft. Feel

the heavy slabs of her in his hands. Smell and taste her. And
toward that end he had resolved to get her into a steaming tub
of water. It seemed impossible, but then everything he had ever
really wanted in his life seemed impossible. His body—and
mainly his back—was a walking impossibility. He was no
stranger to hoping the unhopeable, wishing the unwishable.

"Listen to me, girl," he said, "you special."

"I am?" she said, dreaming over the fact of her sitting here
with this beautiful man, this man that out-manned any man she
had ever seen, even if he was a short thick one.

"The way it is, see, is everybody's got the same thing. It's
just that some got more of it than others."

He saw a kind of shadow pass over her smooth, swollen
features, and she said, "Well, I did think to lose ten pound."

"For you," he said, "a piece of cake."

"A piece of cake," she repeated, actually seeing a huge piece
of cake as she said it. Thick layers cemented together with sugar.
And her stomach, packed with Colonel Sanders, growled and
longed for the cake she saw.

"Lemme just run it down for you. To git rid of what you body
don't want, you got four things to work with." He held up his
hand and counted off on his fingers. "Lungs, liver, night soil
and night rain, which don't count as but one—night soil and
night rain don't—natural elimination."

She had heard of night soil, but never night rain, and she
thought: Billy Bat can even turn *that* into potry. Night rain was
poetry if you didn't stop to think too much about what he meant
by it, and she didn't. She concentrated on his hand.

Billy Bat had been holding up four fingers, and he had folded
down three of them. He had one thickly callused finger left,
held rigidly there between them. "And this," he said, regarding
the finger, "this is you skin. Biggest organ in you body. Biggest
eliminator. Everbody knows you cain't live without you liver.
Think about trying to live without you skin."

He waited, giving her time to think about it. But she did not
think about her skin. She thought about his. Thought about how

smooth and utterly hairless it was. Thought about hugging it. Thought about the huge, leaping muscles under it.

"Cain't, can you?"

"What?" she said, her face suddenly hot with blood because she had drifted on into thinking about tracing his all-over hugeness with her tongue and the thought of doing such a thing to a man had never occurred to her except in the middle of the night in the middle of her bed, alone. She was not prepared for such a thought in the presence of a man.

"Living without you skin," he said.

She felt indeterminant and very weak as though she had lost all the bones out of her body. What was he talking about? What had he been trying to tell her? Whatever it was, she had entirely lost it. All she knew was that she was prepared to believe anything he told her, do anything he told her to do, follow him anywhere.

"And you in luck," he said.

"I know I am," she said, and meant it. She felt like the luckiest person alive.

"What it is," he said, "is I'm a skin mechanic."

"Skin," she said, not following him.

"Mechanic," he said.

"Mechanic," she said.

"Skin mechanic," he said, "is what I am."

He was, of course, no such thing. It had just popped into his head and he had said it, and once he said it, it sounded pretty wonderful. It sounded like the thing he needed to be to get to where he needed to go, so he said it again: "Skin mechanic."

"I don't believe I ever known one," she said.

"It ain't many of us around," he said, "so I can understand you never knowing one before."

What he didn't understand was why he was lying to her. His mama back in Murfreesboro, Tennessee, had not raised him to lie and he knew he was letting his old mama down. He tried to comfort himself with the knowledge that in a manner of speaking what he said was true, but it was not much comfort because something in him knew that in a manner of speaking, *everything* was true. But that was all something he would have to worry about later because his hands were tingling to handle her heft. Her heft was calling to his hands and consequently, like it or not, his tongue, his brain—every cell and fiber of his being— were in service to the need to handle her.

"You said you wanted to lose ten pound," he said.

"I had thought to do it one day," she said. "Maybe ten pound."

"You don't need to lose no ten pound," he said. "You need tonin' and tunin'."

"Tonin' and tunin'," she said.

"If you was toned and tuned," he said, "you'd think you lost ten pound and more."

"I would?"

"I'm here to tell you," he said. "And the secret to bein' toned and tuned is you skin."

"My skin."

"And I'm a skin mechanic."

"What does uh, what does a skin mechanic do?"

"Tunes and tones."

"And me . . . ? What would you do . . . ?" She did not know how to finish, or rather was afraid of where finishing would take her.

"Tone you and tune you, you sweet girl."

"I love it when you call me a sweet girl."

He spread his thick, powerful hands, palms up, and looked at them. "You ain't seen nothing yet."

"I haven't?"

He still stared at his hands. "Them hands hold the power."

"The power to . . . to do what?"

"Tone and tune. Take you to the other side."

She watched him shyly, finally averting her eyes. His voice had taken the tone of a fundamentalist preacher. It was the voice of his father, who was a fundamentalist preacher back in Murfreesboro, Tennessee. It was the voice of ultimate persuasion, filled as it was with equal measures of terror and love.

"You don't know what's on the other side, do you, child?"

"No, I don't."

"On the other side you will know that you are a dear sweet girl. And you will know that you are beautiful. And you will love the only body you ever have to love before you can love all other bodies. It is all body, you sweet girl, and body is all. Body. Think about it, you sweet girl. Body."

"Body?" she said, confused now, eyes still averted.

"Body," he said, and put his hand on her thick shoulder, thrilling at the depth of her fat. "What it is"—and he dropped naturally into the cadences of his father—"is I spent my life in search of body, no sacrifice was too gret to find body, to know body, to be touched by the gretness of body and . . ."

"Potry," she breathed.

". . . it's on account of my life spent in the search of the body that I am today a skin mechanic."

Earline almost said Praise God, but caught herself in time, realizing that would not be appropriate. So in spite of the fact that Praise God certainly *felt* appropriate, she only said in a small, gasping voice: "You can take me on to the other side."

"Then you need to be buffed up, have you biggest organ stimulated."

For him to talk about her biggest organ, have it in his mouth, made her feel faint, but also filled her with a hot pleasure that had its origin in an image: Billy Bat's hand lifting the ruffled skirt of her one-piece and taking the most intimate part of the suit in his brutal bodybuilding hand and massaging it.

"Yes," she said.

"Yes?" he said, astonished at his luck. His hands tingled for the heft of her. His nostrils flared for the smell of her. His mouth salivated for the taste of her. The imminent prospect of the heft and smell and taste of this wonderful, beautiful, free-grazing beast of a girl made him go weak with pleasure. It was the very feeling he had when he came back to his apartment from the convenience store late at night with his car loaded with junk food, knowing that in a matter of minutes he would be safely hidden from the world and free to gorge on all that was forbidden, illegal, and dangerous, at least forbidden and illegal and dangerous to world-class bodybuilders.

"We both professionals," she said.

"We that all right," he said, "you and me." She had told him at some length about her course of study that had led to the degree in Problems of Living. "For proper buffing up, stimulation of you biggest organ, we need wet heat."

"Wet heat," she said, the words impossibly erotic in her ears as well as on her tongue.

"We need that big ole bathtub full of water hot as you can stand it, and you in it," he said. And then as an afterthought: "You sweet girl."

He had seen the tub when she had given him a tour of the bridal bower after they came back from her mama and daddy's place where he did the crab. They had in fact stood for some time, still holding hands, regarding the twin, heart-shaped thrones.

"Nice, real nice," had been his only comment.

And she, strangely unembarrassed with his hand in hers, had said, "Yes, they are. They real nice."

"It's the wet heat that does the trick," he said, looking now off toward the door of the bathroom. Then he slowly turned toward her on the loveseat, their faces very close, his eyes locked on her eyes. "You ready girl?"

"We both professionals," she said in a matter-of-fact voice, "and as one professional to another, so to speak, I'm ready as I'll ever be."

"Gret," he said, "just gret. Toned and tuned you gone look and feel like you lost them ten pound."

"Howsomever," she said, cutting her eyes and looking aslant at him across her cheek.

"Yes?" he said.

"Just exactly what you mean to do?"

"To do?"

She could hardly say it, but she managed to get it out. "When you stimulate my organ . . . my *biggest* organ, that is."

"Wet massage," he said.

Massage? That meant hands. Hands on her biggest organ. She stared at him, squinting slightly in concentration, and then dropped her eyes to his hands.

He saw and understood. "Using a rough surface," he said. "You know, cloth, towel, whatever."

"Oh," she said.

Billy Bat was winging all this, making it up as he went, and he thought he was doing pretty damn good. But was this sweet, beautiful girl—and he did truly think her sweet and beautiful— buying it?

"Let's do it," she said. "It ain't everday a girl meets a skin mechanic and gits a chance to be tuned and toned."

Billy Bat felt the whole inside of his chest lift. She was not only buying it, *she had bought it.*

"Let me go on in there and fill me up that tub and git in," she said.

"All right," he said.

"When I'm good and ready," she said, "I'll holler for you to come on and do it."

The thought of him coming on and doing it struck Billy Bat dumb. He stretched his mouth and smiled at her but did not answer.

"I'll just need me a few things," she said.

"That's fine," he said. "That's real fine. You gone feel like a different girl after you toned and tuned."

She already felt like a different girl as she went over to her suitcase to rummage through it. She spread her feet wide to bend and was keenly aware of her straddling thighs still meeting all the way to her knees, but still more aware of her flaring hips as she bent, aware that her back was to Billy Bat and that he was probably watching, watching her flared and straddling. But Billy Bat was not. He had watched her start to bend and flare, but looked away immediately because he could not bear it. His mouth was still stretched not so much in a smile but in a kind of rictus when she came flouncing by, her own face locked in an expression of grim happiness, with something—what? a robe, towels, he couldn't tell—held close against her chest.

Billy Bat sat listening to the water running into the deep honeymoon tub, his mind filled to overflowing with food he could eat but never keep: strawberry pancakes swimming in butter and maple syrup, half a bushel of M&M candies, grease-dripping sausages laid over with a six-egg omelet filled with lethal cholesterol and covered with salt. His swollen hands ticked in his lap with such urgency that he could almost hear them.

A kind of lilting cry came finally from behind the closed bathroom door which—if he had not been so distracted by images of food that floated not only in his eyes but in his very bloodstream—he would have recognized as a desperate cry filled with resignation. "Billlly Baaaaat! Oh, *Billy!* Come on if you comin'!"

"I'm coming, you sweet girl," he said, rising from the loveseat on his champion, worldbeating legs, gone now, turned entirely into a sickly weakness.

He could not feel his feet as he walked across the deep carpet, opened the bathroom door, and walked into a solid sheet of steam that beaded on his naked arms and shoulders as he leaned toward the sound of water in violent motion slapping the sides of the tub. He moved closer and her red, slightly mottled skin clung to her finely shaped skull and fell down her wide creamy neck and shoulders to . . . to what? Billy Bat strained to see through the thick swirling steam and what he gradually saw and came to understand was that she was wearing her fucking one-piece bathing suit. The gathered, ruffled top of it bound her tightly.

"See you got you one-piece on," Billy Bat said. And then: "You sweet girl."

"Well, Billlly!" she said, her voice still full of desperate resignation. "I couldn't . . . we couldn't . . . you *wouldn't*, not *neked*."

"We both professionals," he said. "We both got trained skills. That makes us different. I thought our skills made us different."

Softly, sweetly, as though she were telling him something intimate: "My skills is in Problems of Living."

His voice harsher than he meant it to be: "Mine's in sompin' else. I'm a skin mechanic. And a skin mechanic is got to have skin. You wouldn't want me to work on the engine of you car without being able to git under the hood, would you?"

Her round bright eyes disappeared under her long lashes and in the smallest of voices, she said, "No, I wouldn't." She submerged, even her head disappearing, and when she surfaced, her eyes still closed, her voice even smaller, she said, "You can git under anything you want to git under." And then in a deep grateful sigh: "Because we both professionals."

And so here he was kneeling beside the tub with both hands draped by thick white washcloths with blue flamingos standing on one leg stitched into each of the corners and Earline still in her one-piece that squeezed her like the skin on a sausage. She had said he could git under it but Billy Bat did not know exactly how to proceed. His experience with women was limited, his interest focused exclusively on those who were joyously and truly fat and that interest extended only to lifting and handling their heft. Billy Bat was by choice a virgin. He had always thought that if a prizefighter could leave his fight in bed, surely a bodybuilder could leave his championship in the same place. He was not about to lose even an ounce of his worldbeating back through the head of his dick.

He put both washcloth-covered hands on the wet smooth hump of her shoulders and rubbed in slow easy circles.

"Mmmmm," she said. "Mmmmm."

The he closed his fists, taking handfuls of fat off her back up into his cloth-covered hands, and pulling ever so gently, but gradually not so gently, finally twisting the fat more tightly. Earline gave a deep moan that had the edge of pain in it and turned her head to look up at him, her eyes open now, round and bright.

"Billy," she said.

"Relax," he said. "Drift and go with it. You in good hands."

"That do smart some."

"No pain, no gain," he said.

"No pain, no gain," she repeated.

"It's the code we live by," he said. "Accept it. Go with it."

"You wouldn't hurt me," she said, her head still turned looking at him.

"I mean to take you where you need to go," he said, and thought: *Where I need to go.*

"But you wouldn't hurt me?" She could feel her whole back lift as the pressure of his hands increased.

"Pain's got nothing to do with it. What you call pain, you'll come to love."

"I ain't never liked to be hurt," she said.

"I want you to relax. Roll your head on your neck. Breathe deep. You don't need to ask if I'd hurt you. You know the answer to that, you sweet girl. You know the answer to that or my name's not Billy Bat."

"Billy Bat," she said, her eyes closed now, her head lolling on her neck, not breathing deeply though, panting rather. Her skin was growing hotter than the hot water she sat in.

"Breathe from the bottom of you lungs. Think about all that is beautiful and safe and natural."

His hands had gone lower on her back, gripping, lifting, probing deeply into her until she could feel the hard, brutally blunt tips of his fingers tracing her ribs under her shoulder blades. He had gone beneath her one-piece and God did it feel good and right. But it also hurt.

"I don't believe I know how to think about beautiful and safe and natural and hurt at the same time."

"Think about a huge green pasture. Try to see it. Can you see it?"

"Yes."

"In the middle of the pasture is a pond of clear, still water, not a ripple in it, like a beautiful piece of glass reflecting nothing except the whitest bits of cloud floating in the bluest sky God ever imagined." She started to turn her head to look at him but he stopped her with his hand. "Still. Be still. Keep you eyes closed. See the pasture. See the clear, looking-glass water. Beside it now. You see a white horse, a proud, young white horse, and just a easy breeze is lifting his mane and letting it fall again and lifting it again. Can you see that? See it all?"

"God, that's potry," she said.

"But can you see it?" he said.

"Yes I can," she said, and she truly could.

"I'm buffing you up now. It's only a matter of time."

He did not say what was only a matter of time, and she did not ask. The rough cloths over her skin were unlike anything she had ever felt. But it was not the washcloths she was feeling now. Billy Bat had long since dropped them. What she felt on her skin that was coming alive with the surfacing of tingling blood was ridges of calluses in Billy Bat's hands. She felt his hands come over her shoulders and slide beneath the gathered top of her one-piece, palm her breasts, and lift them free. She allowed her sight to sift through her lashes and saw her breasts floating there in front of her, long and round and utterly white and, she thought, beautiful. Billy Bat's naked hands were rolling and squeezing them, using long strokes to milk the blood down toward her nipples. And her nipples amazed her. She had never seen them this way before, rigid, darkly engorged with blood, and more than the sight of them was a feeling—again, one she had never before known—as though a mildly charged electric wire had been connected to both nipples and ran directly to the place between her legs. She had lost sight of the green pasture and the mirror-like pond and the white horse. All she could see now was his hands on her, the one-piece shoved down to her navel, his square beautiful hands lifting and holding her beet-red flesh.

Billy Bat's head lifted, his nostrils flared and caught scent of all that his life as a bodybuilder had denied him: pastry, pork chops, fried chicken, thick flaky biscuits awash in butter. Something in him knew that he could not possibly smell what he smelled, but another, deeper part of him knew the steaming air

was filled with what he longed to smell most. And he hefted
the slabs of her and gazed upon what was in his hands with
love and longing.

She looked down and watched his hands on her rounded,
deeply naveled belly—a belly she had hated since childhood—
and found herself loving her belly, her belly now was beautiful
because of the gentle, crooning sounds coming from Billy Bat.
Without thinking, without knowing she was going to do it, she
reached back and caught Billy Bat behind the neck, and with
surprising strength—or perhaps the surprising movement had
simply caught him off balance, leaning as he was over the bathtub behind her—jerked Billy Bat over her shoulders and into
the tub with her. He went entirely under in the deep tub and
came up spitting water. They watched each other, he with the
startled look of an awakened sleepwalker, and she with the new,
deeply felt confidence his painfully gentle hands and the crooning noises out of his mouth had given her.

"A skin mechanic don't, as a regular thing, work in the tub
with a client," he said.

"Client, Billy Bat? Client?" Her eyebrows were arched and
she caught the wet pink tip of her tongue between her teeth.
She released the caught tongue and it ran out long and narrow
and at such length as to startle and amaze Billy Bat. "This one-
piece is binding," she said. "You can go ahead on and pull it
off."

"Pull it off," said Billy Bat.

"You said a skin mechanic needed skin," she said. "A Turnipseed don't do nothing half measure."

He took hold of the suit and pulled. It was tight and it was a
struggle, but he got it off and tossed it over on the floor. Her
belly and thighs rounding and mounding above the surface of
the water there in front of him made it difficult for Billy Bat to
breathe.

Earline closed her eyes and said, "You can buff me up now.
Tone me and tune me as you will."

He went at her with a vengeance, probing, lifting, squeezing, palming the slabs of her heft above the water, staring at it, his face drawing closer and closer to it until he finally touched a dimpled piece of it with his tongue. What he touched with his tongue was so low on her belly that his chin was into the deep nest of her pubic hair.

"Oh goddamn," she said, but the curse sounded like she was crooning to a baby. And she lifted her hips to help him and felt his hard hands slide under her and bury themselves in the young, firm amplitude of her wide cheeks. She felt one of his fingers probing and she spread herself gratefully. But to her surprise and delight, the finger sank between her cheeks and pressed gently, then firmly, against the quilted winking eye of her asshole. She thought it the most loving caress she had ever known, easy and natural and full of caring, and finally without shame or ugliness. In her wildest dreams alone in her bed she had never imagined it could be so.

She reached down and took his head in both hands and raised it from the place it was buried to the ears where no man had ever been. When he looked up over the wide expanse of her, her magnificent breasts floating on either side of her now, his eyes were glazed and unseeing, but his expression was beatific as though he had just been told by Jesus himself that he was going to heaven after all.

She sat up, and as she did, she pushed him upright too, so that he ended sitting between her straddling legs. With his unfocused eyes, but with his blood focused and pounding to the point of bursting, he watched her hook her thumbs in his silk posing briefs and draw them down. And there was the tiny knob of his cock, the only one she had ever seen except for accidental glimpses of her brothers', its sweet and beautifully pink little head bobbing in the water in front of her. She took it in her open hand and it lay there reaching not quite across the width of her palm. The two of them, their expressions like children examining a toy, looked down upon it.

She started to speak, started to tell him that maybe he could teach her to be a skin mechanic, but did not, because they were both watching, transfixed by the miracle happening in her hand. So slowly as to be barely perceptible, Billy Bat's sweet beautiful pink little knob was growing, a great blue vein rising in the top of it, growing and still growing until Earline's eyes were wide and hot with moisture that felt like tears, but was not, was rather the wonder that what she had always heard would happen was happening before her amazed and gladdened heart. Billy Bat, his eyes fixed on his cock like a hunter's eyes fixed on game he meant to shoot, could only think over and over: *A goddamn worldbeater! A goddamn worldbeater!*

She drew him to her and in a skillful delicate little movement, a movement that when she made it she felt as if she had been born knowing it, she flared where he could find her and he dropped into her saddle. And the moment he lay upon her, he knew that this was the finest thing he had ever done, the finest moment he had ever had.

He would never have known when he entered her if her hands had not gripped his shoulders with surprising strength and urgency and a little shy cry had not burst from her lips, lips now swollen and the color of a bruised peach.

Billy Bat hesitated, but her hands moved from his shoulders to the small of his back and pressed with the same urgency they had on his shoulders, and she whispered "Please."

And after some time of violently lapping water, bright shards of it flying over the tiled bathroom, Billy Bat quieted and held her and said, "We fit like two spoons, you sweet girl."

She only smiled and concentrated on the moment she had dreamed of since she was a young girl but had finally come to believe would never happen.

And then later, as she felt the tension building in him just as it was building in her, she said, "We married now."

He did not answer. But he knew it was true, and he knew that she knew it was true. He had always been married to body-building, but when he entered her, he got a divorce. And when he stiffened, howling like a dog with Earline's secret face buried in his shoulder and smiling, the thought occurred to him in that single moment as serious and mysterious as death that he had just given Earline a few ounces of his worldbeating back. And right behind that came the thought that she could have all of his worldbeating back, because she did, in fact, truly have all of him.

FIFTEEN

T hrough the door of Shereel's room, he heard the music she would perform to tomorrow night, ninety seconds of "Street Fighting Man." He waited until the music ended before he knocked. She opened the door standing in her posing briefs, her rib cage rising and falling with effort, and washed down in sweat. Even under her tan, there were bruises of color under her eyes and her lips were thin and leached of color, dead gray, but her eyes were bright and angry. It was game face.

He could see over her shoulder into the room. The tape deck for her music was on a low table she had moved by the window. In front of the ceiling-to-floor mirror Dexter Friedkin had installed, the carpet was dark with her sweat.

"I see Dex got the room put back together," Russell said, unable to think of anything else to say.

"Dex?"

"Dexter Friedkin."

She raised a towel she had been holding in her hand and wiped her neck and face. "Oh, the promoter."

"And the manager of the hotel. A total freak but he seems to get things done. You'd probably like him."

"I don't like anybody," she said.

He regarded her a moment. "I understand," he said.

"No you don't."

"I come close to winning it all, Shereel. You can't go anywhere I haven't been."

"Bullshit. Why do you always bullshit me so much?"

Russell stood very still and watched her. She said he was

talking bullshit, and of course he was. But it galled him for her to say it. She *was* where he had never been before.

As an amateur he had won the Mr. America, but when he turned professional, he had disappeared. He did manage to qualify for the Cosmos, but when he entered he didn't even place. It was because of his skin. His skin was what bodybuilders call *thick*. He had a layer of subcutaneous fat that no amount of sweating, starving, or working could take from between the skin and the muscle. He had size, mass, and symmetry, but he also had that skin, and he could not defeat it. So the skin had defeated him.

And now she, Shereel Dupont, was his chance to make it big. His final chance. And he knew it. He had been looking for a girl he could win the world with ever since he opened the Emporium of Pain. But he had never found her.

That fucking Wallace had *five*, for God's sake. The unfairness of it jellied the very marrow of his bones. If Wallace lost with Marvella, he would win with one of her sisters. It was easy to believe that he might even win with all of them. So anyway you cut it, there was no way Wallace could lose.

But for Russell, Shereel Dupont was the end of the road. If she lost, he lost too. Once and forever, he would lose everything he had given his life to. Everything.

But she could win. She *had* to win. His own reputation, his very life was on the line. She was who and what she was because of him. Couldn't she goddamn see that?

"I'm the one who trained you," he said with considerably more heat than he had intended. "I'm the one who got you here."

"You swung the whip. I'm the one who hurt and sweated blood."

"Exactly," he said.

"Exactly what?"

"Exactly the way it's supposed to be."

"I don't give a fuck *how* it's *supposed* to be."

He had to calm down and let it pass, get on with the job at

hand. He looked beyond her into the room. "You going through the routine, are you?"

"You know goddamn well what I'm doing."

"Yeah, well, I'll come on in and see if I can't help you on a few fine points you may not have nailed down real good."

"I don't need your help. I don't need anybody's goddamn help. What I need is to be left alone."

"I'm not going to get in your way."

"I don't intend to *let* you get in my way."

"Never thought otherwise. Be disappointed if you did."

He walked past her into the room, having to brush her shoulder as he did. He sat on the end of her bed and turned to look at her. She was standing with her back to him, still staring at the closed door.

"How's your weight?" he said, but his eyes from long practice with flesh told him she was tight, right, and righteous. "You need the scale?"

"Do I look like I need the scale?" Shereel said, her back still to him.

"No, but you can never be too careful." He glanced at his watch. "I make it fourteen hours by my watch until weigh-in. What you standing like that for? Don't you want to look at me?"

"I don't want to look at anybody. Nobody but myself."

"I can't ever remember not wanting to see my trainer."

"Maybe that's why you never beat the world."

"There's no need to be cruel."

"This is the time for cruel. The stopper's out of the bottle and madness is everywhere. I can smell the rank craziness in the air I breathe, smell it and like it. There's no son of a bitch here can take me down."

"As far as I know, nobody thinks they can."

"Wallace does."

"Wallace won't be on stage in front of the judges."

"Marvella will."

"Marvella is a slab of beef."

"Marvella is cut to ribbons and you know it."

"A slab of beef cut to ribbons is still a slab of beef."

"She's beat me before."

"Not here. Not in the Cosmos. Tomorrow is your tomorrow, you bought it and paid for it. No slab of beef will take you down."

"I wish I could stop thinking about her."

"Come here," Russell said.

She did not turn from the door, but slowly looked over her shoulder at him.

"Come here," he said again.

She turned and came across the room to stand in front of him. "Russell, I don't need this shit now."

"You don't know what you need." He touched his knees. "Sit." Even with her blood high and more than a little anxiety and even fear in her heart, from long habit of moving to his voice, she sat across his knees.

She felt his hands, his thickly callused hands, touch her back with infinite tenderness, a tenderness she had never felt from him before and a tenderness she would have thought him incapable of. He drew her to his massive chest and one of his hands raised and stroked her hair, stroked it in a manner that suggested to her a father—no, a mother—stroking the hair of a young daughter. Nothing could have surprised her more, not even the entire hotel bursting into flames. She sat still, hardly breathing, waiting. His mouth moved to her ear.

"Stay, work, perform, entirely within yourself." His voice was hardly more than a whisper but firm, strong, a firm voice of strength she had heard only in a scream, never a whisper. And his hand continued to stroke her hair. "Do you trust me? I know how I've talked to you, screamed at you, made you suffer, made you hurt yourself, made you deny yourself everything but breathing." His hand had moved to her neck and gently, with infinite tenderness, traced the lines of her neck, down across her trapezius muscles to her deltoids, his fingers separating, lifting, and massaging so gently that he might have thought her fragile enough to break. "But do you trust me?"

"Yes," she said, and she did, and could not help thinking this is the way her daddy might have talked to her.

"Then believe this. Nobody can beat you but yourself. Shereel Dupont can only be beaten by Shereel Dupont."

She looked away from him toward the wide posing mirror. "I feel like I'm being eaten alive."

"What?"

"Or torn apart, just ripped up. None of this feels like I thought it'd feel."

She was still looking at the mirror, her head turned. Russell took her chin in his hand and gently turned her to face him.

"Talk to me," he said.

"About what?"

"Whatever's in your mind. Whatever's making you talk like a loser."

"I'm *not* a loser," she said with considerable heat.

"Then stop talking like one. You've got one more day to do it. To take it all or lose it all."

"I wish to God my family hadn't shown up. I love them, God knows I do, but they're a total pain in the ass, something I don't need. And especially Nail. I'm worried about him."

"Don't be. Don't worry about Nail Head."

"Anybody with any sense worries about Nail. He only knows one way to take anything and that's by main force."

"What happened?"

"What do you mean, what happened?"

He really wanted to know if she had fucked him. The thought of her fucking him caused a sharp little tear of pain in his stomach. But he didn't dare ask. This was the wrong time.

"It looked like you had him under control the last time I saw you with him."

"Nobody has Nail under control."

"Don't think about it. What the hell can he do?"

"Pretty much anything he wants to do as it turns out."

"What did he say to you? He must have said something to make you talk this way."

"He said I'd win."

"I've told you the same thing. What the hell's wrong with that?"

"I think he means to do something."

"There's nothing he can do."

"It's always something Nail can do. Some good, but mostly bad."

"It'll be all right," Russell said. "I've covered every base."

"Nail can't be covered."

"For the Cosmos championship I can cover anything that needs to be covered. At least I'm not Wallace, I can be thankful for that if nothing else. Marvella's four jive-ass sisters showed up. Wallace is up to his ass in pussy he doesn't need and can't use. If Marvella can keep her shit together and concentrated with those loud-talking, bad-acting bitches around, surely you can hold up to what you're carrying. Christ, you should see'm."

"I saw'm. Met'm in the elevator."

"Did they do their chorus-line routine for you?"

"They do that routine any time, any place. They don't mean anything by it."

"What you've got to get into your head is nobody means anything now. Shut'm down. Put'm out of your mind. Everybody here's got some kind of shit to deal with. Wallace has those four trash-talking niggers and you've got the Turnipseeds and Nail."

"Nail's the only one who has a knife on his belt."

"Yeah, that knife," Russell said as though he had forgotten all about it until she reminded him, when, in point of fact, he had not forgotten it for an instant since the first time he saw it.

"I told him to promise me he'd keep it on his belt."

"What did he say?"

"Said he couldn't and *wouldn't* promise his old mama that."

"Well, shit. Whatever comes down we'll handle it."

"Nobody's ever been able to handle Nail or he wouldn't be alive today."

"Well, I don't wish him any bad luck, but I do wish he'd die a little and get the fuck out of our way."

"Don't talk like that about Nail."

"Here he is making your shit go sour and you tell me not to talk about him like that."

"I grew up with Nail. He wasn't always Nail Head. He was once Harry Barnes. He's my friend."

"Seemed to me he might be more than a friend."

"That's none of your business. And Nail would die for me."

"Everything's my business until this is over tomorrow night. And I wish he would . . ."

"Would . . . ?"

"Forget it." He drew her to him again and started the easy stroking of her hair. "You go onstage tomorrow and remember only one thing."

"What?"

"Remember who you are. Remember that there are posters of you plastered on walls all over this country and half of Europe with girls working to be what you are, dreaming of being where you will be tomorrow night, and there is one of them somewhere who is hurt but working right on through the hurt, paying the price of pain and denial, and the dream of you, Shereel Dupont, is what keeps her going when nothing else could; not even her will, her courage, her ambition to be somebody, only you, what you mean to her, will cause her to stand some day on top of the world, the very best of her kind, and you, only you, will have brought her there. You have made yourself special in a way very few people are ever privileged to know. Hold on to that, keep it in your heart and in your blood."

While he talked he had drawn her ever more tightly against him. And his hand had kept stroking her hair. She felt something coming off him she had never felt before, off his voice, his hands, the heat of his body. And it was a shock to her when she realized it was the purest kind of caring, and concern, and love. And all of it entirely untainted by anything sexual. It made her want to kiss him. And she knew she could have without doing violence to the moment. She could not help thinking it would be the kind of kiss she might give her father.

But she drew back to look at him. "Why are you doing this?"

"Doing what?"

"This. You're petting me, for Christ's sake," she said, smiling.

"Yes, I am, I'm petting you."

"And what you're saying, I've never heard . . ."

"No you haven't, have you? But we've never been to this moment. The time for screaming is past. The time for blood demands is past. Someday, you'll probably train your own champion, and if you do, you'll understand. I don't worry about the game face. You've got it. I don't worry about what's cooking in your blood, I know what's cooking. But there's a time to cook and a time to chill. *Don't* strain tomorrow. Understand. Think about that tonight. *Don't* press. Press and you're dead. Get to the center of yourself and stay there. No matter what happens, stay there, at the quiet, disciplined center of yourself. As the brothers say: This ain't nothing but a thing. Go out and do it."

She pressed herself against him, and then drew back and looked at him, their eyes only inches apart. "I wish you'd talked to me like this before."

"If I had, we wouldn't be here. There's a time for the whip, and there's a time for the scream." He smiled and then drew her to him and held her tightly. "And there's a time to hold you and quietly tell you the truth: You're the best in the world. The world! If it was not the truth, I wouldn't say it. Do you believe me? Do you believe that there is nowhere left for you to go because you are the best?"

"Yes," she said, her lips against his neck.

"All right," he said. "Now get away from that goddamn mirror and go to bed. Don't worry about waking up. I'll wake you up. And I'll be with you every step of the way tomorrow. The only thing I can't do for you is go onstage and win it for you. And when you win, and you will, it'll all belong to you. None of it will be mine, none of it will be anybody else's. You bought it and paid for it in sweat, blood, and pain."

She did not so much stand up from where she was sitting across his knees as he lifted her, lifted her as easily as a child, and set her on her feet. He got up and started for the door.

"Russell," she said.

He half turned to look at her. "Something I missed?"

She was smiling, her eyes hot with the beginnings of what felt like tears. She felt closer to Russell at that moment than she had ever felt to anyone in her life. "Yeah, you missed something," she said.

"And what would that be?"

"You missed ever letting me see you like this."

"I do what I have to do," he said. "It couldn't work any other way. But since you bring it up, I've got one other thing to tell you. No matter what happens tomorrow, no matter what I find it necessary to do or say, or how I say it, you remember tonight. You remember how we had it tonight. You think you can do that?"

"I don't think I'll forget it tomorrow. I don't think I'll ever forget it."

He watched her for a moment. "Get as mushy in your mouth as you want to, but keep the steel red hot and hard in your guts. Okay?"

"Okay," she said, as he was closing the door on the way out.

arvella was lying on a wheeled gurney on her stomach naked but for a towel covering her buttocks, and her four sisters, two on either side of the table, were rubbing her down. Wallace sat across the room with his head in his hands. Of all the things in the world he could have done without, these four girls headed the list. They were magnificent specimens, coming as they did out of the same gene pool as Marvella. They had her bone configuration, and metabolic rate, tending to carry a very high ratio of lean muscle to fat, and like Marvella, their bodies responded to training in a way that was pure magic. What they did not have was Marvella's discipline, her single-minded concentration on the job at hand. They trained hard enough, never missed a day in the gym, but they were unpredictable in every other way. They simply would not listen, or if they did listen, they paid no attention to what they heard. Wallace put his head farther down and let his hands slide over his ears. Jive-ass talking bitches!

He had told them as clearly as he knew how to tell them that they were not to come to Miami to the Cosmos show. He had even given them reasons, for Christ's sake, something he never did to those he trained. Marvella needed no distractions, he'd told them. She needed time and space to chill, to keep her shit together, he'd told them. Stay home in Detroit and train, your time will come, he'd told them. And now here they were without even enough common sense to be sorry and apologetic about it. They had, after all, come on their own money. Marvella was their sister, they'd told him, as if he didn't know that, and blood was blood. Well, fuck it, they were here. He'd have to make the most of it. Maybe it would be all right.

He took his hands away from his ears and looked up. Marvella was on her back now, the towel draped over her hips. What should have been breasts were naked because they were not breasts at all, rather swelled and rippling layers of muscle topped with thick dark nipples that seemed to stay perpetually rigid.

If the sisters weren't here he would have been rubbing her down, the taste of her coming through his hands all the way to his mouth. And the towel wouldn't be there either. The towel was for the sisters, not for him. They were the ones who had draped it over her. Apparently, Marvella had never told them that he rubbed her down naked, had been doing it since she was fifteen years old. There was no part of her he could not and had not touched. And far more than that Marvella and he had an agreement; when she won the Cosmos she was going to spend the night in his bed. She was going to give it up. At long last he was going to mount and fuck what he had so carefully and with such patience managed to build. Now it looked like that was even down the shitter. There was no room to be had in the Blue Flamingo. Not one.

"We can go on and sleep in Sister Marvella's room, just bring in some cots, and if the hotel can't do that, we just make us a pallet on the floor," they had told him.

"The fuck you will. The champion of the world need rest, and they ain't no rest with you four . . . four . . . girls around." He wanted to call them bitches but did not. He believed them to be the future of bodybuilding and they belonged to him. And they were crazy enough to leave him and his gym if he said the wrong thing. He did not know that for a fact, but he did not feel he could risk it.

"You sleep in my room," he had said.

The four of them together: "Your room?"

"My room. Like you said, I'll get cots from the hotel if I can. Ain't possible, then it's the floor. Otherwise, git on a plane and go back to Detroit."

They had not responded to that, only did a little jig-step—
the four of them together—and simultaneously repositioned
their shades on their noses.

And now they were jabbering over Marvella while they rubbed
her down with Rose Bud massage oil.

"You got this locked."

"A lock on this."

"Rest of'm one brick shy of a load."

"But you *loaded*."

"Loaded *and* ready to fire."

"When you go off they all be dead!"

All of them together: "BANG!"

"Buncha laid-out dead motherfuckers."

Marvella had said not a word since she lay down on the table.
Wallace got out of his chair and came across the room to stand
over her. Her eyes were closed, her breathing shallow and regular. That was good. That was real good.

"Dig these guns!" said Vanella.

"Be holding some guns," Shavella said.

They were talking about her arms; the muscles, though limp,
were long and heavy and sharply defined. A blue vein traced
up her forearm, through her bicep, and curved into and across
her striated deltoid. And her color! She was so black she was
almost blue and she glowed like some rare gem dug out of the
earth.

While the four girls jabbered, Wallace went to the phone and
dialed the desk. "This Wallace Wilson." A pause. "Wilson, goddammit, the Wall, Marvella Washington is my girl in the Cosmos." He listened for a moment. "That's better. I need you to
do something for me. Bring four cots and set them up in my
room." Another pause. "You don't need to know why I need
them. Just do it. I could give a fuck where you find them, just
do it. Okay? All right, that's better." He listened another moment. "When? You say when? Ten minutes ago would have
been too late. Have the fucking things in my room when I get
there or I'll have to come talk to you, and try to believe this: *You*

do not want to talk to the Wall tonight. Dig?" And he hung up the phone.

He looked over at Marvella where the four sisters watched him.

Vanella said, "Wall, you be bad, you know that?"

Sassy bitch was mocking him. He let it slide. More important things were on the fire. More important things may be burning up.

"What if we don't want to sleep in your room?" said Jabella.

"Then sleep in the goddamn park for all I care. I didn't ask you here. Or go to another hotel. There's got to be a room somewhere."

"We staying where Marvella staying, and that's the ying and the yang of it," said Starvella, her hands under the towel, massaging her.

"The what?" demanded Wallace.

"The ying and the yang."

"Jesus Christ," Wallace said.

"Didn't say nothing about Jesus Lord, said ying and yang." That was Jabella, who was not just religious, but hardcore, buried-deep religious. She would also win the world one day if Wallace didn't lose her to a fucking convent.

"Stop with the chatter and get out of here. This is my room key." He handed it to Jabella, who was the most trustworthy of the four, which didn't mean she was necessarily trustworthy, but he had to give the key to somebody. "The beds will be there by the time you are."

"We ain't through," Vanella said.

"You're through."

"Your *mother!*" said Vanella. "We ain't back in the Black Magic now. We a long way from home."

"And you'll stay a long way from home and never see the Black Magic again, you fuck with me. Is that what you want?"

"You know it ain't."

"I don't know nothing. Get the fuck out of here."

Vanella looked down on her sister, whose eyes were still

closed. "Got to say goodnight and good luck to sister."

"She don't need a goodnight and she made her good luck in the gym. She needs rest. She needs peace. She needs calm. Now slide out of here and don't let the door hit you in the ass when you leave."

Going out the door, Vanella said, "Your mother, *twice!*" The others followed her.

Wallace stood over Marvella. "Champ," he said softly. The only movement was the regular rise and fall of her rib cage. He gently laid his hand on her brow. Her eyes fluttered and then opened. She had been asleep. She smiled up at him as though she had just come from the happiest of dreams.

"You know what I dream?" she said.

"I think I probably do."

"I dream I beat the world."

"That ain't no dream. That a fack."

"I dream I won it all."

"You just hold on to that dream."

"I hold on."

"How you feel?"

"I feel good. I feel real good."

He slowly and deliberately placed his palm on the rounded hardness of her ass. "You do," he said, "you do feel good."

She looked at him with bright eyes. "Tomorrow night I feel better."

"Yes," he said.

"Tomorrow night *you* feel better," she said, a sly, shy smile touching her mouth.

"Ain't ever man sleep with the finest of the fine, the number-one woman in the world," he said.

"Cain't but one man do that, 'cause it ain't but one woman like that."

"And you her."

"And I'm her."

"Do you believe it?"

"I believe it."

His hand was wandering, touching, lingering in all her secret places. "Why you believe it, girl?"

"'Cause I believe you. You made me special. Nobody else. You took a little black girl, a little nobody black girl, and made everbody in the world wish they was her. But they cain't be. 'Cause they ain't but one me. And you made me the one I am."

He had one of her unbelievable nipples between his thumb and forefinger. He twisted it first one way, then the other, not gently.

"Why you don't come by me?" she said.

He had not heard her. His fingers were listening to the tightness of her incredibly long nipples encircled by dark rings.

"What?"

"Come by me now."

"Now?"

"I'm the same girl tonight I'll be tomorrow night."

"No," he said.

"Sho I will."

"That's not what I meant," he said, wanting to take his twisting fingers from her nipples but he could not make himself do it.

"What you meant?"

"That was not the deal we had. The deal we had was something else."

"The something else was when I was *one*, the *one*."

"Ah, yes, sweet girl, but you ain't the one yet. I take the edge off you blood if I make you the *one* before you are the one and actual *one*. You get to be damp and dirty with the man that made you just like God made Jesus, anything before that can't nothing but hex and conjure against us both. You dig?"

"I dig," she said. "But stop touching me there, God, take your hand off *there*. I ain't nothing but flesh and blood. It's only so far flesh and blood can go, no matter how deep the deal."

"All right, take that head onstage with you tomorrow and cook. You hear me? *Cook.*"

"I hear you. And they ain't seen cook, you ain't seen cook, till Marvella Washington *cook*."

"Take it to'm, Champ. Take it all to'm, Champ."

"I make'm fall down and beg to get from under the cooking I put on'm."

"All right." He nodded toward the open door leading to the shower. "Now go get wet."

She gave him the same sly, shy smile and said, "I already be wet, Bossman, all the way to the knees. I got a wet-on."

He smiled and patted her naked rump. "Stop talking shit and go get a shower and a good night's sleep. When you show up tomorrow, I don't want to see nothing but smoke and fire. I got to go see about those goddamn sisters of yours."

As he closed the door going out, she called to him from the place where she was still lying on the table: "Keep your dick in your pants tonight, mother!"

When Wallace got to his room he heard the sound of a ghetto blaster that could only belong to Vanella, with James Brown vibrating the walls, telling the world, "I don't know karate but I know ka-razor." Wallace opened the door and Vanella looked up from where she was sitting cross-legged on the bed painting her toenails. The ghetto blaster was on the bed beside her and she was wearing nothing but a black bra and black, bikini string panties. Her black underwear made her look even whiter than she was and she was already whiter than most white girls Wallace knew.

"Turn that goddamn thing off," said Wallace, "and put on some clothes."

Vanella lifted a long-fingered hand and cupped her ear. "What say?"

Wallace walked over and turned off the box.

"Now how come that?" said Vanella, arching her sassy brows over her sassy voice.

"Because this is my goddamn room, that's how come that. And go put on some clothes."

"I'll just have to take'm off again, I'm waiting for the shower.

Besides we all know you a champion fucker. I got a long time to wait for your hot beef injection."

"I ought to take you over my knee and spank your ass."

"You do and we both know you'll come."

"Zip your lip on that kind of shit. No more. Do, you'll be sleeping in the hall. Where the hell's your sisters?"

"They making their faces."

Wallace felt a quiet madness stealing into his brain, but it was only to be expected. If he could he'd tie these bitches up and stash'm in a clothes closet until after the contest. The thought had actually occurred to him to do just that. He asked her again about her sisters.

"You going deaf or just what? I already told you."

"Making their faces, you said?"

"That's what I said."

"And exactly what the fuck is that supposed to mean?"

"They in the bathroom paintin' and processin' 'cause we mean to step and juke tonight."

"Like shit," he said.

"Maybe like shit and maybe like something else. Whatever rolls we got to roll with it. Dig? Does that answer your question?" She reached and turned on the ghetto blaster.

Wallace reached for the blaster, a huge thing two feet long and about a foot thick. He lifted it as high over his head as he could and dropped it. It shattered, squawked and squealed, and then went silent.

Vanella stopped in mid-stroke with the tiny brush poised over her big toe and regarded the shards of plastic and twisted wiring before she finished the stroke on her toenail. She had cotton stuck between her toes to hold them apart and she serenely examined her work, her head cocked at a slight angle. Without looking up, she said, "That be four hundred dollars' worth of shit you just stepped in."

"Girl, four hundred dollars won't cover what you've stepped in if you mess this thing up for Marvella. We're not here to play. This is serious as money, and money, little girl, is serious as death. You better start listening to what I say."

There was a knock at the door and Vanella actually walked over and opened it wearing nothing but string bikini panties and bra. The young Cuban standing there fell back a step and cried something desperate in Spanish. There were three other young Cubans behind him, all of them pushing folding beds closed like a hinge and fastened at the top.

Wallace pushed Vanella aside and said, "Bring'm on in and put'm anywhere."

The Cubans pushed their beds into the rooms making every effort not to look at Vanella but unable to help themselves and consequently stumbling over their beds and each other and the other furniture in the room. Wallace saw that they were never going to get the cots unfolded and made up without killing themselves falling and running into each other, so he finally grabbed the one who seemed to be in charge, put a ten-dollar bill in his hand, and said, "Out! That's all, split, go, git the fuck away."

They went backward out of the room, their desperate unbelieving eyes fastened one last time on the incredible white girl who was obviously not white, dressed in less than they thought it possible for a woman to wear.

When they were gone and the door was closed, Vanella smiled at Wallace: "Those poor sweet boys. What a dickhead you are, Wallace. They were only looking. Where's the bad in that?"

"If you don't know the bad in that, I'm not going to tell you. You can't run around naked like that in front of men."

"I'm not naked."

"You're worse than naked, and if you weren't so young, you'd know it."

"Marvella be wearing less clothes than I got on tomorrow night in front of a whole auditorium and on national TV."

"Auditorium and TV is different."

"Seem like you'd splain that to me." She was mocking him again and he knew it.

"I'm not telling you a goddamn thing except to go put on

some clothes, clothes to sleep in, 'cause you ain't going nowhere but to bed.''

"I don't wear even this much to bed, Wallace. I do it naked.''

"That's fine with me. When the light goes out, you can do it any goddamn way you want to.''

"Now, see, we got minds alike. That's what I always thought too.''

"Jesus!'' said Wallace, turning from her and looking dead into Vanella's three sisters coming toward him shoulder to shoulder wearing nothing at all.

Wall thought: Here is Wall, *the* Wall, in the middle of wall-to-wall pussy with a wall-breaking hard-on that I can't do a thing with but hold on to all night and dream of things to come. Well, I've been through meaner shit in my life, but I sure as hell can't remember when.

S E V E N T E E N

At nine o'clock in the morning it was weigh-in for the contestants. The women were being weighed in on one side of the vast Blue Flamingo Convention Center and the men on the other. In both places was a lot of flexing and psych going on, all of it done with seeming indifference to the other contestants present. But of course it was not.

Every man and woman wanted to show what they had brought to the contest, saying in effect: *Look what you've got to beat, motherfuckers. No way. You don't have a chance. At best, the rest of you are competing for second place.*

During the last two or three days there had been a little good-natured ribbing and general grab-ass. Not now. At both weigh-in stations it was as quiet as a church. The only sound was when a contestant's name was called to step on the enormous Toledo scales with a round glass face with huge numbers where the red pointer swung and stopped.

On the women's side Wallace and Russell stared, locked eyeball to eyeball with each other. All the women wore tiny posing briefs, briefs with less cloth in them than any pair of panties ever made. Without exception, the briefs disappeared between the cheeks of their asses, and the women who wore them had hard glassy eyes as though they might have spent the night eating amphetamines.

Shereel Dupont stood calmly beside Russell still wearing her sunglasses and dressed in an ankle-length robe made of closely woven silk that showed nothing of her body so loosely did it fit. While the other women flexed and preened and made every

effort to upstage all the other competitors, Shereel stood so quietly that she seemed not to be breathing. But all the other women
knew who she was, knew what she was holding under that fine
silk robe. They had seen all this before and tried to pretend that
it did not bother them, but it did. They avoided looking at her
much as a bird might avoid looking at a snake.

Marvella had not made an appearance yet and this too was
by design. Wallace did not want her just to walk in, he wanted
her to make a grand entrance. The women were approaching
the scale by weight. The one hundred fourteen and under—the
lightweights—stepped forward first as their names were called,
their weights were noted, and a stiff card with square black
numbers on it was given them. They would pin this to their
posing briefs just to the left of their navels and there they would
wear it until the contest was over. Shereel's class—the middleweights—was next, anything over one hundred fourteen
pounds but not over one twenty-four. The heavyweights would
be last—Marvella's class—anything over one twenty-four right
on up to whatever the girl wanted to weigh.

Shereel's name was called and she walked—a kind of relaxed
amble—over to the scale. Nobody asked her if she wanted to
remove the robe she was wearing, because the silk robe had
become her trademark—or rather, Russell's—and she never
took it off. When she stepped on the scale, nobody was indifferent anymore, nor did they pretend to be. Every eye—including Wallace's—was watching the needle of the scale as it swung
and stopped dead on one hundred twenty-four. A notch-solid
middleweight. It was like magic. Many of these contestants had
watched her weigh in all across the country and she was never
even a fraction of an ounce over or under. A square tag with a
number on it was handed her and she went back to stand beside
Russell, who was now smiling maliciously at Wallace, whose
face was tired and grim.

Russell thought it was because Wallace had seen his girl come
in yet one more time at a weight that was only perfect, but that
was not the cause of Wallace's tired grim face. He had spent a

long desperate night holding his hard cock and listening to pussy snoring all around him while he dreamed on and off of Donald Trump. Not really of Donald Trump exactly, but rather the way Trump acquired things. *Acquisitions.* Wallace had learned the word some time back, at about the same time he became fascinated with Trump. If some was good, more was better. It was the American way. And Wallace counted himself a patriot. And so during the night surrounded by the four girls on their individual cots, listening to their sighs and moans and the rustle of their flesh turning in the sheets, Russell had held fast to his hard-on and to his dream. He had five champions—world champions—and he knew it. He thought Marvella would win the Cosmos four times, maybe as many as six, and then he would bring the other girls to championship form in order of age: first Starvella, then Jabella, followed by Shavella, and finally, finally, to the one he thought would be the best of the bunch, the one no one would beat, the one that nothing could beat but age.

But by the time Vanella was a world champion, there would be franchised Black Magic gyms all over the country, hundreds, maybe even thousands of endorsements for strength supplements sold in gymnasiums and health food stores, and surely a Black Magic line of clothing, both for the street and for the gym, and shoes . . . The list was endless.

And in the meantime, Wallace thought during the long periods he was awake throughout the night, in the meantime Wallace "the Wall" Wilson, who had never been able to be a worldbeater as a bodybuilder, would have won the *actual* world instead. He wanted a yacht just like Donald's, two hundred thirty-five feet long with two hundred and twenty-two telephones on it. He had read about it and those may not be the exact numbers, but they were close enough. They didn't miss by far. In the article he'd read, it said Donald had a telephone for very nearly every foot his yacht measured in length. Was that acquisition? Was that American? Or just what?

And all the while Shereel had been approaching the scale, stepping on the scale, her weight called, and her number given,

all the while this was going on, the proud and expensive things
of the world ticked through Wallace's head: Mercedes, Oriental
rugs, European hotels, a personal cook, a personal pilot for his
personal plane, *a motherfucking personal everything*.

He didn't really feel like smiling but he smiled anyway: He
had the flesh, owned the flesh, that could bring it all home to
him, make it happen.

Inward looking, lost in the thought of *things*, he had forgotten
all about Russell, and when his glazed eyes focused across the
room, he was surprised to see Russell smiling right back at him,
the same triumphant I-can't-lose-and-you-know-it smile.

Russell suddenly lost his smile. The Turnipseeds—all of
them—had come in and the largest one (Wallace assumed the
mother) grabbed Russell, and caught him in a bear hug as if she
meant to throw him to the ground.

"We been upstairs a lookin' at Motor," she screamed loud
enough for Wallace to hear from where he was standing. She
reached back and grabbed Motor by the shoulder and dragged
him forward. "Would you look at him? Would you look at that?
And," she said, still screaming, "you ought to see him neked.
He's shaved it, is what he's done."

Motor was blushing but then so was Russell. Motor dug the
toe of his boot into the rug and said, "I can crab it pretty good
now I ain't got no hair."

"God, I didn't know it was him," said Earnestine.

Turner said, "Gitten rid of that hair lost him near 'bout five
pound I'd say."

"Five pound or not, I'd say it was a improvement," said Fonse,
lighting a fresh Camel off the butt of one he'd just finished. He
looked at Shereel, who had stood impassively through it all.
"You git youself weighed yet?"

"Yes sir, I did," she said, "and it was fine."

"Never doubted it for a minute."

Shereel said, "Where's Nail?"

"He's over with Billy Bat where he's gittin' weighed his own
self," Earnestine said. "Earline made him come with her to keep

Billy Bat calmed down. Don't know what ails him, but you'd think he'd already won everything it is here to win. Just beside hisself is what he is, so Earline asked Nail if he'd come and try to keep him calmed down."

Turner said, "Oh, Nail'll keep him calmed down. He may git'm so calm he's dead."

"Hush talking like that," said Earnestine. "Nail's a good boy."

"Yeah, good at a lot of things and none of'm I'd like to see tried on me," Turner said. "If I ever git to carryin' on too bad, I'd take it as a personal kindness if you-all didn't send Nail to calm me down."

Earnestine opened her mouth to say something but the man sitting at a little table beside the huge Toledo scales called "Marvella Washington," and as if by magic, the double doors leading into the convention center burst open and Marvella strode in looking neither to the left nor to the right and wearing bright yellow posing briefs with so little cloth a pair of gloves could not have been made out of them. And a step behind, her sisters flanked her on either side wearing jumpsuits of the same color, jumpsuits so tight that anybody who wanted to look—and everybody did, even the women—could see their pubic hair curling under the thin cloth.

"Them's the biggest goddamn women I ever seen," Fonse said.

"Them's the biggest *people*, men or women, I ever seen," said Turner.

"Either one of them'd be more than a bed full," said Fonse.

Earnestine reached over and cuffed Fonse on the side of his felt hat. "You hush about big women and beds, you randy old goat."

Marvella, still looking neither to the left nor the right, marched straight to the scales and stepped on. Her weight was called, an even one fifty-five. She took the numbered card in her hand and marched out the same way she had come in, eyes straight ahead, giving the impression of dismissing everyone present—which was precisely the impression the way she walked and looked was calculated to give. Her four sisters, a step behind and on either side of her, followed. On her sisters' backs in black, block letters was the legend:

BLACK MAGIC GYMNASIUM

DETROIT, MICHIGAN

HOME OF MARVELLA WASHINGTON, CHAMPION

The smile on Wallace's face now as he glared across at Russell was one of pure malice. Russell tried to act unaffected but he was, in fact, shaken. Marvella Washington may be big but she was also a miracle and he knew it.

Fonse picked at his teeth with a kitchen match and said, "A hundred and fifty-five pounds my ass. Them scales is wrong or that feller reading'm needs him some new glasses. If that black wench didn't go hundred and ninety, shit don't stink."

Earnestine looked at him hard and said, "Fonse, I ain't tellin' you agin. We off here amongst strangers and I won't have them thinkin' this is a trashy family."

"Maybe not," said Fonse, "but that gal weren't a biscuit away from three hundred."

"Damned if I wouldn't like to see her crab it," said Motor, scratching the left cheek of his ass. He had been scratching all morning, both hands digging variously at his freshly shaven body. He felt as if he needed to fill a tub with Old Spice and get into it, but still and all it felt pretty wonderful to be hairless like other people.

His mother, looking aslant at him, thought his clothes hung in a puny and unseemly way and she missed—much to her surprise—the ruff of hair that hung over the back of his collar like a foxtail. It seemed a body never could be satisfied in this sorry world. All his life she had wished he did not have his hair and now that he'd got shed of it she wished he had it back. She would have to speak to him about growing it back and she already thought of an unanswerable reason to do it. A man could

not very well get up every morning of his life and shave his
whole body. Just think for a minute the shaving cream and razors
a man would need to do that. And because she had hated his
hair so much, and had hardly been able to think of him as her
own son because of it, she reached over, grabbed him, and
squeezed him dangerously hard between her breasts, giving him
a hug that made speaking impossible and breathing more than
a little difficult. When she pushed him back and held him by
both shoulders, she said, "You the sweetest boy a mother ever
had."

"I known you'd like it without all that hair," he said.

"Well, you do look different."

"That's what I said."

"It's more than one way to look at a thing," she said. "It's a
man's nature to have hair."

"Not as much as I had I wouldn't think," he said, digging
first in one armpit, then the other, both of which he had scraped
free of hair in his frenzy of shaving.

"We'll talk on it more later," she said. Scratching the way he
did made her think of a dog that had fleas, but he was still her
son, she told herself, flea-scratching dog or not.

"Here comes Billy Bat," said Shereel.

Billy Bat was coming toward them across the vast hardwood
floor of the convention center holding Earline by the hand, she
smiling, her hips pumping, and behind them, looking as though
he smelled something that suggested an outhouse, was Nail.

Shereel put out her hand and Billy Bat turned loose Earline
to shake it, a power shake with thumbs interlocked as if they
meant to arm wrestle.

"It's all downhill from here, Bat," Shereel said.

Billy Bat was smiling in a way that made Shereel think him
afflicted. "Downhill, uphill, no hill, hell, I don't care," said Billy
Bat.

For a bodybuilder to talk that way just hours before prejudging
could only mean he *was* afflicted. Nail had his knife out cleaning
his nails, but the way he was using the knife made him look

like what he really wanted to do was cut somebody's throat.
Shereel stepped closer to Nail and put her hand on his arm.
"How you feeling?"

"Like I do mostly," he said.

"And how's that?"

"Like shit."

"Nail, try to take it light. This is the day. The only day for
everybody here. You make me worried when you look like you
do."

"Don't worry 'bout me," he said, concentrating on paring a
nail with the razor-sharp blade. "Worry 'bout everbody else."

"That's what I mean. That right there."

Nail coughed up a lunger and spat on the floor. Shereel
watched the arc of the spit and the little splat it made when it
landed on the highly polished floor, but did not say anything.
Nail closed his knife and put it in its case on his belt. And for
the first time since he walked up, he looked directly at her. His
eyes had that off-centered look of craziness that she had come
to fear. It was the look he had brought back from Vietnam.

But when he spoke, his voice was calm and quiet, a kind of
hushed whisper, which made him only scarier to Shereel.
"Never thought I'd live to see it. Grown men tricked out in
women's panties, or what should be women's panties, but of
course they said they weren't, lined up gitten on a scale and
then pinning a little card with numbers on it to their panties.
And ever goddamn one of'm looked diseased, holler cheeks,
sunken eyes, and bodies that looked pumped up by something
to the point they might explode. Wonder what it is a man does
with a body like that? I know what Hitler would've done. He'd
a took ever goddamn one of'm out and gassed'm. I ain't sayin'
that's right but that's dead-solid-certain what he'd a done
with'm."

Shereel started to answer him, say something to ease a little
of the craziness out of him, but Billy Bat's booming voice, a voice
unlike any she had ever heard come out of his mouth, stopped
her.

"Mr. Alphonse, sir, I have come to ask for your daughter's hand in marriage."

All of them turned to stare at Alphonse, who in turn stared at the glowing end of his Camel cigarette. Stared at it for a long time before he finally looked up, pushed his felt hat back on his head with his thumb, and said, "Say you have?"

"Yes sir."

Fonse examined his cigarette again but this time not for long. His wife, Earnestine, had gone gray in the face and looked on the point of fainting.

Fonse said finally, "Which one would you be askin' for?"

"Why, Earline, of course."

"Yes," said Fonse.

"What?" said Billy Bat. He didn't know what he expected but he thought a longer response than a single word would be more appropriate.

Again, Fonse only said, "Yes."

Earnestine flung herself on the body of her huge daughter and they both burst into tears and little shrieks of joy.

Turner said, "Now don't that beat everthin' all to hell. Come all the way down here to find you man." He took Billy Bat's hand and they shook. "Looks like we gone be brothers."

Fonse, lighting a fresh Camel, said, "Don't know as it's ever been one in the family zactly like you." He put out his hand and Billy took it. "Hell," Fonse said. "Everbody got to look like something."

When Earline had finally untangled herself from her mother's embrace, Shereel came to her and kissed her. "Tonight when all this is over we'll have a real celebration. There's not much I can do now, though. I'm so proud and pleased for you but I've still got a contest to go through."

"To win," said Russell, pulling Earline into a massive embrace and feeling himself sink into what felt like a full foot of her fat. Russell couldn't help but wonder what arrangements had to be made for Billy Bat and her to get together. How the hell would a man ever *find* it? He guessed he would never know. It was not just the sort of thing that you come right out and ask a man about.

Motor was simply too amazed to speak. He just stood there looking first at his sister and then at Billy Bat. Billy Bat was not the best-looking man he had ever seen. But he was a *man*, a trifle short and thick maybe, but a *man*. He just could not believe his sister had managed it. Jesus, to his knowledge, Earline had never had but one date in her life and that was to Franklin Funckwell, nicknamed and universally called Little Funk to distinguish him from his daddy who was called Big Funk. Harelips ran in the family. Big Funk had one and all six of his sons had one. But not one of them had one to rival Little Funk's. It looked like somebody had hit him in the mouth with a hatchet. It was he, Motor—not making fun but out of genuine curiosity—who had asked Earline when she come in from her date how that mouth of his felt when they kissed. Earline had burst into tears and the subject never came up again, and as far as anybody knew that had been her last date.

"Well, Motor, ain't you gone welcome Billy Bat to the family, him right now almost being a brother and blood kin?" said Fonse.

"I shore am," said Motor. He took Billy Bat's hand and pumped it for all he was worth and then turned to embrace his sister, who surprised and shocked him by hissing into his ear: "This'n got a right pretty mouth, don't he, you slop-eating son of a bitch?"

Motor fell away from her as if she had struck him.

Fonse said, "You ain't got to look so poorly about it, Motor, sisters git married ever day, praise the Lord."

Earnestine balled her fists on her enormous hips and demanded, "Just what the hell you mean by 'praise the Lord'?"

"I didn't mean a goddamn thing except what I said, it just so happens," said Fonse. "I believe this trip is done ruint you disposition and I also believe it is about time us menfolk had a little drink to celbrate the occasion."

"You ain't never had a *little* drink in you life and you know how I feel about all that," Earnestine said.

Fonse looked at Billy Bat. "If you ain't found it out yet, son, I'll let you in on a little something. It's two kinds of people in this world: them of us that wants a drink and them that don't want us to have one. But this is the first youngun of mine to go ahead on and tie the knot and I mean to mark it with a drink."

"Go and be damned then," Earnestine said. "Take a drink if you got to but don't you go and git drunk with me off from home like this amongst strangers, and them tourists at that. You do and you can make you a pallet on the floor, 'cause you ain't gone be in no bed of mine."

Fonse was about to say something back to her when Shereel reached out and touched his arm. "Don't get to carrying on, for God's sake, I've already got too much to deal with as it is."

"She's right, Earnestine," Fonse said. "Kinda trashy for us to git into it right here where she's about to go and be somebody."

"Suits me just fine. I don't have to talk to you about nothing. You know how I feel about things."

"God knows I do," Fonse said.

"Don't start, goddammit," Earnestine said.

Billy Bat stepped between them. "I cain't drink none myself, of course, but the hotel lounge is right down there about thirty yards from where you check youself in."

Earline said, "You might as well know it right now, Billy Bat, I'm just like Mama. Lips that touch likker will never touch mine."

"Honey, I ain't never had a drink of alcohol in my life," Billy said.

"How goddamn mortally depressing," Nail said.

"But," said Billy Bat, "that don't say I wouldn't be proud to step down to that lounge with you."

"Lounge, my ass—'scuse me Mizz Earnestine—but I already seen the lounge they got here," said Nail. "Just like ever other lounge I ever seen, nothing but glass and plastic. I'd as soon drink my whiskey in a drugstore. As it turns out, I got two fifths of Jack Black behind the seat of my pickup truck."

Billy Bat said, "I'd think that whiskey'd be a trifle hot. It ain't but about a hundred and ten in the shade out there."

Fonse snorted, hustled his balls, and spat on the floor without taking the Camel out of his mouth. "Billy Bat, whiskey's got to git to the tempature of you guts to make the jump to you blood. Ice don't do a thing but make it wait. I'd say Nail's whiskey's just about right to swaller." He paused, took his cigarette out of his mouth, and examined it. "'Nother thing, too. Now that you gone be family, we got to do sompin' about you name. It cain't be no bats mingling with the Turnipseed blood."

Shereel, who had been shifting from foot to foot in a tension-ridden little dance, said, "You can settle this without me. I'm going to the room till prejudging. I've got to be alone. The time is right here, right now."

Russell said, "I'll get you an hour before show time, Champ. We'll go backstage and let'm see what the real thing looks like. I'll sit with you if you want."

"I want to be alone."

"I'll have some quartered oranges and quartered apples sent up," Russell said. "No more than a quarter of either every half hour. And no water."

"I think I know what to fucking do," Shereel said.

"*Dorothy!*" said Earnestine.

Shereel looked straight at her mother and did not blink. "I'm sorry but Dorothy's dead. It's *Shereel* time. Her time is here. Her time is now."

"I don't understand," said Earnestine, "but you my youngun and I love you."

"I know you do," said Shereel.

"We all love you, honey," Fonse said.

"Just take it to'm, Champ," said Russell. "Just take it to'm. There's no way you can be beat."

Shereel looked back at Russell as though she meant to speak but she did not. Without saying anything to any of them, she turned and walked away.

"I wish it was sompin' I could do," said Earnestine.

"Me too," said Earline. "Don't seem right, her bein' alone at a time like this."

"This is the way she does it," Russell said. "This is the way she wants it. She'll go up there, close all the blinds, put a damp cloth over her eyes, and fill her heart with hate."

"Great Godamighty, what a thing to say," said Earnestine.

"There's no other way," Russell said.

Nail, who had taken his knife out and was testing the edge of the blade against his thumb, said, "Little like going to war, ain't it?"

"You'll never say anything truer," Russell said.

EIGHTEEN

Backstage at the enormous convention center was a riot of color and movement and a babble of tongues, German, Italian, Spanish, and most of the other major languages of the world. The contestants, men and women, in their varicolored posing briefs were pumping up and greasing down, oiling their blood-engorged muscles until they held just the right sheen to catch and hold the overhead lights once they went onstage to compete. Their trainers were with them, along with members of the press and photographers from more than three dozen muscle and fitness magazines. The privileged members of the competitors' families who had managed to get backstage passes moved among the popping flashbulbs, and moved too among the athletes themselves as they pressed and squatted and rowed through the heavy air, heavy and hot because the air conditioning was off backstage to help them heat up with the light weights they were using in high repetitions, light weights which nonetheless banged and clanged when they were dropped on the matted floor.

Off at one end of the large backstage area, near the end of the heavy blood-red velour curtain, stood Nail Head and Alphonse with his two sons Motor and Turner. Every now and then Turner would glance around the end of the curtain where the busy drone of the audience, restless and angry sounding, broke like a wave. Motor had unbuttoned his shirt nearly to the navel, and his glance traveled continuously from the tanned, hairless, and nearly naked bodybuilders to his own incredibly white and equally hairless stomach where it mounded slightly below his chest. Fonse was the only person backstage wearing a hat, and he nervously shifted from foot to foot as he reached up to touch it with first his left hand and then his right. Nail's eyes did not seem to focus on anything, but neither were they glazed—hooded, rather, and inward looking as he stood without moving.

Billy Bat came toward them with Earline at his side holding a bottle of oil in one of her very tiny and very fat hands. Beads of sweat stood across Billy's broad shoulders and his deep chest. With each step he took heavy wings of muscle flared from his back as though he might flap and fly away, half man, half bat. His face, unlike the other bodybuilders', was relaxed and smiling. But for his extraordinary body, every muscle of which had swollen drumtight with rushing blood, he might have been a man out for an afternoon stroll, so easy and relaxed was his stride. Earline was every bit as wet with sweat as any of the competitors and her bright red face was tight with worry so intense that it looked like rage or maybe even terror. Her thin sweated dress clung deeply in the creases of her fat until she appeared almost naked. But she seemed to be unaware of how she looked, or simply did not care, as she alternately patted and fanned Billy Bat's shoulders with the end of a towel she had hanging about her neck. Billy Bat seemed not to notice what she was doing with the towel, but from time to time he turned to glance lovingly at her as they came across the floor.

Billy Bat stopped in front of the nervously shifting Alphonse and said, "How you doin', Dad?"

"Not 'Dad' yet, son," said Alphonse, "not till the I-do's git said. And I'm all right but I'd be a sight better if I could smoke me a Camel ceegret, maybe about a carton of'm, but as long as I know I got me a pack as close as up there under my hat"— he reached to touch his hat with both hands—"I believe by God I can make it." He looked at Earline. "Dammit all, girl, stop with that towel!"

Earline said, "You ain't got to be cross, Daddy. My nerves have got to have something to do with theirselves."

Billy Bat kissed her lightly on the cheek. "You doin' fine, you sweet girl."

Turner, who was looking around the edge of the curtain again, said, "Jesus, if it ain't a houseful out there."

"Sounds like a crowd at a football game," said Motor, examining the prickly heat that had cropped up on his stomach when he applied Old Spice aftershave in an effort to quit itching.

"Yeah," Nail said, looking at nobody, "thank God I got on the outside of some Jack Black before you told me about this prejudging bullshit."

Billy Bat said, "Now, Nail, you could still be settin' out there in you Chevy pickup drinkin' if you wanted to."

"Not hardly," Nail said. "It ain't but one time to do this. I told Dor . . . *Shereel* that I was with her, stuck clean to the bone, and I mean to make good on my promise. But that don't mean I don't wish I wasn't on the outside of a quart of that whiskey behind the seat of my truck."

"And I could burn me up a few Camels right now, by God," Fonse said.

Billy kept his good-natured smile. "If you want to drink and smoke, it's got to be sommers else. I told you all how it was."

"Yeah, you did," said Nail. "You told us how it was, how all of it was."

And Billy Bat had told them. Standing out in the parking lot, the men passing the bottle in a brown paper sack, Billy Bat had explained it all under a bright sky out of which the sun beat with relentless heat.

When they got to Nail's Chevrolet truck out in the parking lot, Nail Head had unlocked a door, reached behind the seat, and got a brown paper sack with the neck of a bottle sticking out of the top of it. He uncapped the bottle, turned, and dropped onto his haunches in the partial shade of the bed of the truck. Alphonse and his two sons squatted side by side in a single line to get part of the shade. The four men had fallen into their hunkered positions, sitting squarely on their heels, as if they had been planning and practicing the way they were going to do it all morning. Billy Bat leaned against the open door and watched them quietly.

"Son," said Fonse, squinting up at Billy Bat, "you look like a goddamn *Ay*-rab I seen on the TeeVee."

"My tan's peaked," said Billy Bat. "Cain't afford no sun." He had a long-billed cap on his head with the word FORD on the front of it. But he had first draped a towel over his head before putting on the cap, and he had pulled the towel across his face and around his neck. The long-sleeved white shirt he was wearing was buttoned all the way to his throat and at his wrists, and he kept his hands in his pockets. Only his shaded eyes were visible as he looked down upon them where they squatted. "I got my tan *balanced*," Billy Bat said. "I wouldn't want to come out here and throw it off."

But nobody was listening to Billy Bat now. All four men had gradually brought their attention to bear upon the naked neck of the bottle. Nail lifted it toward Fonse. "Go ahead on," said Nail. "Press this to you face and you'll feel better."

"Never take the first drink out of another man's bottle," Fonse said. "Bad luck. But if you be good enough to take the newness off it, I believe I could stand me a taste."

"Well," Nail said, "since you put it just like that, I'll bubble it a few times."

"Thought you might," Fonse said.

Nail turned the bottle up and the others watched his throat jerk once, twice, three times. Billy Bat moved away from where he was leaning on the truck door and stood straight up after Nail's throat jerked the fourth time before he brought the bottle down and stared thoughtfully at the neck of it. "Now that right there," Nail said slowly and softly as though divulging a secret, "is whiskey."

Fonse said, "You gone let a old man squat out here in the heat of the day and die of thirst?"

"No sir, I'm not," Nail said, and passed him the bottle.

Fonse wiped the lip of the bottle almost daintily on the front of his shirt before taking a long pull at it and passing it on to

Motor, who was next in line. Nobody said a word until it got back to Nail, who drank the same amount as he had before and at the same speed.

Billy Bat tightened the towel about his throat and turned his back to the slanting sun. "Don't mind my saying so," he said, "you gone be too drunk to see any part of the show you drove all the way down here to look at."

Nail said, "If I weren't a drinking man, I don't know as I'd have much to say about what somebody else could or couldn't do with whiskey. But since you made Earline a happy girl, I'll tell you this for nothin': I can git drunk and confused as a ten-dick dog right now, and be straight as a plumb line by eight o'clock tonight."

Billy Bat dropped to his heels the same as the others had done, putting the open truck door between himself and the sun. "Be too late then."

"Sign said the contest was at eight o'clock," Turner said. "Nail's right."

"Nail's wrong," Billy Bat said. "Who's won and who's lost is settled at prejudging."

"Say what?" said Nail, who was about to drink but took the bottle down and stared at Billy Bat instead.

Billy Bat said, "I told the others *some* about the contest, how it works, but I'll tell you *all* of it because I know how you feel about Miss Shereel."

"You don't know a goddamn thing about how I feel about nothing," Nail said.

"I know more'n you think I know and I can at least tell you how the Cosmos works," said Billy Bat, "if you'll just slow down with that bottle. Ain't no use me talking to a drunk."

Nail passed the bottle carefully to Fonse, looked off for a moment at the horizon, and then back to Billy Bat. "You gone marry into the Turnipseed family, you gone have to learn not to be a asshole. You gone have to learn to talk right for starters."

"I come from the same part of the country you do, old son,"

said Billy Bat, shifting on his heels. "I'll talk any damn way I please."

"We may have to go into that another time," said Nail.

"We can talk about it anytime you want," Billy Bat said.

"Didn't say nothing about talking, said we'd go into it."

"Any time, any place," Billy Bat said.

Alphonse, who had been following the talk with his good ear, put his elbow into Nail's ribs hard, and wheezed a laugh before he slapped his own knees with both hands. "Damn if I don't believe I like this boy."

"They say it's good blood up there in Tennessee," Turner said.

"It might be something to him at that," said Nail, taking the bottle being passed back to him. He took a short sip. "That easy enough on the bottle for you?"

"You can do anything you want to, Nail. I just said I'd tell you if you wanted me to."

Nail smiled and he could feel the whiskey in it. Half of the smile was whiskey. The other half was that he thought he probably liked this boy, too, liked him in the way Fonse had meant. He didn't take a knee. He bowed right up. Well, talk was cheap. Maybe somewhere down the road they'd find out what was in this Billy Bat. And maybe they wouldn't. That could wait for now. For now he wanted to find out about this *thing*, whatever the hell it was.

"Tell me," Nail said.

"Well, first of all, the women go first."

"Like I sometimes say," Nail said, "it's always something to be grateful for. Ain't a hell of a lot that embarrasses me in this world. But damned if I don't think watching a bunch of men struttin' their stuff in panties wouldn't just embarrass the hell out of me."

"And that's because," said Billy Bat quietly, "like *I* said earlier, you ignorant."

"Yeah," said Nail, "so you told me. We'll git into that later. Tell me about what Shereel's in *now*. Tell me *all* of it, while I just tongue along on this bottle. Can you lay it out for me simple and straight?''

Billy Bat adjusted his towel and hunkered a little lower on his heels. "I can. I can lay it out straight for you."

And he did. "At the beginning all the girls come on stage at the same time lined up shoulder to shoulder. They relaxed at this point, you see. The head judge tells them to take a quarter turn to the right. They stand thataway for a little. Then he tells them to take another quarter turn. Their backs are to the judges now. They still standing relaxed. He keeps doing that until the girls have turned all the way round and they now facing the judges again. The judges been comparing, checking for symmetry, how one body part balances and fits with another body part. They looking at skin texture, checking how thick the skin is—it ought to be thin—for how much fat's between the skin and the muscle, how free and clean one muscle stands from the muscles beside it and joining it."

Billy Bat's voice was quiet and even, a kind of monotone, as though he was reciting something he had memorized. And while he talked the bottle passed slowly up and down the line. At some point, Nail got another bottle from behind the seat of his truck as Billy Bat talked on. Fonse smoked one Camel after another in a single-minded passion, as though he were in a contest himself, a smoking contest.

"Then the girls leave the stage and come on one at a time for free posing. They do it to taped music they've decided on themselves. They don't git but ninety seconds for that part. After everybody's done that, all the girls are brought on at the same time again and lined up at the back of the stage. The judges call the girls, two at a time, three at a time, down to the front of the stage and ask for a certain pose—it could be a double bicep lat spread, or quadricep, or abdominals, anything—and when the judges call out that certain pose, the girls down at the front of the stage all hit it and hold it until they told to do something else. The judges are comparing then just like they been doing before.

"The judges got scorecards and at every step of the way, they score each girl. When it's all over, the head judge throws out the high score and low score on each card and averages the others. High number wins.

"Now here's what I wanted you to know. After the prejudging, the winners in ever class have already been selected. The winner of the overall—the best in show—has been selected too. *But the women—and the men too far as that goes—never git to know who's won and who's lost till after they free pose at the night show.* What I'm saying is, all everbody does at night is come out and do their ninety seconds to their music. After that's over, the winner of each weight class, all of'm at once, is called onstage for what's called a *pose-down.* One of these girls is gone be Ms. Cosmos, the best in the world, win the overall, you see. When they called out for the pose-down, they just turned loose up there to do whatever they want to do. A girl might do a hamstring and calf, 'cause that's one of her strong suits she thinks, so she pops a pose to show it off. A girl standing next to her is allowed to step right in between her and the judges and hit the same hamstring and calf to show that hers is better. It's a real dogfight, and they go at it like dogs a fightin'. Damn do. After all that, the winner's named."

Nail had stopped drinking and had taken the bottle out of the sipping sack. He stared at the label a long quiet time as though trying to read something that did not quite make sense.

Finally he said, "How come they try so hard at night, if the thing's already been settled?"

"It's a off chance that somebody can make somebody else fuck up and change the winner. They think that anyway. Hell, I even go into the night show thinking the same thing myself. We all know it ain't a chance in hell of that happenin' but we keep holding somewhere in us that it *could* happen. But at this level of competition, it ain't a one of us don't know the damn thing's over after prejudging."

"That's the sorriest way to do anything I heard of recently," Nail said.

"Sorry enough," said Billy Bat. "But if we want justice, we gone have to die and go to heaven."

"Not all of us," Nail said. "No, some of us don't have to go to heaven."

"I wouldn't natchally say sompin' like this," said Fonse, "but these ain't natchal times." He looked directly at Nail. "I'm gone have to ask you not to cause no trouble."

Motor, who had his shirt up and was examining his hairless stomach, said, "Might as well ask shit not to stink."

"Keep a civil tongue, dammit," said Fonse.

"Forgit it, Fonse," Nail said. "I ain't studying a civil tongue."

Turner, who had the bottle now, said, "Don't pay him no mind. Motor ain't got good sense. Any man that'd shave his whole goddamn *self* has got to be about two quarts low in his crankcase."

Fonse held out the bottle to Nail, but Nail shook his head. "I think we ought to put the stopper back in that jug." He glanced at the watch on his wrist. "It looks to me like about two hours before Shereel is right in the middle of her trick of shit." He gestured toward the bottle Fonse still held. "So I don't think we ought to kill that soldier. He'll keep till later."

Fonse had cupped his good ear to hear the last of what Nail had to say. "Now, by God, these is strange times. You shore you all right, Nail?"

"We got the rest of our life to git drunk. I think we ought to be straight for this thing Shereel's got coming."

"Well, hell," Fonse said. "I thought that myself from the beginning, but I think too much of you to set out here and watch you git drunk by youself."

Nail said, "Ain't ever man'll take drinking whiskey as a duty of friendship. But that daughter of yours needs us. Even if she has turned butch on me and twisted the family name on you."

"Run that by me again," said Fonse, cupping his ear.

"Never mind." Nail turned to Billy Bat. "You said something about a head judge. Now why is it he's called the head judge?"

"It ain't because his dick's the longest," said Billy Bat,

wrapped up to and half over his eyes now.

"Billy, son," said Fonse, taking his Camel out of his mouth and examining it while he talked, "you'll know more how things are later on. But for right now, could you talk straight to Nail Head? Could you oblige me on that? I'm too old and this whiskey feels too good to have any kind of commotion out here in the heat."

"Sure, Fonse," said Billy Bat. "This sun's addled me. We ain't got no sun like this in Tennessee." He looked at Nail. "The head judge's the one who calls for turns and poses from the contestants, he totals the other judges' cards—it's seven judges in all. Did I say that? Is. He votes along with everbody else and his vote's not suppose to count any more or any less than the other judges."

"You say *not suppose to*. What's the truth of it?" Nail asked.

"The truth of it is I don't know. I know what I *think* and what most of the bodybuilders I know *think*, but the truth is something that I cain't say."

"What is it you think?"

"The head judge is the most experienced judge. He's the best-known judge. And wait'll you see the one we got for this show. Cain't miss the sucker. Bigger'n a side of beef and never wears nothing but white. White *everything*." Billy Bat shifted easily on his massive haunches. "The judges talk things over together constantly. You see their heads go together down there at the front of the stage all the time. When something's close, ever judge is talking for his side. Now if it was *one* in *seven* that was the most experienced, best known, and in this case, the biggest, what do you think would happen if he thought one thing and the others thought somethin' else?"

"It'd come down on his side," Nail said.

"I *think*," said Billy Bat.

Nail said, "So whatever happens, we can lay it at his door."

"I wouldn't go as far as to say that," said Billy Bat.

Nail looked at the bottle in his hand and started slowly screwing the cap on it. "I would," Nail said.

Fonse watched Nail turning the cap down with a certain sadness. "You ain't even gone have another *taste*," he said, "before we go?"

Nail handed him the bottle. "You and you boys go ahead on," he said. "I cain't use another drop till this is over."

Fonse immediately started taking the cap off. "I got a feeling it's gone be a long dry day."

While Fonse and his boys took one last drink, Nail said to Billy Bat, "It comes to me that it's strange you squattin' out here in this parking lot, not even drinking, just watching us drink, when Shereel is up yonder in her room by herself gitten ready, doin' all them things Russell said she was gone do. Is it your habit to jack around like this and not run tight like she's doing?"

Billy Bat let his towel down to answer and he was smiling. "Normally, I'd be doing just what she's doing, but like Fonse says, these ain't normal times. Normally, I'm tight as Dick's hatband, but today I'm loose as a goose. I never met Earline before, you see. She's changed everythin'. I think she's ended all this for me. I'm gone take her back to Tennessee where I got a little land and a piece of a Ford dealership. Didn't tell you that, did I? Do, though. And once I git'er up there where I come from, we'll see if we cain't have us some younguns. Man needs a family. Am I right or am I wrong?"

Nail did not answer but Fonse, who had been taking one long last pull at the bottle, brought it down and, after he'd wheezed a moment, said, "No more'n he needs air to breathe. I already given you my blessin' and I give it agin. Lot of things I been but I ain't been a grandpa yet."

Billy Bat threw the towel back over his face and spoke through the cloth. "I'm gone do the best I can today, go full bore. It's the way I am. But after Earline, this thing just don't mean what it used to. She changed the whole thing quicker'n it'd take to tell it." While he talked, the bottle had been capped and put back behind the seat. "You boys about ready to go back in yonder?"

"Can we go backstage where she'll be gittin' ready?" said Nail.

"Oh, hell yes," Billy Bat said. "Way they been treatin' all of you, easiest thing in the world." They were all up and moving across the parking lot. "It goes without saying, though, you cain't drink or smoke back there."

"We'll be all right," said Nail.

Motor said, "Put Daddy where he cain't smoke and he might bite like a dog or otherwise behave unseemly."

"Fonse'll be all right," Nail said. "We'll all be all right."

But backstage now, with Shereel about to appear any minute and Fonse nervously touching his hat and the whiskey wearing off and him beginning to feel the strong call from his guts for another drink, Nail was not so sure that he would be all right. Something in him felt like he would never again be all right. It was a feeling a little like the one he'd had as he climbed the steps to board the plane leaving Vietnam.

The whole backstage area suddenly went quiet and Nail realized that everybody was looking at something behind him. He turned and there was Shereel in an immaculate white silk robe with Russell holding her arm. Nail's eyes met hers and her face showed no sign of recognition, no smile, nothing except a contained, relaxed calm. As their eyes met, voices in rhythmic syncopation burst from the other end of the curtain: *Out of the way! Stand away! Move away! Children, this be Marvella day!* Nail turned just in time to see Starvella, Jabella, Shavella, and Vanella—all wearing bright red elastic tights from ankle to throat—make an aisle, two sisters on a side facing each other, to frame Marvella dressed only in her posing briefs, which were the same bright red as the elastic tights. Tiny drops of glistening sweat mixed with oil clung to her brilliantly black skin. And Nail thought: *Jesus that ain't just big, that's fuckin' scary.*

N I N E T E E N

Shereel looked across the wide backstage directly into the eyes of Marvella Washington and smiled. Marvella Washington smiled too, showing a mouthful of wide white teeth and red gums. They balanced there in each other's unblinking gaze. Shereel knew that Marvella's sisters were chanting again in unison but whatever they were saying came to her as only a kind of loud buzz. It did not register as words. It had nothing to do with her. She knew Marvella was there, and she knew this was the time. She and Marvella were alone now. And she also knew that barring some unthinkable accident, one of them would win the world and one of them would cease to exist. Coming in second was by far much worse than not coming to the contest at all.

Shereel consciously took her arm out of Russell's massive hand. He would be at her side, and he would talk to her. She couldn't do anything about that. But he no longer had control, none at all. He could force her to come in wearing a white silk robe, and Wallace could force Marvella to make her entrance behind her huge, chanting sisters, but for the rest of the way she and Marvella would be as alone as they would be when the first shovelful of dirt dropped on their caskets.

As if on cue there was sudden motion and a babble of voices mixed with the jarring clang of iron on iron as the other competitors continued pumping up. But Shereel could feel the oblique and furtive glances everywhere around her as she raised her right hand to the button at her throat.

"You feeling all right?"

It was Nail. Shereel had to cut her eyes away from Marvella's to focus on him where he stood at her side.

"We'll talk about how I feel later," she said.

"I told you I'd help," he said, "and I will."

"You want to help?" she said.

"Yes."

"Then stay out of my way and let me work."

"Work then," he said, stepping away from her.

"You handled that just right," said Russell, keeping his voice low. "Exactly the right thing to say."

She felt the smile go stronger on her face, and felt, too, her blood leap with exhilaration. Of all the places on the face of the earth where she could be standing, she was standing precisely where she most wanted to be.

"Yes," she said to Russell. "Stay out of my way and let me work."

His voice still low in her ear, Russell said, "I'm with you. You need, you ask. Otherwise, it's all on you." Then in a voice too loud, startled and startling: "TAKE IT TO'M, CHAMP! LET'M SEE WHAT IT LOOKS LIKE!"

Her fingers flew down the row of buttons and the robe slid off her shoulders onto the floor.

Somewhere there was a low whistling intake of breath, somewhere else there was a groan. Marvella had dropped flat-backed on a bench under an Olympic bar with twenty-pound plates and was doing a long sequence of rapid prone presses, snorting through her nose each time at the top of the press as her elbows locked out. Her sisters, two on each side of the bench, grunted point–counterpoint as she worked.

Shereel had warmed up in her room, and Russell had applied a light coat of oil to her skin. She went over to the squat rack to start the pump that she would take with her onstage and as she walked over and put her shoulders under the bar, she felt something move in her that was very nearly an audible *click*, a click that always felt like a bolt sliding shut, sliding shut and locking her in with herself and locking everybody else out.

She put her shoulders under a bar that Russell had hurriedly weighted for her. It was exactly one hundred ten pounds. She stepped away from the rack and slowly eased into the first squat, breathing deeply as she sat into it, going down until her hamstrings were parallel to the floor. She moved deliberately, breathed deliberately, and concentrated herself entirely in her legs, feeling her quadriceps start to flush with blood, then her hamstrings, and finally as she moved steadily and easily under the weight, her calves. The secret was not the weight of the bar but the quality of her concentration and the number of repetitions she did. She kept her back flat, her head up, and focused, trying to imagine she was all legs. As she slipped into the fifteenth squat, she could feel the muscles in her legs separately and distinctly, one from the other. She could feel her quadriceps divide above her knee, could feel them rise to stand thick and hard under her thin skin. A faint sweat had broken all along the surface of her skin when she heard her daddy's voice. She heard it and understood it and ignored it, because it could not touch her where she was now.

"She don't look like the same youngun," Alphonse said. "It's the first time I seen her out of that bathrobe and I didn't reckon on this."

"You seen Billy Bat," said Nail.

"Yeah," said Alphonse, "yeah, I did. I ain't talkin' about Billy Bat."

"This is what they do, Fonse."

"What *happened* to her?"

"You cain't git to look like that by accident. She did it to herself. She made herself into somethin' else."

Shereel set the bar back into the squat rack and turned to a low bench where Russell was standing with a thirty-pound dumbbell in either hand. As she went onto her back on the bench, she briefly saw Fonse and Nail and Motor and Turner standing very still and close together. Fonse had both hands on his hat. Nail had his knife out but unopened. Turner's jaw was slack. Motor stared straight ahead, but one of his hands was inside his shirt on his slightly mounded and hairless stomach. Shereel thought about, felt, and focused on her pectoral muscles supporting her tiny breasts as she went into a set of flies. On her back, the dumbbells above her, she eased her hands out and down, feeling the weight stretch her chest over the deep breath she had taken and held. As she brought the dumbbells back together above her, she slowly exhaled and closed her eyes. Behind her eyelids she could see where the muscle attached to her sternum, see it divide and work and swell. God, it felt good. It felt like the best thing in the world. When a light bruised ache started spreading under her breasts, it felt even better. This was *it*. This was the only day there would ever be. The sweat was heavier, hotter, and Russell touched her with a towel. She pumped on.

From far away, Fonse's voice came to her, followed by Nail's and then Motor's.

"I don't know as I like this."

"I don't know as it matters if you like it or not."

"Likin' or not likin' ain't got nothin' to do with it. A little like this hair of mine. Once ittas gone, ittas gone. I wisht for it back the first time or two I was neked. Wishin' didn't change a goddamn thing."

"Don't cuss back here amonst these goddamn strangers."

"Forgot myself, Daddy."

Shereel had moved into standing, behind-the-head presses with a bar and focused now in her deltoids, felt the veins swell and trace little blue designs over the skin of her shoulders.

Russell's voice came softly from somewhere behind her. "It's not going to be long now if you want to get into your seats."

"Turner, see if you ma and Earline's out there to the seats."

"I looked oncet awready. They was some of the first out there."

"Well, Earnestine said the seats was the place to see this thing from and she didn't have no bidness back here. By God, she was right. I don't know as I like seein' my youngun into nothin' like this right here."

This right here is the best abdominal wall in the world, thought Shereel, as she bounced on a slant board, doing crunches until the ridges of muscle in her stomach caught fire and burned. She crunched them, burning hotter and deeper.

"Let me dry you off and oil you down. It's time." Russell's voice came from a far place. She kept her eyes closed and focused harder on her stomach. *"Now."* She opened her eyes and stood up, feeling strong and hot and good.

"Les us go on out there with Earnestine and Earline. I cain't watch this."

"Don't know as I want to watch it either," said Nail. Then: "Shereel."

She moved her eyes and Nail leapt into focus, that strange crazy smile he had brought back from Vietnam on his face.

Nail said, *"Get some!"* And he was gone.

Russell's hands were calm and easy on her body, and his voice, when it came, was the same calm, steady, and confident voice he always had when it was time to go head-to-head in competition, time to do it. "You've bought this and paid for it. Go pick it up and take it home."

The call had come for the competitors on the PA system. None of the women had to be told what to do. These were professionals and they had won their knowledge over hard years of competition. Shereel stepped away from Russell and fell into line with the other middleweights. There was a buzz of voices, hostile and threatening, a buzz that Shereel by an effort of will never allowed to turn into words that she could understand. A lot of the women talked to one another, cursed one another, threatened one another, put a general bad mouth on one another when they lined up to go on and the talk continued even after they were onstage. Right out there under the lights with the audience applauding and screaming, a brilliantly smiling girl, her lips barely moving, would say: "Tiffany, you come-drinking cunt, you've lost your legs." And Tiffany would come back: "Look at me, bitch. Look at me and eat your fucking heart."

But Shereel never talked, not even to respond to something

said directly to her. Russell had told her that was the best way. Stay within yourself. Control is the name of this game. Control *every*thing. *Believe* you can control everything. Believe it and you can *do* it. Believe it and it is the truth. Shereel had no way of knowing what Wallace had or had not told Marvella, but Marvella did not talk either. Her response was always with her body. She could break your back and your spirit with her body. And she knew it. Say something to Marvella and she might throw out one of her magnificent legs, relax it so that the thick muscles swung with her movement, and then flex it so that every muscle leapt as though it meant to come off her leg. It was startling, almost unbelievable.

The women were lined up by divisions now, ready to go on and win it all, or come up dry. In each division, first place brought $25,000, second $15,000, and third $10,000. The overall winner, Ms. Cosmos, added another $25,000 to her first $25,000. But $25,000 would not cover the expenses of a single woman here. The only winner was the one who went home with the title. Everybody else was down the shitter to nowhere land. That's the way Shereel thought of it, because that's the way Russell had always told it to her: The loser's down the shitter to nowhere land. That was true in any contest, but nowhere was it true in the blood-and-bone way of the Cosmos.

The audience was already clapping and cheering when the lightweights filed out, and after them the middleweights, but when Shereel took her first step out under the burst of brilliant lights, a wave of sound took her, broke over her and kept breaking, unlike any she had ever heard. Belligerent in its intensity, it did not even sound like applause as it came to her out of the vast darkness of the convention center and it joined her as vivid in its feeling as a raw nerve, joined her and lifted her with the certain, always startling knowledge: *They love me.* And the raw nerve of the audience's love forced her so deep inside herself that she felt if she wanted to, if she *needed* to, she could isolate every single cell of her body from every other cell of her body.

"Just stand relaxed, ladies."

Shereel suddenly saw him, the head judge speaking into a microphone there where he sat below the edge of the stage. She saw him with a singular vividness, a massive black man with a round, shaved head that sat neckless on unthinkably thick shoulders. Everything he was wearing, coat, tie, shirt, was immaculately white.

"Relax," he said again, his voice mellifluous, soothing, his heavy black eyes directly on Shereel, or so it seemed to her, as she gave herself up to his voice telling her, telling *her*, not *them*, to take a quarter turn to the right.

She followed his voice through the quarter turns until she was facing him again. She deliberately did not look at him now, only followed his voice. "Don't play to the judges," Russell had told her time out of mind. "It can kill you. Just do your job. Don't *look* like you're enjoying yourself. *Really* enjoy yourself." So she looked out into the darkness and followed his voice. She knew the audience was wildly applauding and cheering, but mostly she did not hear it. Sometimes it impinged on, exploded into, her consciousness, but mostly she followed his voice and did her job and really did enjoy herself.

She had never been more relaxed and ready and at one with her music when she came out to do her ninety-second routine to "Street Fighting Man." She hit every pose on the right note. She was a champion. She knew it. She was a worldbeater. She knew it. *The* champion on a stageful of champions. She knew it. Nothing could go wrong. She knew it. When her music ended as she hit the last pose and held it, she gave herself over to the thunderous applause that beat in her ears before finally beating with her heart in her blood. She was pure body, the bodiness of body, and in perfect control.

When she came offstage, Russell was there to touch the sweat off her face and body with a towel and reapply oil to her skin. He talked to her while he did it, but she did not listen. She smiled at him as though he were an idiot child and whatever he was saying made as much sense to her as an idiot child's babblings would have made as she waited to be called back onstage for one-on-one comparisons. That was where she knew, just as everybody in the convention center knew, that Marvella Washington and she would be called together. She only waited for the sweet, soothing, mellifluous voice to take her where she most wanted to be, next to Marvella, just the two of them hitting and holding the same poses while the judges decided who was better, who was *the* body.

When the call came, there was again the abrupt change in the audience's reaction when she stepped onstage, the wildness, the uncontrolled exuberance went a notch higher until it was a kind of clanging of voices that reminded her of the gym, and it was all directed at her. She lined up at the back of the stage with the other women, her eyes focused out into the darkness, and waited and listened for her number to be called.

Numbers were called and women, in pairs and threes and sometimes fours, went down to the front of the judges, and hit the poses they were told to hit. Shereel did not watch. She focused on the darkness. Then the head judge called it.

"Seventy-seven, please."

Shereel stepped away from the other women and went to stand alone on the lip of the stage on the very edge of where the darkness started. She held her smile, stood relaxed, and waited. She did not know Marvella's number. She had made a conscious effort not to know it.

"And twenty-one, please."

Shereel did not see Marvella standing beside her. But she felt her. A huge, hot presence. And now that the two of them were alone at the center of the stage just above the judges, the audience thundered and roared. People were calling to her, begging. People were calling to Marvella, begging. Shereel felt herself on the edge of an abyss. This was the ultimate test. After this, the contest would be over. A whole terrible afternoon and evening would have to pass before she would know the outcome for sure, but the actual test was upon her now.

"Double bicep back pose, please."

Shereel turned to put her back to the judges and to the baying voice of the audience, and as she did, she came face-to-face with Marvella, deliberately standing as close as she could get, trying to dominate. It was always a surprise when she got this near Marvella. No matter how many times she did it, it always shocked her. Brutally and beautifully monstrous in size. Inevitably, Shereel felt surrounded when Marvella was close enough to touch. Marvella, from her height, looked down upon her, wide teeth and red wet gums flashing. It seemed to take forever to make the full turn so that she could no longer see Marvella. But she was finally there and alone with herself again. She hit the double bicep back, but also put a taut, lean hamstring flex on her leg and felt the diamond point leap from her calf.

After the first pose, she was home free, relaxed and working easily. Shereel listened to the smooth, almost crooning, voice of the head judge and moved to it as though it were music and she a dancer. And as she moved, a palpable sense of victory touched her, and she knew there was not another woman in the world that could beat her on this stage under these lights on this day.

And then the head judge was saying, "Thank you. Step back, please."

The voice of the audience followed them back to their places with the other women. The show momentarily stopped because the head judge could not make himself heard. It was only after Shereel was standing still that she felt the sweat running on her skin and felt, too, the sweet constriction of her lungs under her heaving rib cage. There was nothing else in her life to compare that moment to.

She focused on the far darkness and waited.

When she came offstage with the other women, popping flashbulbs blinded her, and she was off her feet, caught up in Russell's arms, and she could hear him bellowing over and over: "You did it you did it you did it." From the far corner of the curtain, she saw Nail, and behind him her brothers and daddy.

Then Nail had her, his head bent close to hers.

"What do you want to do? What?" She could feel his lips at her ear.

"Room," she said, being pushed and shoved by the swirling crowd and blinded all over again by flashbulbs. *"My room!"*

"Turner, Motor," called Nail.

Her brothers opened the way, people bouncing off them, as Nail led her out, his arm about her shoulders. Her daddy, already smoking, was behind her, kicking and punching and butting anybody that got close enough to hit. When she got to the elevator, Turner and Motor cleaned it out, and suddenly it was very quiet, as though they had gone underwater. It was only then that Shereel saw that Russell Morgan was with them, and that he no longer looked happy. Her daddy put out the Camel he had been smoking on a sign that said smoking was against the law in the elevator and punishable by a fine of $500 and no more than six months in jail. He had lost his hat.

"I lost my hat," said Fonse.

Nail held her tightly against him and did not answer.

Russell said, "This is not the way it's done. We ought to be downstairs. We—"

Nail's closed hand came up and a silvery blue blade leapt from his fist. "Everbody shut the fuck up. *Now.*"

They rode the rest of the way in silence except for the whispery sound of the elevator shaft. They all watched the blade of Nail's knife, even Fonse.

When the elevator stopped, they followed Nail, his arm still around Shereel's shoulders, down the wide hall to her room.

Once inside, Nail said, "How do you want this played? You want us out of here?"

"In a minute," said Shereel, and she was smiling again for the first time since she left the stage.

"We ought to be downstairs, celebrating, talking to reporters, getting pictures," Russell said.

"I'll celebrate when I have something to celebrate," Shereel said.

"It's done," Russell said, "money in the bank."

"It's done when the judges say it's done," she said. "There's time enough for pictures and reporters then. I—"

Russell cut her off. "Since when did—"

"Shut up till she finishes," Nail said.

"I've gone over this a million times in my mind," she said. "I know how I want to do it. I need to be alone now, and very quiet, very still." She looked at Russell. "Send up some orange juice so I don't cramp out there tonight, and a bowl of ice. Knock on the door an hour before show time."

"The door's behind you," Nail said. "Don't slam it. Fonse, wait in the hall for me. I only need a minute."

"You, too," Shereel said.

"I've got something to say to you," said Nail.

"I don't want to talk and there's nothing I need to hear."

Nail only said again, "I've got something to say to you," as he closed the door behind Fonse, the last to leave. He turned and stood quietly looking at Shereel.

"What?" she said.

"Help," he said. "My help."

"Can I say it once and be finished with it?"

"Always," he said. "This is Nail you talkin' to."

She sighed. Her smile went softer. "Nail, do you think I'd want a championship that came on the blade of your knife? Do you think I could rest easy with that?"

"No," he said. "Only askin'. You name it. I'll git it done."

"You promise? No matter what?"

"Yes."

"Leave it alone. I want it, but it's got to be mine when I get it. Walk away from it. Can you do that?"

"It's done," he said, opening the door and closing it very quietly behind him.

Shereel put out a fresh robe and posing briefs for the evening show and had just come out of the shower when there was a knock at the door. She slipped into the robe and opened the door. A bellman was there with orange juice and a bowl of ice.

He would not take money for it, nor would he accept a tip. He was young and very handsome with fine long lashes over his liquid brown eyes.

"You were very beautiful there today," he said. "Good luck the rest of the way."

"Thank you," she said.

He said something softly to her in Spanish and was gone.

She sat on the side of the bed and drank half a glass of orange juice which she did not really want, but she knew she needed the potassium. She put the glass down and took a cube of ice into her mouth. How good the water felt, falling on her uneasy stomach. She felt like she wanted to vomit, had, in fact, felt like that since she came off the stage. Nerves, she thought. Over what? It's done.

She lay back on the bed and carefully put her head on the pillow. She felt somehow brittle, easily broken, as though she had to be careful with herself. She closed her eyes and smiled at the notion that she, a worldbeater, could be brittle, easily broken. But the smile was an effort and she felt it leave her face.

The thing that scared her was that she did not have any options, any alternatives. Her whole future, the rest of her life, rested squarely on today. This notion had occurred briefly to her before but she had been able to resist it. Now she could not resist it and that scared her.

On one side of the ledger was winning and its consequences. Maybe something was possible between Nail and her. But only if she was Shereel Dupont, Champion. She had loved Nail since she was just a girl, but she wanted nothing to do with him as Dorothy Turnipseed, typist, from Waycross, Georgia. He chewed up Dorothy Turnipseeds without even thinking, without ever tasting them. But he could not chew up a Shereel. Shereel Dupont, Ms. Cosmos, was somebody, somebody to reckon with. As Ms. Cosmos, she saw her name on gyms, on food supplements, on sportswear. It was easy to see that name written across the sky.

On the other side of the ledger was the alternative to winning. And she did not know, could not imagine, the consequences of not winning. That side of the ledger was not only blank, it was dark, like the thick dark of the convention center where the howling voice of the audience came from. Behind her closed eyes in an effort of will, she tried to look away from that dark, look away from what she did not know and could not imagine. But try as she would, the dark stayed and she kept very still and forced a deep steady rhythm on her breathing.

She did not know she had slept until the key in the lock awakened her. She drew the robe she had been lying in more tightly about her, and tried not to remember what she was thinking of when she fell asleep.

"I got you thirty minutes earlier than I said I would," Russell said. His voice was irritable. "Every photographer and reporter in the hotel has been asking for you."

He had lost control, and she thought he knew it. Too fucking bad. "They can have me when the judges announce I'm Ms. Cosmos." She picked up her posing briefs. "Put my music on and turn it as loud as it'll go while I get a shower."

He looked at the tape player and then at her. "This is not—"

"This is not the time to talk to me. *Do it.*"

She stepped into the bathroom and slipped out of the robe. She turned the water very hot and stepped under it. In a moment "Street Fighting Man" broke over her with the water, and with her eyes closed she concentrated on seeing the moves she made with the music, on *feeling* the moves she made with the music, focusing on herself, there under the water where she stood very still.

She came out of the bath already dressed in her posing briefs and went to stand before the floor-to-ceiling mirror where she carefully started to apply oil to her skin. She would smooth it on slowly and evenly wherever she could reach before handing the bottle to Russell so he could do her back.

Russell watched her from where he sat on the edge of the

bed. "Jesus, I wish we could have done this without your family," he said. "What a fucking nightmare."

"But we didn't," she said without looking at him. "We couldn't."

"It only made everything about twice as hard."

"Bullshit."

"You just don't know. I thought Earline was going to have a breakdown when Billy Bat came on. You should have seen that. You really should. If it had not been for your mother, she would have probably wrecked the whole contest. Hadn't been for Earline, though, your mother would have been up here with you. Your daddy too. Took both of'm to keep Earline in line. Jesus. Your brothers got so excited over Billy Bat—especially Motor, the one that shaved down—and excited over Earline acting out, that they started butting heads. Christ, I never saw anybody do that, butting their heads together and slobbering like dogs."

"Common in Waycross, Georgia," Shereel said, smoothing oil over her shoulders. "Common way of showing appreciation and excitement by young men in the rutting stage of life."

"In the rutting stage? Is that what you said? Rutting?"

"That's what I said."

"I won't even comment on that."

"Good."

Russell snorted through his nose and went to look out the window. "You didn't used to be so quick-lipped."

"No, I didn't used to be," she said.

She held up the bottle of oil, still without looking at him, her eyes focused rather on her body in the mirror, on the muscles sliding, locking and unlocking, under the oiled shimmer of her skin. He came to her and took the oil out of her hand and started working on her back.

"For somebody winning the world," Russell said, "you damn sure don't seem very happy."

"I haven't won it yet. And I've got the rest of my life to be happy, as Nail would say."

"He's something else that worries me."

"That's allowed," she said. "It's all right to worry about Nail. That just means you've got good sense."

"I don't know why I'm even talking to you," he said.

"I don't either."

He was silent, smoothing oil now down the backs of her legs and over her calves. Then: "Fonse said Nail was out in the parking lot sitting in his truck drinking whiskey. It's only about a hundred and fifteen out there. If he wants whiskey, why doesn't he go to the bar?"

"Nail doesn't much care for bars."

"Not a hell of a lot he does care about, is it?"

"You'd have to ask him about that."

"I don't want to ask him about anything."

"Not talking to Nail about anything seems like a good plan to me."

He stood back and looked at her carefully. Then he turned her and looked again. "You ready to go down and finish it?"

"Yes."

He took her shoulders and made her look at him. "All right, so we've had a few differences. Forget all that now. Act like a champion. Walk like a champion. *Feel* like a champion. I'll do everything I can. You want something, just ask me."

"Keep everybody away from me until it's over."

"I will," he said. "No problems there."

But there was some problem there. Not only was Nail backstage, his face flushed and chin set, his eyes red, but the whole Turnipseed family was there, too. Fonse had a Camel in his mouth, but it was not lit, which he had to keep pointing out to people who told him to put it out.

In a voice too quiet, too controlled, Nail said, "The next one says anything to you about that Camel, Fonse, slap the shit out of 'm. Slap the shit out of 'm and then get out of the way and let me have it."

Shereel, although she had been trying not to, was watching

him. It wasn't what he said to her daddy, but the too quiet, out of place, crazy voice that made her move around Russell and go to him.

"You're not going to ruin it this close," she said, making it a statement, not a question.

"No," he said. "I'm not going to ruin it this close."

"God, you should have seen Billy Bat," said Earline, looking as though she might throw herself on her sister's neck, but only did a little light-footed dance instead. "How come you been hidin' in you room, for God's sake?"

"Just the way I needed to do it," Shereel said. "Are you all right?"

"Right as rain. Billy Bat's gone . . ."

Her mother gently moved Earline out of the way with her still talking and stood looking at Shereel. "Honey, you looked . . . looked like nothin' I ever seen before, just beat all . . . this whole thing just beats all I ever seen before."

"Thank you, Mama. I've got to get ready now."

She went to the squat rack to go through the same routine she had gone through before, but she didn't go as hard this time. This was only a show for the paying audience. The judges' cards were already marked and it was done. So Shereel only did a few repetitions with each exercise and stretched until she was pumped and hot. Marvella stayed on the other side of the back-stage and did not look at her. The four sisters, wearing purple Spandex tights, seemed subdued and did not chant in unison or leap about disrupting things, but only watched. Wallace leaned against a wall behind the bench where Marvella was working. It was the first time Shereel had seen him, although she knew he must have been there all along. He had his face inclined toward the floor and when he looked up, he looked very serious, the way he might look—Shereel thought—at a funeral. Well, it was gut-check time for everybody, those that had a shot at winning as well as those who had no chance at all.

The first division, the lightweights, started being called one at a time to do their ninety-second routines to music. Shereel did not watch. She stretched to stay hot and kept her back to the stage. She never heard the middleweights called, but felt Russell touch her with the towel and say quietly, "You're up, Champ."

It was difficult to hear her music over the noise of the crowd, but she knew she was hitting the poses exactly because the audience became more and more hysterical, so that when she finished, she felt very strong and good and confident. As she was leaving the stage, she turned and raised both fists over her head.

"You were only perfect," screamed Russell to make himself heard over the cheering that had followed her backstage.

She went directly to a corner of the backstage and faced into it. Russell stopped beside her and lowered his head to hear her.

"Keep everybody away until the pose-down," she said and saw him nod.

The noise backstage and the noise of the audience were mixed and meaningless to her now that she was locked in with herself and waiting for the very last thing that would be demanded of her. It was possible, many bodybuilders said, for the pose-down to reverse decisions the judges had already recorded on their cards. But Shereel did not believe you could win back in the pose-down at night a contest you had lost earlier at prejudging. Neither did Russell.

But he always told her: "That doesn't mean you can dog it, take it for granted, and walk through it. When you're out to win the world, you give everything *everything* you've got. Why take chances?"

So she took no chances. Ever. She closed her eyes and pressed the ends of her fingers against her temples. She told herself there was only one more step to take. It would be over. Ended. Once and for all. She stood very still and forced herself to breathe evenly.

Shereel heard the name called for the winner of the lightweight division and heard the girl give a gaspy, triumphant yelp. Then she felt Russell touch her with the towel.

"I know," she said, not turning, but standing very still in the corner where she stood.

When she heard her name, winner of the middleweight division, she thought, *there it is,* and turned and went out under the brilliant lights where the voice of the crowd, in wave after wave, washed over her. She raised her arms, fists clenched. She never heard Marvella's name, only the clapping and foot-stomping and hysterical cries of the audience rise in volume and intensity. Then she felt Marvella beside her.

The tiny lightweight, her close-set blue eyes bright and manic, as though she had just received the best news of her life, or the worst, stepped directly in front of Marvella and hit a crab, all the muscles of her body, from head to heel, leaping and holding, quivering, sweat running. A stunned look came on the lightweight's face as she held it. Marvella, relaxed and smiling, glanced briefly at the girl holding the crab, and then moved one of her legs out so the girl had no alternative but to see it. With the forefinger of each hand, Marvella pointed to the relaxed calf of her extended leg. Then in a flex too quick to see, the calf exploded into a configuration unlike any Shereel had ever seen. And with that magnificent calf, Marvella defeated the lightweight, maybe even humiliated her. Shereel could see the defeat taking place in the attitude of the lightweight's body as Marvella pointed and the crowd thundered and the calf, steady and rock solid, seemed to grow even bigger. The lightweight shivered; her pose went softer. Marvella only pointed and smiled.

Shereel had not moved, but she had been gradually isolating her abdominal wall, feeling the blood rush there and the barred rows of muscle tighten. The wild applause grew more intense and it took a long time before Marvella understood the collective gaze of the audience had shifted. Marvella stepped down and in front of Shereel, but before she was ever set Shereel was already moving.

And so Shereel and Marvella were finally into the place that had no rules, into the place that may or may not affect the outcome of the contest, into the place that may or may not be meaningless. Whatever one of them did, the other tried to go it one better, to upstage it, to defeat it. As though dancing to a music only they could hear, they responded one to the other. The light-weight was there, but no longer really into it, posing rather on the edges of the space controlled by Marvella and Shereel.

Shereel concentrated on her own body and the darkness and the wild noise of the cheering crowd coming out of the darkness, concentrated until it was over. And it was over very quickly, or so it seemed to her. Coming offstage, she no longer felt strong and confident, only exhausted. Released suddenly from the tension of posing, she had no notion at all how she had done. Marvella went apart from her and waited with her sisters and Wallace. Alphonse's cigarette was still unlit but he was holding a kitchen match now as he stood quietly between his sons. Earline was over with Billy Bat where he had been warming up with the other men. But the men had stopped now. The whole backstage was quiet and still, waiting. Nail came nearer to Shereel, but he did not look at her and he did not speak. His eyes were very red. Russell took her arm and held it tightly, and she let him.

The lightweight's name was called as the third-place winner. There was no surprise in that for anybody backstage or anybody in the audience. There was a muted, restrained applause. Then there was utter quiet, a silence that Shereel could feel on the surface of her skin. Everybody waited for the next name, because the next name would end it. The next name was second place, and that would leave only Ms. Cosmos.

Shereel heard her name and did not move, could not believe it. She felt Russell's hand drop away from her arm, and a sound came from him as though he had been struck. Marvella screamed and her sisters went into a blurred dance to the rhythm of their clapping hands.

Shereel went out under the brilliant lights to acknowledge second place. There were catcalls and boos from those who loved her and thought that she had been wronged by the decision. But they were soon drowned out by those that loved Marvella, their hysteria rising to an intensity unlike any other during the contest.

That hysteria was the last thing Shereel remembered until she was coming off the stage. She knew she must have stayed for pictures, and that she must have flexed and smiled and probably even congratulated Marvella, but she remembered none of it when she found herself offstage with Nail facing her, his bright bloodshot eyes locked with her eyes, his face calm.

"What?" Nail said.

"Out," she said.

Nail put his arm about her waist and she was moving. She briefly saw Russell in a far corner, his hands holding his bald sweating scalp. Awash in shame and loss, she looked at the floor as people bounced off Nail, who was sweeping them away from her with his free arm as he bulled his way to the exit.

In the elevator, she took a deep breath, raised her head, and looked at Nail. "It's over and losing wasn't so bad after all," she said but her voice sounded strange in her own ears. Nail watched her and did not speak. "I have to get myself together. A bath. This oil." She gestured toward her body and the oil. "Clothes on. Oil off and dressed." She could feel the smile holding her face like a clenched hand. "Celebrate."

Nail did not speak in the elevator. Or in the hallway. Or at her door. She turned down the top of her posing briefs and tore off a small piece of adhesive tape. A key came off with the tape. She unlocked the door and turned to him with the key in her fingers.

"You took your room key onstage with you?"

"Come for me. In forty-five minutes," she said. "You come. Nobody else. Key."

She gave him the key. He stood looking at it lying in his open palm. Then he looked at her for what seemed a long time. Finally, he said, "This is the way you want it?"

"Yes," she said.

"You're sure?" he said.

"Yes, I'm sure."

"Okay," he said.

She had the door opened when he said, "Shereel." She turned to look at him. "You're a champ. You always been a champ."

She went on through the door and did not answer. Nail stood watching the closed door for a moment, and when he did move, it was only to step back and put his back against the wall and slowly slide down it to hunker there on his heels. He glanced at his watch, and when his eyes raised, he stared at the door in front of him and did not move.

Nail smelled cigarette smoke, and Fonse was squatting there beside him. He did not know how long Fonse had been there. Fonse took the cigarette out of his mouth and looked at it a long time.

"Earnestine is down with Earline," Fonse said. "They both wanted to come up here with me. I thought no. I thought ittas better for them to stay down there with Billy Bat."

Nail said, "It's better for them to stay down there."

"I thought it might be."

Fonse smoked, and they watched the door in front of them.

"She all right, I guess," Fonse said.

"She said she was gone take a bath," said Nail.

"Take her a bath," said Fonse.

"That's what she said."

Fonse put the butt he was smoking under his shoe and then took a long time to examine a kitchen match before he got another Camel going.

"I don't guess," Fonse said, "I might ought to knock on that door."

"I don't think so," said Nail. "Not now."

"That's what I thought." Then after he had carefully ground out his cigarette on the carpet in front of him and made little designs in the ash left there: "I don't reckon that Russell feller's been by."

"No," said Nail. "I don't much look for'm."

"That's the way I had it figgered, too," said Fonse.

"Why don't you go on down and be with Earline and Earnestine. They need you down there. I'll wait up here."

Fonse stood up and Nail stood up with him. "I prechate this, Nail."

"You take care of Earnestine and Earline."

"I will."

When he was gone Nail went back onto his heels and waited. He looked at his watch now and again. Finally, he looked at his watch, got up, and opened the door with the key. He took one step into the room and pushed the door closed behind him with his foot. He stood very still a long time before he turned his head and saw Shereel through the open bathroom door. She was in the tub and her face was turned away from him. The water she was in was incredibly red. He walked over to the tub and lifted one of her arms. At least she had the courage to do it right. The incisions—thin, the work of a razor—were parallel and ran up her wrist from the heel of her hand. He put the arm back into the water, and stood looking down at her. The last option. The one open to everybody.

He remembered being on a helicopter in Vietnam that picked an army major out of a firefight. He was the only one left alive in his command and he was covered with blood even though he was not wounded. His eyes had been bright and his face calm, much as Shereel's had been, and he put a .45-caliber pistol in his mouth and blew his head off while the helicopter was still rising out of the jungle. Nail would not have stopped him even if he could have. The major had lost every man in his command, had lost everything that made him an officer, had lost it all, and the last option was his only option.

Nail took Shereel out of the water and put her on the bed and wrapped her over with the sheet. He locked the room door behind him and went first to his own room and then to the front desk. The lobby was crowded and Julian never saw him until Nail was standing directly in front of him holding out the key.

Nail, keeping his voice low, said, "Call a doctor. Tell'm to git a stretcher and bring it. You got that?"

Julian, very pale now, the key caught tight in his trembling hand, said, "Yes sir."

"You do this right and don't fuck it up," Nail said.

"No sir," said Julian.

Nail smiled, and the smile made Julian shiver with a delicious horror. "You ain't a bad sort, Julian, if you studied more on you nose."

"Studied on my nose, sir?"

"Where to put it. Where not to put it."

"Oh, I understand, sir. I *do* understand."

"I hope so, Julian. I hope you do. I got somethin' else you can do for me, and I don't want any conversation about it. You think you can do that?"

"Anything," said Julian. "But do you think I should call the doctor first?"

"It ain't no hurry about that."

"But you said to bring a stretch—"

"No conversation, goddammit. Remember?"

"Yes sir."

"I want the room number for the head judge."

"I can give it to you, but he's in the bar now."

"In the bar?"

"The show's ended. I saw—"

"All right," Nail said.

As Nail turned to walk away from the desk, Julian said, "I'm sorry about Ms. Dupont."

Nail stopped and took a long time to turn and face Julian. When he did, he said, "You nose."

"Yes sir. Sorry."

Nail went into the bar and ordered a double Jack Black straight up. He drank two more before turning to look across the room to the place where the loudest talk was coming from. The head judge, glowing like a light in his white suit and shirt and tie and shoes, was sitting in a corner holding court in front of a semicircle of huge young men and women.

Nail ordered another Jack Black and sipped. It was not long before the head judge stood up, drained a tall glass of what looked to be orange juice, and walked toward the restroom. Nail followed. In the restroom, the man stood at a urinal. Nail washed his hands until the head judge finished and stepped back and pulled his zipper up. He came to the basin beside Nail, turned on the tap, washed his hands, and bent to splash water on his face. Nail put the barrel of the .357 into his neck. The exposed hammer clicked loudly against the tiled walls when Nail cocked it with his thumb.

"Stand up," Nail said.

The man stood up, the whites of his eyes flashing as he looked down at the .357 under his chin.

"My wallet's inside my coat. Left side. There's a Rolex on my left wrist." His voice was curiously high and thin and a twitch had started in his upper lip. "That's all I have."

"That ain't all you got."

"Except for the change in my pocket." Huge, isolated drops of sweat had appeared on his face.

"Don't talk," Nail said. "Back into the far stall." The man backed into the far stall, guided there by the pressure from the .357. "Now, in case you ain't ever seen one of these, it's a round in this thing as big as you thumb. Move, and they won't even find you goddamn head." The man's eyes had stopped blinking. They had not blinked for a long time. Nail reached in his pocket with his free hand and brought up the fragmentation grenade.

"What's that?" said the man.

"The end," Nail said. He caught the pin in his teeth and pulled. He spat the pin out of his mouth and a piece of tooth came with it. He forced the grenade behind the man's belt and turned it loose.

"Why are you doing this?" the man said.

"Because you head is up where I can see it. Because you wear white."

"I don't understand," the man said.

"I don't think understandin' it's ever been necessary," Nail said.